CHICAGO PUBLIC LIBRARY
SULZER REGIONAL
4455 N. LINCOLN AVE. 60625

R01908 93884

D1787504

A Room in the Woods

A Room in the Woods

Patrick Drevet

Translated by James Kirkup

QUARTET BOOKS

First published in Great Britain by Quartet Books Limited 1991
A member of the Namara Group
27/29 Goodge Street
London W1P 1FD

English translation copyright © by Quartet Books 1991
Originally published in French,
copyright © by Editions Gallimard 1989,
under the title *Une Chambre dans les Bois*

A catalogue record for this title is available from the
British Library

ISBN 0 7043 2781 3

Typeset by MC Typeset Limited, Gillingham, Kent, UK
Printed and bound in Great Britain
by Dotesios Printers Ltd, Trowbridge, Wiltshire.

A Room in the Woods

Translator's Note

I first became aware of Patrick Drevet's work when I read his remarkable novel about the relationship between a teacher and a mysterious, sullen adolescent pupil in *Le Visiteur de Hasard* (Gallimard, 1988), which I reviewed favourably for the *Times Literary Supplement*. I went on to read his other works, of which *Le Lieu des Passants* is the author's own favourite. *Une Chambre dans les Bois* (Gallimard, 1989) is Drevet's sixth novel, and I was attracted to it because the theme of the growing love between a boy and a young man was strangely similar to that of my first published novel, *The Love of Others* (Collins, 1962). Drevet's novel, which he admits is autobiographical, also contained scenes that reminded me of my wartime experiences as a lumberjack in the forests of the North Tyne and the West Riding. I reviewed this novel also for the *TLS*.

So when I had the good fortune to be commissioned to translate *Une Chambre dans les Bois*, I felt I could do so with authority. Drevet's impressionistic and subtle style does present difficulties, but it is a joy to read, and the story is deeply moving. There are brilliant descriptions of the lumberjacks' life in the forests of the Jura, excellent portraits of individuals and of the boy hero David and his older friend William. The novel is set in a small town in

France during the Algerian conflict, and the tensions of that period are well evoked. But it is the passages that describe the meeting, the dawning friendship and the passionate love of the two protagonists that are the most beautiful in their purity and conviction. There are several erotic descriptions, done in great detail, with a total frankness and a brave innocence that make them among the finest examples of this kind of writing in homosexual literature. Despite their striking realism, these erotic passages are curiously chaste, almost reserved.

In translating this outstanding novel with its very individual style, I have been helped immeasurably by the encouragement and advice of the author himself, whom I should like to thank here for his friendship and support. In a dedication he wrote for me in one of my copies he kindly says his book has become mine. I hope our English readers will find it is true.

I

The young boy, the person haunting my memory, is silhouetted against the black lacquer of a 203 on which he is leaning, just next to the door hinges. The car's bulging roof is gleaming like a mirror behind his nape. A lacy border of inverted and shrunken fir trees curves round the edge of the pool of light, in which the entire sky is captured. The reduced lighting of the setting sun's rays only serves to emphasize his clear-cut features, the lack of texture to the skin that one senses is pale beneath the orange-tinted surface. The even radiance, just muted enough not to dazzle, nevertheless contains a diffused luminosity that brings out the sheen of the eyelashes, the eyebrows and even the scalp under the cropped black hair, spiky, disposed in a lively movement extending the spiral of a forelock where the brow meets the temple. The eyes are wide open, and the incandescent sparkle at the periphery of the sombre irises, that are looking to one side, helps to accentuate the wild, harsh, moody impression created by his gaze.

I have no trouble placing him: he has come with his mother sent to bring the wages to the lumberjacks employed by the firm where she works as a book-keeper. It is she he is watching, some way off, surrounded by male figures who almost seem to be paying court to her. He has refused to join them. He is getting restless. He doesn't like her to linger, he disapproves of her complaisant attitude. His displeasure is directed chiefly at the foreman whom he knows and whose obsequious manners raise his hackles. As on all occasions when this man meets his mother, he treats her with a suspect solicitude, seeking every opportunity to get close to her and put his hands on her arms, on her shoulders, upon which he exerts pressures that disturb the young woman without at the same time making her want to get away from them. The foreman's ability to turn his mother's head has made the boy look upon him as his enemy.

He turns his eyes away, unable to repress a shrug of his shoulders. He looks down at his sandals that in an angry gesture he scrapes on the packed earth of the dirt road. Opened up for the lumber business, this road overlooks the old farmhouse now made over to the loggers. The rough gravel of the embankment supporting the road extends down almost to the foot of the building that seems to crouch beneath its immense roof with the pointed gables. The boy's gaze, following the roof-ridge and the house's lines of perspective, is bound to turn back once more towards his mother, but suddenly his attention is deflected by a sense of someone else's presence.

Indeed, framed in one of the two windows in the façade he is looking down at, he sees the seated figure of a young man. He gives a start, and blushes. The young man is looking at him, but without insisting, with an indifferent air. He is sitting cross-legged, his back against the window frame, one of his knees hanging over the window-sill, the other raised to support his arm. The darkness of the room behind him creates a ghostly background; the massive blocks of stone that brace the opening in the masonry, the broken shutter that hangs askew on the one hinge still holding, underscore by contrast the solid physique of his body but above all it is his hair that catches the attention: of a straw-coloured blond that in places seems to brighten into lighter tones, it descends in a long, curving lock over the forehead, thus increasing the volume of the skull and narrowing the face that appears ageless, set as it is in a fixed, arrogant expression. At the end of the arm held horizontal by the knee on which it is hanging, the wisp of smoke from a cigarette keeps twisting and snaking round the slackened hand.

'David!'

As if, dispersed by the breeze, it was coming from very far away, his mother's coaxing voice, drawing out the first syllable of his name and muting the second so as almost to make an elision of the final consonant, partly distracts the boy's attention concentrated on the young man. Like some gentle reprimand, it even makes him afraid that they have discovered the reason for the absorbed look on his face, and his anxiety to disguise this by putting on a dreamy expression detracts from the keenness of the final glance he cannot help casting towards the window, as if he were hoping desperately to receive some signal from it; though not to make sure of intercepting a returned look, but simply in order to take away with him something conclusive, something memorable.

'These gentleman want to make your acquaintance,' the young woman explains, intrigued by his absent air. 'Let me introduce David,' she says, immediately turning round in a twirl that makes her ponytail swing up and balloons her frock – for a second its pleats form a spiral before falling back into place.

The four men are watching the boy approach.

One of them moves towards him. He brusquely shoves out a hand.

'I'm Mario,' he says, patting with the other hand his chest that reverberates with a dull sound. 'But they also call me *Il Buffone*,' he adds, stepping back, twisting his features into a comical grimace.

One of the two other lumberjacks, young but already bald, whose childlike face seems at odds with his impressive corpulence, starts arguing with his workmate in Italian, and all that can be grasped of the brief altercation is the word *commediante*.

Mario lowers his face towards David.

'You know the story of the Seven Dwarfs?'

He straightens himself and points in the direction of the bald young man.

'That one there – he's *Il Brontolo*, Grumpy,' he translates. 'Known as Alberto.'

Alberto's deep, gravelly voice again gives vent to invectives: '*Istrione! Coglione! Stupido!*'

The young woman interrupts this flow, and turns David towards a man in a cap whose weather-beaten face breaks into a smile.

'Mr Quintarelli often asks me how you're getting on,' she says. 'He knew you when you were just little.'

'*Sì! Sì!*' the lumberjack says, nodding his head.

He removes his cap. Kneads it in his fingers. As if he were afraid to offend the boy by his bad pronunciation, he is reluctant to speak.

'Don't you have a son the same age as David?' the young woman goes on.

The man again nods his head, then sighs. He decides to try to explain, in phrases somewhat distorted by his accent, that this son is causing him a lot of worry, that he doesn't like going to school, that he does just as he pleases. '*Un testardo! Un testardo!*' he repeats, beating his forehead with his fist.

Mario asks him why he doesn't call his son over. 'It's like he feels afraid to show him to you,' he continues, turning back to the young woman. 'He'll never be prime minister, that's for sure, but he's a good lad. Mr Dieter can vouch for that,' he adds, turning towards the foreman who nods in approval. 'He'd do the work of the four of us if we didn't stop him. *Allora, lo vuoi, chiamare?*' he says, pressing the man to call his son.

'*Mah! chiamalotu!*' Quintarelli replies, throwing up a hand in the air in a gesture of irritation.

'*Padre snaturato!*' Mario accuses him, and he takes a few steps towards the slope that descends to the farm.

He puts his hands to his mouth to make his voice carry. The name 'Renato' re-echoes from side to side of the blind valley. Reduced to its final syllable, its diminishing echoes seem to be swallowed up in the depths of gorges lost in tenebrous distances, imparting a magical aura to the owner of the name, and making his presence immanent, limitless. David tries to distinguish those points in space from which he feels the name rebounds with the effect of a mischievous response. His eyes search the cover of the forests that are spreading a black stain over the slopes, almost expecting to make out the shape of the one who is as it were playfully withholding the manifestation of his presence. Finally he thinks of looking towards the rear of the building that he was just now overlooking but whose façade is now hidden from him. He feels tense with expectation. Again he hears the voice of Mario shouting: 'Come on, Renato, are you deaf or what?'

A sloppily dressed youth appears round the corner of the farmhouse. He frowns, looks up at the group standing at the top of the slope. In an instinctive gesture of defiance or self-defence, holding his right arm bent horizontally, he covers his mouth with the back of a hand daubed with machine-oil while the other scratches an itch on his thigh. This stance parts the front of a skimpy sweater revealing a chest where braces are wrinkling his checked shirt unbuttoned down to the navel. His socks accordioning over his heavy workboots combine to give this apparition an utterly miserable appearance.

'We've got visitors,' Mario shouts to him. 'They want to say hallo.'

The youth pulls himself together, awkward in his hand-me-downs, betraying the nervousness he feels in all his body. Gradually he takes a deep breath, and his two rigid arms held to his sides and the expression on his face all conspire to convey defiance.

'*Vuoi venire?*' his father shouts, threatening to bring him up by force.

Renato begins climbing up the ramp without bothering to hide his displeasure. He keeps his eyes fixed on the pebbles in front of his boots, giving the impression that he finds it hard not to kick them out of his way. His stiff hair rises in rebellious spikes whose tips have been bleached by the sun.

'He's crazy about machines,' Mario explains to the young woman. 'There's nobody like him for patching up old broken-down crocks. Just now he's working on ball-bearings for the truck. Hey, Renato,' he shouts, turning towards the boy and moving an imaginary steering-wheel, 'are you ready for the San Remo rally?'

Renato stops a few paces from the group. Raising his chin slightly, he considers David and his mother. His long eyelids give him almond-shaped eyes, a cat-like, disquieting look. The contraction of the muscles pinching his lips at the same time give them a pout marked with little lines. The young woman goes up to him.

'I'm glad to make your acquaintance, Renato. Do you like lumberjacking?'

His father places a hand on the boy's neck. He introduces *la signora* to him and it is obvious he is asking him to behave politely.

The boy parts his lips. He shrugs his shoulders.

'You have to do something,' he says.

His voice is surly, a little husky. The young woman turns towards David:

'Aren't you going to say hallo?'

They are both equally reserved, with set mouths, jaws tight, pale with distrust, each attempting to scare the other. The two youths are weighing each other up and neither will take the first step. Mario comes between them. He looks from one boy to the other.

'Eh!' he exclaims, raising a finger, 'they're the same age, the same height! Which one's the soup, and which the polenta?'

In order to compare their heights, he makes them approach one another but then gives up the attempt and tells them to shake hands. They do so unsmilingly, tense with instinctive rivalry, withdrawing as if jolted by an electric shock. Mario plants himself right in front of David, face to face, quite close. His staring eyes, their whites crisscrossed with small veins, the knotted lines on his forehead, the specks of his badly-shaven beard that make his cheeks blue, and the outline of his thick lips give him a repulsive look that nevertheless is transformed by the naïve expression on his face.

'Now then,' he says to David, 'what do you say to coming and spending your holidays here with us?'

'He'd be too much bother for you,' the young woman objects.

'No more than Renato!' the lumberjack replies.

'Not a bad idea,' the foreman comments.

Unconscious of the cool air the breeze is bringing

from the woods, he has slipped his thumbs under his braces, on a level with the buckles that attach them to the front of his dungarees, and the set of his arms folded thus accentuates their muscularity: the tapered forearms shaded by cross-hatchings of hair, biceps whose bulges stretch the skin to a whitening membrane that allows the azure delta of veins to shine through, massively blocked shoulders bursting with packed muscles that sturdily buttress each side of the neck's thick column. His voice rings out again, with a grave note, re-echoing:

'Renato won't mind having a companion. David will get a lot of benefit from an open-air life.'

His eyes do not linger on the boy: he looks at the young woman whose features grow tense.

'Well, what do you think, David?' she asks.

Dieter, pointing his chin at the yellow tractor parked at the edge of the road, adds that he makes the trip every day with the Latil. It will be no bother for him to pick up the boy in the morning and take him back at night. David lowers his head. But lifts it again almost at once to say he would like to accept the invitation. Mario is jubilant. Already he is thinking up a programme of fun and games for the boy. Quintarelli gives his approval. Renato says nothing but his eyes, fixed on David who ignores him, gleam with vindictive spite. The faint lines that had appeared on the young woman's brow do not disappear. She thanks them one and all and gives as an excuse for cutting short their farewells that it is getting late.

Dieter accompanies them back to the car. He tells her not to worry: David will be in good hands, for he will look after him himself. He makes her turn back and look at him, so that he can see her face.

'Yes, I'm wrong to worry,' she admits. 'But you know, he's all I have.'

She gives him her hand, throws her head back a

little, gives a shake that frees her ponytail caught in the opening of her frock, and gives him a forced smile.

The fields are vibrating to the frantic stridulations of the grasshoppers. David has reached the 203 whose elegant rear reflects on its rounded parts and on its chromium detailing the luminosity that is focused upon it as if caught in the burning circle of a magnifying glass. On the other hand, the farmhouse, in its hollow under the embankment, is already sunk in the darkness rising from the earth, and only the reflective nature of the blocks of stone allow him to distinguish the outline of the façade beneath the darkling mass of the roof. At present the windows pierce the wall with two black holes like empty eye sockets. Both are open on the same dense shadows. Within the window where the young man was sitting, not one ray of light, not the slightest movement that might reveal his presence.

The lumberjacks stand out like shadow puppets on the misty background of the twilit wooded slopes. Renato is going back down to the farmhouse. David just has time to glimpse, through the car's rear window, the movement of Mario's arm waving goodbye. Then the silhouettes vanish behind the bank that a bend in the road brings across his field of vision. The circle of the mountains moves away, jerking to the bumps of the 203, and is black against the indigo of the sky which in its turn is occulted by the drawing-in of two high curtains of fir trees closing in on the blind valley.*

---

* The French word *reculée* is used specifically to indicate a certain type of enclosed valley in the mountainous Jura district of south-east France. The *Petit Larousse* defines it thus: 'A profound Jurassian valley with vertical walls, ending in a cul-de-sac at the foot of a limestone escarpment, often referred to as "the end of the world".' (*Translator's note*)

II

For a long time, the real remains a dead letter for an individual, and then, one day, it becomes incarnate in a face that suddenly arouses the senses and the mind in all their force. In David's eyes, a young man he had barely glimpsed has focused the world's light on the place he inhabits.

   Since David's arrival, at dawn, he has had no chance, being with Dieter and Quintarelli outside the farmhouse, to do more than pass by him. The young man was leaving the ground floor living-quarters and, surprised by the sight of the boy, he had halted on the threshold, his body turned sideways, his head full-face. In the heavy blond lock covering his brow, the curve of the hair with its stiff points had momentarily frozen on the spot the sudden hesitation. The twist of his neck slightly tilted his face. The part turned outwards revealed smooth lines from the temple to the square jaw, while in the other the shadows mixed with reflected light emphasized the bulge of the chin, the hollow in the cheek, the arc in the deepset socket that half-circled the eye and separated the lower lid from the high, slanting cheekbone. Something fragile seemed to inform that distant physiognomy, something candid, questioning, almost apprehensive – a kind of irresoluteness that could be perceived in the rather thick, slightly puffy, somewhat pale lips with their well-blocked contour.

And then, he had stuffed his hand in the pockets of his khaki dungarees and walked away. So it is for his sake that David has come back to the forest. Though he cannot approach him yet, for the moment it is enough for him to know that an encounter is not far off.

Whether in order to keep him away from dangerous jobs, or to let him make friends with a boy of his own age, Dieter has put him in the hands of Renato whose task it is, away from the tree felling, to trim away the masses of tangled branches on which lies a fallen fir. But the young Italian turns out to be rather cross-grained. A sullen animosity sets him against David. Forced into inactivity, the boy squats cross-legged on the tree stump. He watches his workmate and keeps trying to get a conversation going as he strips the leaves from a hazel wand. The path he is unaware of having chosen nonetheless helps him to discover the words he needs to make his way along it.

'Do you never go tree-felling with the others?'

Renato straightens, his hair falling over his eyes. In the open neck of his shirt flicker points of wet light.

'I'm not here to watch them,' he answers.

The leaf David was pulling off the wand tears between his fingers.

'They don't give you any other jobs?'

'I'm preparing the ground for the timber waggons.'

His lips twist in a sudden grimace. David beats the wand in front of him: it whips the air like a switch.

'Don't try to tell me you're indispensable,' he says. 'They're not going to wait for you to start dragging out the timber!'

'You'd better shift your arse somewhere else,' Renato says. 'Your shorts are all over resin, I'll bet. And the unbarked trunk could jack up.'

He changes the bill-hook from his right to his left hand, spits on his palm, adjusts the handle again, waves the tool in front of him to test his grip on it and, after a short pause, attacks with a sharp blow the end of a branch that he starts to pull, first with brief jerks, then uninterruptedly, disentangling it and dragging it further off into the undergrowth where the rustling of foliage in fits and starts indicates the youth's wrenching progress.

Silence falls over the forest's unfathomable depths that the colonnade of trunks transfixes in a vibrant immobility. A new tension concentrates the stillness, so that the yell that suddenly rends it rebounds against its confines in slower and slower, ever-decreasing echoes, followed by a tremendous grinding roar that is transformed into a sort of lacerating squeal; fibres are cracking, something sighs, groans, explodes and drops. Leaves threshing, twigs snapping, scratching, then the dull detonation of the trunk crashing to the ground, followed by the final snarls and mutterings between its rebounds; then silence, once more, less dense, less dumbstruck.

'No need to ask if it's the first time you're in a forest!'

Renato has come back, and, perched in the nest of twigs and branches, is weighing up David who is still all ears.

'What about you?' David counters, making an effort to adopt a calm tone of voice, 'd'you spend your holidays here every year?'

Renato turns his head aside: the bill-hook is again yapping away. David keeps on at him. He asks the youth if his father always works with the same crew. Renato stops chopping a moment to explain that as the lumberjacks are self-employed, independent, teams are made up depending on available labour.

'But you've known Mario and Alberto a long time,' David goes on.

'Must have.'

'And the other one?'

'What one?'

'Him – the blond.'

'William?'

David has difficulty in concealing the emotion that the disclosure of this name arouses in him, a name whose syllables clearly evoke in him the image of the young man almost as vividly as if he were there before him.

'Oh, him. He's not a lumberjack,' Renato reveals.

He pauses a moment before getting down to work again.

David is turning between his fingers the slim hazel wand, now leafless. He cannot resist asking another question:

'You know where he comes from, this William?'

'Why don't you ask him?'

The power of a first name that – through its sonorities suggestive of a gentle temperament, an harmonious face, a seductiveness we transpose upon the person who bears it or through the echo of qualities that it awakens in our feelings and in our memory – invades our consciousness, arouses our desire, prepares an evolution towards a possibility we did not know we were waiting for. Marvellous, too, through the warmth and intoxication it communicates to us, ominous as the formula of some dangerous remedy, it presents us with a secret of which it is always both the lock and the key.

David savours, trembling, the power that Renato has unknowingly accorded him, not the power to gain access to the intimate being of the young man of course, but at least the power to look upon him, to inhabit his consciousness, to possess his image. Without a name, he was nothing but a fugitive apparition, a snapshot that left him teased by the itch of an enigma. From now on, he does not know him any better, but the person seen in the flesh takes on a depth, nuances, the defined contours of a real being, with its sensibility, its density, its past life. He becomes accessible and David feels, in the capability he now carries within him, even without intending to take advantage of it, to call to him, to make him turn round or set his eyes upon the caller by shouting that name, a pleasure that takes his breath away. Curiously too, the physical qualities that are all he knows of William are crystallized in these syllables that lend them individuality; he has the feeling that they bear within them his blondness, his languorous walk, to which are added, further deepening the personage, all those resonances that the gentleness and the foreign accent of their sonorities instil in him: something like the charm of solitude, of exile, of grief.

Rustlings of foliage and shouts coming from the depths of the virgin forest burst the bubble of the dream in which David is lost, and he jumps. From the dungarees and the gesticulations of his arms, he recognizes Dieter in the distance, but hesitates over the identity of the person following him. Although the young man has just been the subject of his daydreaming, the fact that he has not overcome the confusion the thought causes, and also the sensation of being caught at a loss, too suddenly, without being allowed the time to prepare himself for this encounter, make him hope that it is not he. But it is he all right, the one he is thinking of, the one he realizes he is seeing in his khaki dungarees, with his rather heavy step, and above all his mane of blond hair, so distinctive. But under the flash of a shaft of sunlight the bald pate has created this illusion, and now that David recognizes Alberto he is disappointed. He stands up and takes a few steps along the fallen trunk before jumping to the ground, swipes the branches here and there with his hazel wand, in a careless manner. The foreman and Alberto just pass by. Once again the air takes on its profound immobility.

'He's keen on your mother, is Dieter, eh?'

Renato has taken him by surprise, and David requires a few seconds before he can react.

'Why d'you say that?'

Renato puffs out his chest.

'Otherwise I don't expect he'd have saddled himself with you.'

He bends down again towards the branches that he starts lopping off with even greater energy. David clenches his fists, seeking a retort that doesn't come, lowers his head, takes a few steps, finally gives a violent swipe at the long grasses at his feet.

'So I suppose,' he says, 'that it was Dieter who signed on William?'

The reply bursts forth among the sharp blows of the bill-hook that Renato does not find it necessary to interrupt.

'I wouldn't think so.'

'Why?'

'Dieter's only a labourer. He mucks in with the rest of us, even though he likes to act the boss.'

'Then what is William's job, if he's not a lumberjack?'

'Same thing as me. He'd be here if it wasn't you. And we'd have finished this job long ago.'

'He's learning the trade?'

Renato, who has stuck the point of the bill-hook in the end of a branch, draws himself up.

'Is this an investigation or something? You making an inquiry?'

Angrily pulling out his bill-hook then drawing himself up again, he looks David up and down.

'We don't like nosy-parkers here. Mind your own business!'

Again, there is the staccato attack of the bill-hook, barely muted by the foliage that accompanies the clearcut sound of the blade with a rasping, human, expressive voice. Soon, as if they are the distant echo, axe blows are heard from the depths of the woods. Producing a deeper tone, indistinguishable from the moaning notes of the trunk they are battering, they seem to be taking the part of a continuous yet independent bass, counterpointing the blows of the bill-hook by underscoring its higher-pitched register, its nervous intensity, its compactness. The air all around their pulsations is charged with expectancy. Time seems to draw itself out, makes a pause, lets its slowness be felt. At the edges of the clearing or beneath the sunshafts that stab the shadows, the leaves of the thickets try to aspire, lacquered by the excess of light they take like a gleaming fixative. Silent, or revealed by the drone of their flight, sometimes outshone by the opulent and virtuoso dancing of a butterfly, the intrepid insects attempt their wavering approaches.

In the common living room, when he gets the first opportunity to approach William, I cannot imagine David except with eyes lowered to his plate, incapable of bringing himself to steal one glance at the young man, but on the contrary anxious to attract as little attention as possible, to make himself invisible, transparent. The pointless expectancy a certain person can provoke in us is something we cannot experience without a feeling that it must be visible to all, that it is exposing us to ridicule, laying bare our thoughts, revealing more of us than we know ourselves.

But to the timidity the boy senses within him in relation to William is added the unexpected feeling of oppression created in him by the absorbed ambience of the meal, the loaded silence of the lumberjacks, the imprecision imparted to their gestures and their features not so much by the semi-darkness as by the nature of the inner debates they are conducting with themselves, that withdrawal of energy to an inmost limit of their nerves, into the soft relaxation of their blurred flesh, each one lost within himself, enraptured by the universal ecstasy of the body in the torpor of noon.

On the other hand, this is the time for the reign of things and insects that take on an hallucinating high relief: the fruits, the dishes, the breadcrumbs on the boards of the table, the buzzing of flies, the screeching of nailed workboots on the stone-flagged floor, the chiming of forks and knives on the china plates. Only Dieter, seated to one side on his chair, the shape of his head and shoulders silhouetted against the halo of the window, lets his voice be heard in the drowsy air. He is recalling Indo-China, the expeditions in the rice fields, the bivouacs under the mangrove trees, the violence of the combats, the tricks of the Viet-Minh, the clammy atmosphere. He seems to be mumbling aloud his still recent memories, all to himself, between two mouthfuls, two gulps of wine. Yet the orderly manner in which they are presented suggests that he is studying his effects, never giving up hope of capturing the others' attention, which, very skilfully, he is conducting towards some edifying or treacherous climax that in the end does indeed drop anchor: as far as he is concerned, he at least has done some fighting, he can be proud of his youthful exploits.

Between Quintarelli and William, Renato is dismembering a bunch of grapes held level with his face in a negligent hand, his elbow on the table. The faint crunch of the seeds between his teeth attracts the attention of David who detects a hidden smile in the movements of his lips while he is chewing. Perhaps some joke exchanged with William has come to mind, but the young man's proximity would be enough to justify Renato's self-satisfied and even infatuated air. Sharing his aura, he benefits from the magnetism conferred upon William by his maturity, the serious expression on his face, the tension that imprisons his shoulders and his nape as in a pillory of glass. Yet Renato could never arrogate to himself the attractive force that remains the young man's sole prerogative, that has its source in the energy underlying it and culminating in his blond hair. Probably William senses David's insistent gaze coming diagonally from the other end of the table, but he does not show it, he preserves the distance inherent in his character, one hand supporting his chin, the other tracing hieroglyphs among the breadcrumbs.

I discover him through David's eyes. No boy I have ever known could serve as the inspiration for his appearance. He is the product of precise requirements whose exigencies I am unable to pinpoint, and if I were to succeed in listing a few of them they would not be sufficient to justify the specificity he presents. But there is no doubt that William represents in part the realization of a synthesis of traits and characteristics peculiar to those older boys whose faces – from childhood into adolescence – haunted me for many years. Withdrawn, solitary – or become so from the way I looked at them – they had a family resemblance in their manner of walking, in the way they kept themselves apart with a kind of loaded deliberation some secret imparted to their comportment, and that I envied them for. They stood out not so much by their uncommon physical attributes as by a contained force, by that even-tempered disposition that made them so intimidating.

All the same, the power of attraction they exerted over me could not fail to be linked to my intuition that here lay a sensibility flayed alive, which explained their sullen air, compelling them sometimes to adopt a disdainful attitude, making their eyes smoulder with a somewhat uneasy tremor. The tortured lines of their lips bore witness to a hidden well of sadness or discontent that provoked in me generous impulses I despaired of ever being able to give way to. Lacking the key to their kingdom, I had to satisfy myself by merely looking at them. I expected that any interest they might be inclined to show in me could only increase my stature. And if they were to condescend to look upon me, if they went so far as to smile at me, if they accorded me the favour of a few words, then I was so overcome, I could barely manage to enjoy the existence their attention proved was mine, at least in their own eyes. In the belief that I had become the object of an expectancy that I could only succeed in disappointing, I longed to run away, to hide, to disappear; unless, overwhelmed by happiness, made ecstatic by this sudden increase in the enhancement of my feelings, I was only conscious, in my breathless distraction brought about by my pounding heart, of the need to master my emotions in order not to faint clean away.

Such is the nature of the emotion I see David preparing to confront. It is all still submerged in his ignorant flesh. Only the intuition that he is venturing out of his depth forewarns him that he is letting himself in for some severe castigation. No matter. When he observes how the companionship of the young man instils such self-confidence in a radiant Renato, he is stimulated by a desire to share it too.

His mother was probably calculating that a single day spent in the forest would be enough to discourage him from returning there. Seated at the end of the table, she studies her hands laid one on top of the other before her, white on the white surface of the formica. The presence of Dieter, who is setting down the glass of wine she has poured for him, and the way he looks so fixedly at her disturb the young woman, make her feel slightly giddy. Nevertheless she manages to turn towards David who is leaning against the sideboard, facing the foreman and exhibiting impatience in the way he is jigging one leg.

'The town is organizing a course of swimming lessons,' she tells him. 'The young people in charge of it are real sporting types. It seems to me to be an interesting project. Don't you want to take part in it?'

David moves away from the sideboard. He stops jigging his foot, his lips are trembling. The shame she arouses in him by treating him as a child is perhaps waging a losing battle with the confusion he feels as he realizes the violence of reactions that have never before set him against his mother to this extent. She is stupefied.

Dieter shakes with silent private laughter. Under the mask of sunburnt weariness, his radiant face resuscitates the boyishness of his features, their vigour, the attractiveness of their bold lines. The thin moustache with the uptwirled points moderates his somewhat self-righteous expression with a touch of irony, though it is really his whole face that is made finer, as if magnified by it: the nose's rectitude, the fold at the corner of the lips, the dimple their smile makes in the cheek, the zigzag lightning line running across his temple. He advances his hand, in a movement pregnant with all the tenderness he intends to use in laying it on the young woman's shoulder in an effort to calm her down, to absorb some of the nervous agitation that racks her, to lend her support, give her guidance. But, either as the result of indecision or sudden doubts, he does not carry through his gesture, and has resort to words instead. His voice, following through the tentative movement, produces, because of the carrying power of its intonations, a sort of protective envelope.

'David is in just as safe hands with me in the forest as with the coaches at the swimming pool: you have no need to worry.'

The young woman quivers, does not dare look into his eyes.

'I'm not criticizing you,' she says. 'I'm just worried that he might be a nuisance to you . . .'

'I don't make any exception for David: he has to muck in with all the others!' – Then, turning towards the boy and giving him a wink, adds: 'You'll get him back home with the muscles of a champion boxer – won't she?'

The young woman still cannot calm her fears. She doesn't like David to be in the hands of the lumberjacks; she is afraid that these daily trips will make the days too long for him, and for Dieter, who has his own family to take care of. However, torn between her son's obstinacy and the foreman's obliging attitude, she is already won over: she is putting forth arguments to salve her conscience, and in a tone lacking in conviction – she even lowers her voice and leaves her sentence unfinished. Dieter slaps his thighs and stands up. He shoves his chair under the table, leans with both hands on its back and studies the young woman, who still seems distressed.

'I'll see you out,' she says.

Standing up, she stares into the face of the man who is watching her. It seems as if there is now some understanding between them, they look serious. Dieter moves away, lets her pass in front of him, follows her with his eyes. Before proceeding after her, he suddenly turns to David. He advises him to have an early night. He reminds him that he has to get in good shape so as not to forfeit Renato's esteem. He feels confident of being able to help David to hold his own against that raw youth, and, in an encouraging gesture, he shakes his fist. For a moment, the bare arm sketches in the light an image of knotted blocks of muscle. Then suddenly there is vacant space again, with its inertia, its lack of depth.

It presses against the brilliantly smooth surfaces of walls, doors and cupboards, against the flat table top its perfect, homogenous transparency. The excess of luminosity, the brilliance that ceaselessly menaces the eyes with its sharp shafts, the cutting edges of the lines defining objects hurt the sight, force themselves upon his vision, provoking symptoms of migraine. It is with a strange detachment that David now considers each of the elements in this room that is nevertheless so familiar, but in which his eye only takes in whiteness upon whiteness.

The voices of the foreman and the young woman who are still in the corridor re-echo in the room as if, coming from outside the walls, they were the voices of missing persons, memories of voices, the voices of unknown passers-by. They are clearly audible but too entangled with their own echoes for David to be able to gather anything more than rhythms, modulations, sudden crescendos, languorous relapses in which they seem to become extinguished completely. In Dieter's measured bass accents, the blood-red of his viscera seems to make itself heard together with the solidity of his flesh, the robustness of his body, all of which persist in expressing his insistent purposes, his obsessive underminings of the will, his barely-controlled impatiences at once contained by the obsequiousness of reiterated and soothing acquiescences. The reserved tone of the young woman's replies make her voice sound a little faint, never completely free of that silence she carries within her, and into which, sometimes, she retreats.

The two voices pursue their game, prolonging it for a period that to David seems interminable. From time to time they stop talking, and then the less restrained tone with which they start up again seems to indicate that formal goodbyes are being made; but then they gradually return to the tempi of renewed effusions, to that regular rhythm that drags on endlessly, and the boy is brought back to the whiteness of the kitchen, to the sharp outlines of the furniture on which his gaze seems to be continually cutting itself, to the vacuity of the lifeless space. On those smooth surfaces the light becomes neutral. It is no longer anything more than a crude, bald, tactless illumination, an absence of shadow, uniform and flat, indifferent, a reflection of light but not of the light itself kept out behind the curtains.

III

The next day, I seem to see David standing at the edge of a clearing. He is watching the group of lumberjacks whom the sudden appearance of Dieter, furious that they should not have waited for him, has interrupted in their preparations. David's hair, one with the shadow of the undergrowth, discloses a forehead whose pallor suggests something obstinate in him. The smoothness of the skin, the absence of clear-cut features show him to be going through that process of development which is slowly bringing him to fulfilment but is still leaving him somewhat unfinished. Already there are signs of a metamorphosis: the shading of fine down on his upper lip, the straight lines of the dense eyebrows that anxiety tends to draw together.

In the same way as William's, but in a less mysterious fashion, David's face is too summary, too much his own for me to be able to recognize in him the boy I once was. With the passage of time there is an effect of distanciation: we carry our childhood within us like a legend. We can no longer identify ourselves with its hero, we never see ourselves except as someone else, the mastery of language dispossesses us of the emotions it allows us to give names to.

At the heart of the dark green depths, William's blond hair gleams with a muted brightness. He is struggling with the knot on a hank of rope he is loosening. The breadth of his shoulders, the strength of his neck, the sturdiness springing from the narrowness of the hips are in contradiction to the fiddling details of this insignificant task and are thus revealed simply as themselves, in their own right, without any other purpose than to display their tranquil aura. As if he had sensed the insistence of David's gaze, William looks back at him. He does so without moving, without modifying anything in his posture. David simply realizes that William's eyes are fixed on him, neither questioning nor hostile, a look without depth, entirely absorbed in whatever it is watching, open to everything. The young man's face betrays no feeling, he is not seeking to communicate anything; his expression is mute, it is empty: but the vacancy it evidences gives promise of total adaptability.

Dieter informs the team that they must proceed to another section and is already on his way, but after twenty metres or so he stops, turns round, waiting. Mario cannot refrain from giving the tool-chest a good kick before bending down to grab the leather belt and pass it over his shoulder. David takes advantage of the confusion and makes use of shadows, concealing branches, bushes, foliage, in order to move nearer to William.

Now he is only two steps away from him and keeps his head lowered, hands gripped behind his back as he slouches along. He is too close for such an attitude to betray hesitation, fear, timidity. William, who is carrying the loosened hanks of rope slung across his chest, is having trouble gathering together the chains and hooks he still has to pick up, but it never enters his head to ask help of the boy whose presence, so marked right at the precise moment he needs his assistance, disconcerts him. David sees the young man bent down, putting out his hand to the ground, but forced to hold on to the ropes that threaten to slip from his shoulder. David grabs the chains. They smile at one another. William starts walking. David follows him, trailing behind him the chains whose dull jinglings fill the undergrowth with the gurgling of a stream.

Renato is waiting for them, axe over one shoulder and bill-hook in hand, looking at William in astonishment. Behind him, the lumberjacks are thrusting their way into the shadows, often impeded by thickets, and looking, among the tall trunks, like dwarfs. Quintarelli's axe, the saw blades carried by Alberto send out flashes of bright, brief reflections of sunlight on their metal surfaces. On Mario's back the tool-box has the appearance of some phosphorescent object that his walk causes to shine off and on like a lantern.

'He really doesn't know what to do for the best to put himself forward as the boss,' Renato says of Dieter.

William asks him to go on. There is nothing to be heard now but the rustling of leaves beneath their feet, the crackling of snapped twigs, the chinking of the chains that in the soft mass of silence plough this sonorous furrow, singular and tendrilled like the coloured flame that twists in an agate.

David has done no more than exchange a furtive smile with William. He does not understand the reasons why this stranger has from the start shown himself to be possessed of such power, but simply being allowed to follow him, to savour his nearness, is enough to excite him. Not only does he take care not to increase the distance between them but moves even closer so that he has to watch out and not bump into his back; and whenever they get to places where they are halted by a slowing-down of those ahead, he almost presses himself against William and is overwhelmed by his proximity. Everything about him astonishes and reassures him.

William has the use of a motorbike. Around mid-morning, Dieter had sent him on an errand. He had still not returned by the end of the midday meal. So David was not interested in following the crew into the forest that day. He noted the disorder in the dining room, the piles of unwashed dishes. He suggested that he should stay in the farmhouse to tidy the place up. His offer had been well received. Renato had remarked snidely that it was young ladies' work more suited to his abilities.

Now he has finished clearing up. His long wait runs counter to the innate patience of things, the stillness weighing down upon the walls, the unbearable self-assurance of plants rejoicing in their perfect insouciance. That calm in which all existence has its being, marking our sensibilities so deeply that later, at moments of overwhelming terror, we feel a nostalgic longing for it.

His lack of occupation then leads him to a furious self-criticism – his features, his bad points, his weaknesses. He is in despair over his unmuscular calves, all scratches, the bony protuberances on his knees, his thighs' spindly slenderness, the thin, reddened wrists. He sees himself as deformed and a traitor to his real self when he thinks of the openness and ease of William's body or even Renato's. He starts to regret the situation he has put himself in and that reminds him of the plight of some small child who has been punished and made to stand in a corner. He thinks that in the company of others he would not feel such boredom. A queer sensation of grains of corn running between his thumb and index finger, swarming over his hand, rushing up his forearm and making his elbow tingle sharply prompts him to get moving.

He reminds himself why he is there. He listens for sounds from the road, striving to construct in his mind an image of William zooming along on his motorbike, his body folded in the Z-shape of a lightning flash, his blond forelock fluttering its yellow flame on the vague background of the forests. He wishes he could simply by taking thought eliminate the distance that separates them. He does not investigate the reasons why he has chosen him. He is filled with the curiosity the young man arouses in him.

But this image is mingled with memories in which William is associated with others, with Dieter, with Renato, and the questions worrying David give way to the emotions they arouse in relation to the young man. The lumberjacks too, whose looks and gestures he recalls, take their turn in occupying his thoughts, then are brushed away, leaving his gaze to stumble over stones, to wander among the spaces between the furniture, to glide over the flagged floors whose smooth unevennesses have been swept clean and fresh, to take in the spaciousness of the room he has put in order again, immobilized as it is within the order that holds it in suspense, as it does him as he waits.

The door leading to the lumberjacks' room gives him the idea of visiting it, but he realizes that this is not the place he wants to investigate. Now or never is the chance to enter the young man's den, the room he alone occupies, and where David saw him for the first time, sitting on the windowsill. If it affords no revelation of his mystery, at least his belongings will reassure him as to his reality.

Soon he finds himself in the stable, situated in the other part of the building and, as the splashes of grease on the hard earth floor would seem to indicate, it is being used as a garage. A stair to the right of the entrance leads to an upper floor. David does not succeed in discovering the signs he is looking for, the footsteps he would have liked to follow in on his way up. He is trying not to be clumsy, not to trip on the treads, not to disturb anything in the grooves of the disjointed planking, but the floor creaks at almost every step he takes, and the grains of corn rolling between his boot soles and the resounding wood make squeaks that take on a life so removed from his own, they seem to be caused by someone else's footsteps. Then, having reached a long corridor and having passed an abandoned room piled with rubbish, nothing stands between David and the room occupied by William except this door whose split panel is traversed by a long slash of light.

More from a desire to keep on the alert than not to betray his presence, he is careful not to make any noise. Also, the fear of leaving traces of his visit keeps him from touching the walls as the imbalances caused by his excessive caution provoke that possibility during his progress. In front of the door, he still does not know if he can bring himself to push it open. A final scruple restrains his hand, but it is also that sense of indecision that, once the necessary steps have been taken to effect some plan, leaves us at a loss, stupefied by the audacity it has needed, exhausted by the energy expended to realize the project we no longer feel able to carry out, and for a moment David remains immobilized in time, lucid and as it were suspended, his gesture frozen, as if he were letting himself be swallowed up by time, as if he were wandering in a state of confusion where he is gradually losing the motivation for his actions.

The crack in the panel is sufficiently wide for the eye to perceive a broad section of the interior: part of the window, the corner next to it, the bare plaster of the wall that is bumpy and stained by humidity (unless it is a remnant of faded colour from a formerly pink coating of distemper), then the sombre skirting-board covering the angle where floor and wall meet.

The unlocked door gives beneath the pressure of his hand and opens on the landscape contained in the window, then on the corner and the patch of wall already seen through the crack. Finally, appearing at the same time as a collection of clothing hung on nails, an ordinary pneumatic mattress on the couch in the corner, and on it a sleeping bag with a khaki cover. In an alcove in which some planks have been fitted to create a sort of bookshelf, William has placed a few objects: an alarm clock, a toilet case, a pair of gloves, a knapsack, magazines. At the end of the mattress, a pair of tennis shoes whose forms concentrate the light: the white canvas and the rubber reinforcements on the heels and the toecaps appear as under a magnifying glass, the texture more or less stretched to the shape of the foot, the criss-crossed laces undone parting the uppers on the limp tongue.

Absorbed in his comings and goings between these objects, David is unable to carry out his intention, which is to touch, through their mediation, the presence of the young man. He finds he is impeded by the motionless order to which William's absence reduces his modest possessions. The peaceful character of the room and everything in it is in no way affected by his intrusion, nor does it protest such an incongruity. He loses all consciousness of fear, he forgets the peculiarity of his behaviour, he allows himself to be won over by the sense of irreality the objects' indifference confers upon him. He turns to the window, he walks over to it, he is out of this world now, abandoned to his ecstasy. He checks the point of view William had on him that first evening. He could wait for his return there, sitting on the sill, copying his posture. He is astonished by the immense calm he feels at his absence from his room. He hopes that the young man will delay his return. He thinks of the latent uncertainty one feels each time one is going to meet someone again. Sometimes it only takes an hour for us to realize that someone no longer means anything to us.

On a corner of the table, isolated in its own brilliance that drips down its sides, the wineglass left there by Dieter still seems to vibrate with his energy, shine with the radiant planes of his skin, copy the tremor of his smile. The purplish crescent left by the dregs of the wine as well as the impress of his lips increase the effect of some living relic produced by this glass, which in itself is sufficient to evoke the foreman's vivid presence.

Turning his eyes away from it, David meets the look his mother is fixing on him. The slightly tense lines on her forehead give her an inquiring, rather worried physiognomy. The fixity of her eyes gazing into the boy's shows the effort she is making to fathom the nature of his reactions that seem to be causing her some remorse. Her look is already veiled with the hint of a denial, its insistence announces a protest, but then it grows troubled, betraying the disarray the young woman feels in the face of David's expression, which is neither suspicious nor condemnatory but withdrawn, become opaque, and showing no less discouragement than her own. 'You're not eating?'

An interrogative intonation for this statement which cannot disguise an anxious curiosity, soliciting some conciliatory sign, some words of reassurance. David lowers his eyes, looks at the contents of his plate and dutifully finishes what is left. The chime of his knife and fork against the porcelain, the ring of his glass when he sets it down on the table – these trifling sounds accentuate the impenetrability of the distance between his mother and himself. He is probably trying to forget the strange expression he has just caught in her face, as if it were the face of a stranger, but the reflex reaction that rejects this image continues to stiffen his attitude.

'Did Quintarelli's boy seem more communicative today?'

The subject of her question does not seem to be really at the centre of the young woman's preoccupations. Anyhow, she does not wait for a reply, but hastens to add: 'And is Mario still clowning?'

She gives a smile, hoping that the memory of the talk and gestures of the lumberjack will have some effect on David and drive away his obsessions, break the tension that makes him so stubborn, and encourage him to speak. But David keeps silent. He even exhibits some irritation at the sound of that voice to which impatience lends a discordant vibration. He cannot stand his mother's obstinate attempts to start a conversation in order to disguise her uneasiness, to have recourse to words in order to furnish the silence that would still remain just as empty, and to divert the gloomy presentiments hanging over them.

'Won't you tell me what you've been doing?'

He shrugs his shoulders. He notices the way her fingers toy with her bread, crumbling it and rolling the crumbs. Vexation wrinkles the skin on the young woman's forehead, arches her eyebrows. She gets up, as if something had made her jump. She goes to the radio standing high up on a corner bracket. With one hand on her hip, she waits until the still voiceless expiration coming through the fabric covering the loudspeaker gives way to loud crackling sounds, then she adjusts the wavelength, turns down the volume, and the strains of violins exuding a treacly melody that cannot free itself from the catarrhal hoarseness's eructations invade the room, whose space is rasped by their handsaw teeth. Their steely points grate and set the nerves on edge like the screech of blackboard chalk.

The high-pitched notes of the automatic chimes that herald the start of the broadcast news hold the attention of the young woman who wrinkles her brows and prepares to listen. She stops in mid-air the gesture she had begun, holding David's plate in one hand, suspending the other over the baked custard: she is armed with a serving-spoon with which to attack it.

After the usual formalities, the broadcaster's nasal tones deliver the news at top speed and in a voice pitched higher than normal, as if he were shouting in order to be heard better. The ceaseless sizzling of static seems almost to embody the distance it has to cover, to situate its origins beyond the earth, in a sidereal blackness pricked with flickering particles and, as if one were only perceiving the echo of the voice, it keeps fading and returning and fading again in an oscillation that sounds like the reproduction of wave patterns on the surface of the oceans. These fluctuations maltreating his delivery add to the tone – now authoritarian, now hysterical – an almost tragic coloration. David's mother stands there totally absorbed, but she slowly lowers the spoon to the custard where the cut opened by its edge in the caramelized surface lays bare the yellow, gelatinous substance that at once slides into the hollow of the serving-spoon and clings to it. With the same precautionary slowness, as if the slightest clumsiness would draw down wrath upon her head, she lifts the portion she has manoeuvred on to the spoon, raises the quivering, many-faceted shape, transfers it to the plate on which she carefully deposits it, then returns the spoon to the dessert dish to scoop up the syrup and enrobe the portion on the plate with it, not once but twice, always just as slowly, as delicately, solemnly.

The disembodied voice is now in full flood, rattling on with a regularity that allows no pause between phrases and homogenizes his discourse. As every word he utters is recharged with a supplement of energy, his voice appears always to have more to spend, and as it gradually swells, progresses through more and more ample periods, linking up the words faster and faster, until it sounds as if it is attaining successive plateaux, like the voice of someone in the grip of mounting anger. In the room saturated with its reverberations it creates a nervous agitation that makes the objects shrink into themselves, seems to exasperate them so much that the light appears to be vibrating all round them. Just as one contracts to the onset of cold weather, David rounds his shoulders, draws his elbows in to his sides, cannot envisage any communication except with himself. His own home has become foreign to him, and as for the dessert, that nevertheless stands witness to the affection in which he is held, he stares at it wobbling on his plate as if it had suddenly moved out of his reach or as if he himself had relinquished the faculty of appreciating it, was no longer able to take pleasure in this taste of cream, sugar, vanilla and caramel so softly presented by the stuff when it melts in the mouth.

Despite the feeling of shame it gives him, a reflex left over from infancy forces him to raise his eyes to his mother, to seek for her assistance. She has not helped herself: she is sitting there motionless, her hands placed flat on either side of her plate, her body tensely arched, her strained throat all tendons, her head turned towards the radio to listen, her face a mask. Another voice has succeeded the first, more distant, submerged in a denser drizzle of crackling static supplemented from time to time by salvos of applause or interrupted by shrill vituperative chants. David asks what has happened. With a movement of impatience, the young woman jerks her head away, stands listening. Then her face relaxes but retains its concerned expression.

'There's been another bomb attack,' she said. 'Many dead. Don't you want your dessert?'

Her eyes stare at the boy, open wider as she scans his face, trying to find there some accord that has now become impossible. She stands up, begins to clear the table; the sharp, quick noises she makes with her crisp little movements are damped by the persistent screeching of the radio. She cannot suppress a shudder.

'It'll all end badly,' she predicts.

She carries the dishes to the sink. The opening in her dress accentuates the fragility of her neck swept by the curling end of her ponytail. Everything around her looks just as fragile, isolated, precarious.

David goes to the window. The streets are empty. The asphalt turning blue. Under the plane trees in the square there is not a breath of wind. The town, kept at home by the broadcast voices that converge in one lugubrious echo among the house fronts, has abandoned its alleys to the swifts. Their swooping flight, like showers of filings, keeps spreading their piercing cries all over the street.

IV

Today, David is seated at the table next to William. In the half-light, the animation that the shared meal and brief conversational exchanges confer on heads lowering and rising, bare arms stretching and glistening serves as a cover for his presence now unembarrassed by the consequences of his reserve but liberated in a kind of rapturous light-headedness. The rapidity with which has been realized what only yesterday was just a dream is making his head swim.

Renato, given by his father a job that took him away just as William was coming back from the pump, left the field open for David who, never having left the young man's side all morning, felt entitled to follow him. Before sitting down next to him in Renato's place, he had a moment's hesitation, especially as the latter, suddenly reappearing, was hurrying to claim it. David would never have had the nerve to argue with him about it, but Mario, sitting opposite, delighted to have him seated in front of him, urged him to take the place on the bench, as did Quintarelli, who accompanied his welcoming smile with a meaningful nod of his head, and even William, whose back and nape, expressionless, showed he was resigned to having a new table companion. Renato could do nothing but clench his fists and sit down opposite his father in the only remaining place.

Their being brought together delights the lumberjacks, for it takes the boy away from Dieter and strengthens their crew; and though William persists in remaining silent, in keeping his distance, he seems, through his very taciturnity, to be in charge of the boy, to be preparing the ground for him, to be sponsoring him in a curious way.

At table, Mario redoubles his intermediations, bending to one side, then to the other, playing all at one and the same time host and waiter, serving-maid and lady of the house. He flourishes the wine bottle, fills the glasses, inspects the contents of everybody's plate, presses second helpings on them. He lends his gestures an expansiveness appropriate to the ambience of some festive dinner party, without ever losing the thread of the conversation in which he talks twenty to the dozen. In the full flood of his tirades, he takes visible pleasure in giving play to the varied registers of his voice whose supplies of breath sometimes have difficulty in supporting such expenditures of passion. He addresses his monologue to no one in particular: an impulse sprung from the depths of his being finds its only release in this grandiloquence, a sort of chant through which pours an irresistible longing for music and celebration.

Like those people who have no illusions about themselves or because of fundamental humility dwell apart from life, by a willing self-disparagement also; who exist in fact through the procuration of happiness to which they feel they themselves have no right, Mario has indeed already shown himself anxious, this morning, to help David get closer to William. Renato had again left David on the sidelines while he was clearing the undergrowth with William. Mario had pretended to criticize them for inefficiency and had offered to lend them a hand, claiming that they would never manage without him. By dividing the labour, he paired with Renato, and, ignoring the protests of the latter whose anger was making him insolent, left David working with William, assigning tasks that required their collaboration. Thus it was that David had not left the young man's side all morning.

At first, this companionship created embarrassments. The care they took to avoid looking at one another only resulted in making them more aware of one another: if David kept on waiting for instructions or orders, William remained out of countenance by David's confidence in him, and, having no intention of seeking his help, continued working as if the boy was not there. Then, by the lucky chance of a clumsy mistake that made them both laugh, a blunder by David that brought William to his assistance, or difficulties in manoeuvring a branch, they forgot to keep watch over themselves, and exchanged glances with hints of amusement. Their gestures were in harmony, and William was able to bring himself to advise David, giving him brief suggestions to which he lent the possibility of an option on David's part, as if he were afraid of wounding him by issuing too precise orders. Their jobs cut them off from the others, and it also kept *them* at a distance. There came moments, the silence becoming more intense caused them to notice it, when the shyness they had felt at the beginning would return, even more painful than before. William would look at David. Under the thick blond forelock his steady gaze seemed to intensify the blue of his eyes. David would look at William, letting himself be dazzled by his blond beauty, self-forgetting in the contemplation of his rather tough features.

Displeased at being ignored, Dieter finally lets his presence be felt. His chair creaks as he shifts his weight in it, the hobnails of his boots make the flagged floor screech: he clears his throat.

'Did you hear the news?'

They all turn towards him. Leaning forward, elbows on thighs, he is examining his hands, turning them this way and that, playing with his wedding ring that he keeps pushing down to the base of his ring finger. He looks up at Quintarelli.

'It's going to be civil war all right.'

Mario and Alberto exchange glances to see if they have to take the foreman seriously. The latter keeps looking at his hands. The grave tone of his voice takes on a lugubrious note:

'There was another bomb attack yesterday. And this is just a beginning let me tell you.'

A smile twists his lips, an access of indignation lifts his shoulders at the same time as a little whistling breath escapes from his nostrils.

'The plans are well laid. There's no two ways to go about the downfall of a country. I know what I'm talking about. I had all the time in the world to watch them at work, over in Indo-China.'

Holding out an arm, he points a finger, indicating beyond the walls and the mountains an enemy who, surprised by his gesture, would at once take cover.

'Because they are all the same, it's no use kidding ourselves . . .'

Anger lifts his head on his upstretched neck; the hairs stand up on his weatherbeaten flesh that gleams like metal. His lips struggle to get out the flood of words that jostle for release and to which their impediment now lends a crisper sonority, as if he were lisping:

'Only their tactics are getting more sophisticated. It's child's play to stir up the Viets or the Wogs: a bit of lolly here, a bit of lolly there, a lot of fine talk about liberty and Bob's your uncle. But what their aim is now, is to sow discord among the French, you mark my words, and them as will fall into the trap are not lacking, beginning with that bunch of buffoons in Parliament who waste their time passing the hat round. A pretty sight, I must say!'

Opposite David, Mario is showing signs of impatience. His fingers are drumming on the table. Dieter's voice has slipped into a rhythm that suggests he is now well away.

'They should be kicked out on their arses, the bloody lot of them. We've got their ticket, they've shown the kind of stuff they're made of: no more order in society, no more ideals, the young 'uns with nothing but fuck on their minds.'

The hammered rhythm his delivery gave these last few words seemed to have been put on for the benefit of some precise individual.

'We're not capable of keeping an army together. The conscripts skedaddle, they just have to pull certain wires. They'll not be troubled, the authorities close their eyes. And as they're not overburdened with a sense of honour . . .'

There is a gathering tension that threatens to explode at any moment. But Dieter forges ahead:

'It's what they call having bullshit for bollocks.'

Proud of the effect he has produced, he pulls in his belly and puffs out his chest. He rummages in the haversack lying on the floor beside his chair. He bites into an apple after having polished it between his palms. A look that Alberto casts at William convinces David that the young man was the object of this attack. Apparently he has taken it without flinching but his forearms are trembling, planted on the edge of the table, their muscles are working under the effects of other contractions than those caused by the movements of his fingers occupied in picking the seeds out of a handful of grapes. He suddenly stands up, steps over the bench. His face expresses nothing, he looks absolutely serene, a little distant. He walks away, his hands in his pockets, unhurried, with supple ease that lends his figure an insolent nonchalance. One could have almost sworn that, sensing Dieter's gaze behind his back, he slowed his walk, taking pleasure in answering him simply by the splendour of his person.

In the farmyard now David is drifting dreamily, aimlessly. His head lowered, his arms loose at his sides, dragging his feet, he barely disturbs the general torpor of the afternoon. He gives the impression, as he dawdles at the heart of so much immobility, that he is exhausting the small stock of energy informing his listlessness, and even losing part of his substance. From time to time he seeks the shade of the coach-house. He sits on the block used to sharpen blades of bill-hooks and axes, but does not stay there long. He returns to the sunlight on the yard where once more his footsteps seem to sink into the earth and bring him automatically back beneath the lean-to roof.

Mario has not touched the dirty dishes. He has gone to the bedroom where the others have followed him one by one, Renato among them. David has avoided Dieter's company: he had rushed blindly out of the dining room, with the vague idea of having to do something to repair the damage, to safeguard his own presence in the place. And now he is putting it off, obsessed by the idea of going up to William's room but incapable of bringing himself to do so.

It is not so long since I felt myself less bound by scruples of that nature. Age and experience armour us with various ruses for approaching someone. The sense of our common miseries and the ability to renounce it all in the event of incompatibility put into perspective, even when desire is involved, the true importance of an encounter, depriving it, true enough, of the poignant character, torturingly voluptuous, that the pangs of misgiving invest it with. It is not without nostalgia that I recall the nervous agitation aroused in me in anticipating the moves, the words, the gestures I proposed to employ whenever the occasion presented itself to approach the person I was unable to stop thinking of; or whenever I experienced the urge to do so, and found myself on the verge of surrendering to my longing. The passage to the act demanded of me something more than the negotiation of the distance between us: it entailed disturbing the tranquillity of existence, struggling against the current that is the universal harmony of things, battling against an inanimate mass which, like some enormous pneumatic mattress, would keep on pushing me back.

The possibility that I might have a chilly reception or be made to look an idiot caused me less anguish than the prospect of an acquiescence following which I would not know how to conduct myself: I only surmised that I should once and for all be confronted by the real, without the possibility of resorting to any kind of self-defence, unable to envisage any form of retreat, finding myself stripped naked, with nothing to offer.

In those borderline situations such as the one in which David now finds himself, it would nevertheless so happen that my desire was stronger than everything. The accumulated tension would act as a propulsive force, and I would take the plunge, as David suddenly does, with trembling legs, with pounding heart.

He enters the stables. In the shadows he distinguishes patches of brilliance that suggest the curving chromium tubes of the motorbike, the blissful orb of the headlamp. The powerful odour of sawdust and hayloft makes him pause at the bottom of the steps. He is still allowing himself the option of beating a retreat, so he goes up the stairs without making any noise. At the end of the corridor stands the door to William's room, so tight shut, one might almost say it was bulging under the pressure of a presence it is having difficulty in containing. Blocking the perspective made even deeper by the half-light, and whose vanishing traces radiate from each of its corners, the door still seems to be situated a long way off, inaccessible as a door in a dream, not so much giving an impression of sealing up the interiority it protects as of being enthralled by the introspective, painstaking, silent inner activity over which it stands guard, and which it obstructs like the head and shoulders of a spectator in a front row at the theatre. If it were not for the crack that slashes the upper panel and lends it a gleam of that keen, slightly perfidious attention seen in a cat's eye, the door would appear inert, obtuse.

David thinks he is still far away from that door panel when he is separated from it only by a thin layer of air he just needs to break with his hand in order to knock on it, but suddenly it seems to him that distance is impenetrable, or is confused with the space that always exists between the conception of a gesture and its actual realization. He loses his way, gets bogged down in it, exhausts his strength attempting to connect the notion of knocking with the muscles he has to call upon to perform the act.

However he notices that the sharp light glinting through the crack in the panel is alive with nictitations, as if something opaque and mobile lay at the perimeter of its source. David draws nearer. The crack imprints itself on his face – a ribbon of light that gradually narrows until it becomes no more than a fine incandescent vertical streak coming to rest exactly upon his eye.

The young man, standing at a distance from the window, three-quarter length, legs straddled, torso arching, is outlined against the wall that is freckled with stains, impregnated with rusty rivulets left by the damp. He stands with arched back, chin lifted, eyes closed, and a slow rotation of his pelvis imparts a languorous undulation to his body. The tension lifting his face seems to be making it strain upwards towards some other face. His whole attitude appears to be one of prayer. A faint crooning accompanies his oscillations, like a low moaning, a lament.

Compelled more by respect than by fear, David draws away. He retains a clear image of a figure bent backwards, trapped in the tightly-stretched folds of the khaki dungarees, abandoning itself to the lurchings of a willed intoxication, obedient to the memory of a litany that carries him away in its embrace. He sees again the tangled spikes of fair hair, the quicksilver line accenting the outline of the nose, the curve of the smooth chin, the thrust of the Adam's apple. This image would be enough to nourish his daydreams for a long time, but some force impels him to take another look.

Planted there on buttressing legs as if he were confronting an audience with this provocative pose, William is jerking his hips, making this pendulum movement as if to free himself from a harness, to extricate himself from a hole, to work himself free of some clinging sheath that refuses to release him. The zip fastener gapes open in an elongated V on his torso. The light emphasises the contrast between his smooth skin and the material's coarse wrinkles. Elbows pressed to his sides, William is plunging his hands into his crotch, where, with slow, deliberate manipulations, they are kneading some obscure mass. His features are deformed by grimaces. His closed eyes form two soft, deep, mysterious long stains. The lock of hair, flung over the thrown-back head, reveals that surly, severe side of his nature David had always suspected.

For a moment, David is conscious of being granted something he had always felt the need for, independently of William. He had long since been searching for this scene from which, without foreseeing what it might represent, he had expected to receive some profound shock. He could not have asked for anyone better than William to give it to him. Nor could he have received a more explicit revelation. He finds himself confronted with the vision he had longed for, but too quickly and in too absolute a way not to feel taken aback by it now. The coincidence that offers it to him is something of a miracle, giving his vision the suspect aura of chance, and augmenting its power by the impact of fatality.

He watches the young man whose movements are becoming more unrestrained. He sees him adopt a more exaggerated stance under the shot of pain that, coming from between his thighs, is flooding his chest. The young man is writhing as if to diminish its force, or, possibly, to provoke it further. Hips jutting out, he rocks back and forth, contracts his belly muscles, and his palm seems to make the taut flesh shiver as if it is being stroked with a feather. Higher up, his other hand squeezes the nipples, caresses the fullness of the shoulders from which he is dragging the top of the dungarees. His face exhibits intense concentration. He scowls, his lips are parting, his features now suggest he is on the rack, now relaxed, as if illuminated.

The rocking and rotation of his hips now take on a more expansive intensity. His quickening breath leaves his mouth in a panting hiss. The outline of his ribs appears on his flanks, as well as the arc of the thoracic cage, beneath which the abdominal wall contracts, forming a hollow haunted by shadow. The young man, his erect member dragged out of the opening in the zipper, gives it thrust upon thrust in the vice of his clamped fingers. Sliding in his fist, the weapon keeps darting the tip of its empurpled piston, vibrant, delivered from its foreskin that the back-and-forth agitations of the hand wrinkle then stretch to tearing point. Under the garrotte of the fingers, a whole network of veins and engorged blood vessels maps the long cylinder of muscle.

Spreading his legs a little further, and bending them at the knees, he arches his spine, shoving out his chest and countering its thrust with an incurving of the loins, momentarily giving his figure the contorsion of a votive statuette, then, with a violent jerk, driving his hips forward as if he was wanting to pack his whole being into his brandished sex. He grits his teeth, the column of the trachea swells in his bared, abandoned neck, the jaw muscles stand out under the ear, the meanders of an artery are embossed on his temple.

The deep-seated rolling of his haunches accelerates. It seems to respond to the beat of some pulsation beyond himself. He can no longer dominate the to-and-fro of his hand on his sex and does not know how he could stem the increasingly powerful contractions that are convulsing him. Carried away by this galloping stallion, for a moment he seems to be going mad, and hoarse little cries interrupt the panting rhythms. A sudden impact almost lifts him off the ground, and, as if seized by a violent impulse to vomit, makes him arch downwards over his tool, itself arched in the opposite direction under the bonded fingers that are throttling it at the root. His head drops forward, mouth wide for a shout released only after a gush of hot candle-wax spurts from the engorged muscle in a great jet of foam transfixed by the light, as if hanging there suspended a moment. Further jolts keep forcing from the tip of the strangled engine great clots of that sap that propulses pearl after pearl, sliding and snaking over the fingers, with breaks in which its flow is swollen by tears.

Raising his head, William, using prolonged pressure, is busy squeezing out the last oozings. Convulsive shudders signal the final spasms. He gazes down at the lump of swollen flesh in his fingers as if it were something that no longer belongs to him. He takes a handkerchief out of his pocket and wraps it round his prick. Despite these precautions, he cannot attenuate the scorching sensations caused by the friction of the rough cloth on his member. Unwrapped again, the cock is jewelled by the light that emphasizes the tooling of the veins and its fish-like shape, that still keeps its stiffness. It oscillates horizontally above the dangling metal tag of the zip, where there are glimpses of tufted hair shining like fine wood shavings. As if endowed with an existence all its own, like a baby dandled on its mother's breast, it wobbles from side to side as it appears to let itself be carried off by William when he turns towards the window, takes up a magazine David had not noticed on the windowsill. The young man's silhouette stands out like a shadow puppet against the brilliance of the day, moves back into the centre of the room, leaves David's field of vision.

David can still follow the soft tread of William's bare feet. He catches the rustle and slap of the magazine tossed on a shelf, the dull sound of a body collapsing. Then all is silence, and, in the dusk of the corridor, among the smells of sawdust, soot and grime, as well as in the sense of numbness like that experienced in an attack of fever, not unconnected with the feeling of blissful fullness happiness brings, he hears nothing more than the dull, slow pounding of his own heart.

This evening, he wastes no time in going up to his room. A great burden is weighing on him. He feels bruised all over, as if he had been beaten. It has nothing to do with physical fatigue, even though he does feel dead-beat, even though his skin has an aching smart, as if it had been subjected to rough treatment. It is caused, he is sure, by the protracted turmoil unleashed within him by the knowledge he will henceforth be the depository of.

Until now, he had only been able to surmise, but now he knows, he has seen with his own eyes. No, he has not been shocked; has he not already begun to detect within his own body an annunciation that kept urging him towards self-discovery and inspired him to turn to William? The young man has revealed to him the power, the importunity, the impetuosity of that annunciation, he has demonstrated to him the awesome pantings, the scorchings, the abrasions, the groaning sighs, the gulping breaths in which one cannot avoid plunging in response to that call whose fulfilment is a collapse into a simulacrum of death.

Stretching his arms and arching his back, David slips off his shirt whose taut fabric strains against his shoulder-blades, grazes his hips. He frees his arms from the sleeves one after the other but he keeps the shirt on his knees. His face expresses a wonderment from which it seems he cannot shake himself free. Behold, he has had before his eyes the revealed form of Man. Before his gaze filled with the startled innocence of some young wild beast, the most fascinating creature in all creation has divested itself of its envelope, has cast the coat of its outer skin, has forgotten its distrust and its dissimulations; it has opened its raiment and revealed the flexible outlines of its secret flesh, it has lifted up its voice in the communion of light and shade to cry out the enrapturing harmonies of its body's abundance, it has rendered its message even more accessible by its movements that underscored the melody's hoarse modulations and unveiled the mysteries of the chant's elaboration as it was conducted through the unending developments of its phrasings and re-echoings.

David has witnessed that. From that vision, he has retained something to be held in safe keeping – something like the secret of the world. He draws from it the sense of a benediction that reconciles him with himself. But this grace burdens him with a responsibility for which he doubts he possesses the necessary strength and dignity. Already he feels himself to be as ancient, as wise, as mysterious as the walls guarding the intimity of the young man, as mute as the trees and the mosses that are the confidants of his preoccupations and his memory, as full of awareness as the moon and the stars that were present witnesses of his story long before he was, and to which has been granted the power to follow him always.

He regrets not having obeyed the compassionate impulse that drove him towards William. He waited for him in the stable, near the motorbike – whose seats and streamlined metal his hands have timidly stroked. When he heard from upstairs the creaking of beams indicating that William was getting up, he had felt relief rather than fear. But gradually, hearing his footsteps running along the corridor and then descending the stairs, making him realize that another meeting was imminent, he was seized by an insurmountable anguish that was not far from panic.

William noticed him, and drew near. In the half-light, David could see his eyes, experience the condescending sweetness of a smile. William asked him how he liked the motorbike, and plied him with other questions, a note of amusement trembling in his voice. David did not succeed in finding his own voice, for he was beyond words. He could not take his eyes away from that profile he had seen just a short while ago, head thrown back, jaws set with torment, then the face radiant in the vertigo of some exquisite sensation, finally the features racked by a monstrous effort that compressed all his muscles, swelled his veins, wrenched open his jaws on parted lips – and now he was experiencing a sort of distrust at the sight of this handsome mask, lacking that former wild abandon, which the young man turned towards him.

In the dusk of his room where the furniture seems in retreat against the walls, the mirror on the wardrobe door stands out as a pool of reflected light and appears to be waiting, to be calling to him, urging him to confide in it. From the place where he is sitting, the boy can see himself reflected full-length, clearly outlined on the sombre background. Not caring to examine himself more closely, he followed the swooping circles of the swifts high in the sky. As if one part of his attention had not given up verifying what the looking glass had shown him, he returns to it, despite the reticence he feels. That boy seated, naked, pale, his thighs half covered by the folds of a shirt which his hands pull over his stomach, the scared gaze, the trembling lips, all surprise him as much as he, too, seems surprised within the glass. He considers the smooth forms of the muscles outlined beneath his skin, but which still lack volume. A kind of vexation lends a hint of bitterness to the line at the corner of his mouth. With a fingertip, in a hasty, self-conscious movement common to gestures that one attempts for the first time, he smoothes one of his eyebrows whose irregularity suddenly displeases him. He does the same thing with his hair which he tries to flatten at the front where there is a rebellious lock. His face defies all his efforts. He turns his eyes away from it then immediately brings them back to the reflection as if, by attempting to catch his face unawares, he was wishing to see himself as he appears to others, but is incapable of snapping the bond between himself and his image. He explores his features, perhaps hoping to discover their provenance, and regretting that nothing in his cells and in his blood can help him get closer, even just a little closer to William.

He stands up, leans out of the window, and is enveloped in the warmth and the dusty smell exhaled by the walls, the trees, the pavements. There are couples exchanging polite nods in passing. He hears the shouts and laughter coming from a group of youths gathered in one corner of the square, under the plane trees. He raises his head and looks at the mountain peaks that dominate the town, reddened by the fires of the sunset. From down in the valley, piercing successive layers, he can hear the tinkling sounds of the river running over the pebbles.

V

The distribution of the various tasks this morning has once more placed David in the company of Renato and William. At some distance from the rest of the crew busy sawing the branches of felled trees, they have been ordered by Dieter to pile up the logs scattered over a certain section, where they are beginning to be covered with mould. They work in silence, in the rustling of leaves crushed underfoot, in the acrid smell of earth broken up by the dragging of tree trunks. The widely scattered logs allow them on occasion to wander among the trees. When they pass under them, they receive from the rays slanting through the forest dimness, a douche of light from which their figures seem to take fire like torches.

    Not bothering with Renato, who himself ignores him, David is waiting for a chance to join William. Taking advantage of their comings and goings, they could hardly fail indeed to find themselves close to one another, even though the nature of the job makes it difficult for them to meet and above all to stop and talk. One of them would have to wait for the other or to change direction, to attract his attention with an obvious gesture, a word, a look inviting a closer approach. David supposes that William would never think of taking such an initiative. As he does not suspect how perspicacious William's casual glance at him can be, he does not appreciate its significance, so there is nothing in it to make him take heed or to worry about it.

His figure appears, disappears, reappears among the trunks. It almost blends in with the vegetation, for it disturbs nothing of the calmness of branches and foliage in the broad current of cool air that circulates between the trunks and above the thickets. Even the glint of his blond locks seems to become part of the shimmering of spots of sunlight scattered on the leaves by the slanting shafts. The noises he makes are absorbed in the continuous rustling of vegetable life, they do not intrude upon the stillness emanating from the tall, straight trunks, from the irresistible movement of their growth, scarcely grazed from time to time by the soughing of a yielding branch, by the grinding of bark, by a snapping of twigs, an impact, the dull, soft sound of something falling on the pine-needled humus.

David cannot help anticipating that the young man might deflect his course towards his own. Emotion makes his heart start pounding when he sees him moving in his direction, and even more so when his breathings, the rubbing of the legs of his dungarees against one another, the crack of logs as they knock together in his arms, the rustling of grasses or branches he brushes past bring his body nearer, make his presence felt. David, disguising his watchfulness by the care he pretends to give to the collection and transportation of his own logs, is always expecting William to be on the point of bumping into him.

The young man disappears, reappears. The weight of the logs causes him to arch his body backwards, and in order to avoid tripping over obstacles he cannot see he lifts his feet higher in an exaggerated way, giving his walk a somewhat military appearance. Sometimes he allows himself a breather and stands with hands on hips examining something or other in the grass at his feet. David only needs to move a few paces to be able to observe his silhouette among the tree trunks. The illumination, though shadowy, picks his figure out with a precision it could never have in the diffused, dusty light of open territory. A flexing contour clings to the elasticity of his limbs whose forms are enhanced by the lurchings of his hips: an overwhelming sensation of massively structured flesh animated by a force that exploits all the density of its solid substance surges from the broad arch of his shoulders, from the parentheses of his arms curving on either side of his torso, from the ample bulges the dungarees mould here and there from slabs of muscle all along his thighs, his supple flanks. William, relaxing his vigilance, is now lost in daydreams, and the other personage whom David had caught unawares in his room, throbbing with the dedicated will to make ritual offering of his entire being, manifests himself again in the released body, the averted face.

David cannot turn his gaze to the grasses at his feet, to the leaves that brush his face, to the branches and the trunks of the fir trees without receiving intimations of a tension forever on the verge of explosion in their shapes, in their consistency, the irrepressible and terrifying vigour that holds them erect, floods their tissues, stretches their fibres, engorges their veins and cells. Everything in the upsurging of the oozing, mossy trunks evokes that intumescence of matter, called upon to overload its mass, transported by the torsional rigidity that dilates it. Even the knots on the logs communicate to his hands the sensation of power kept imprisoned in the ligneous fibres, the vertiginous force that persistently irradiates the inflexible contours of the timber.

At last he resolves to reach the pile of logs at the same time as William is unloading his armful. The latter thinks he is asking his help. The boy's perseverance in following him gives his attachment a gravity that disturbs William, who feels it invests him with an important responsibility to fulfil a hope, an ideal he does not wish to represent. But in the end he turns towards David. Under his blond forelock, the eyes show the irises starring the pupils with their blue paillettes like a bunch of needles. It is almost impossible to endure their corrosive force and no less impossible to look away from it.

David approaches with his armload of logs. At that moment, a rapid flickering of the eyelids serves to efface that perfidious tension in William's face: he lowers his eyes, shifts his weight to the other foot, and the first hint of a smile draws his lips to one side where their corner is lifted into the creased cheek. He raises his head, seizes one of the logs David is offering him and with a swift swivelling of the torso casts it on top of the pile where he steadies it before turning back to take the next one.

Renato now appears and calls to William. He indicates David with un upward jerk of the chin:

'Found someone to serve mass for you?'

He gives a few bursts of forced laughter, that make his shoulders heave. William's bewildered expression prompts him to explain:

'Don't you see? He looks as if he's offering the altar cruets.'

William gives him a faint smile then gives David a brief but significant look as he lifts the two logs of wood that remain in his arms. They move away together, to the annoyance of Renato, who looks after them with a spiteful expression on his face. David would like to start the dialogue this companionship seems to invite, but cannot think of anything to say. All his faculties are absorbed by the unique perception he now has of the world ever since he heard the rhythmical rustling of William's footsteps at his side, the faint squeakings of the stiff cloth rubbing on his skin, the warm energy radiating from the flesh of his palms swinging in the shade a little lower than his hips. The young man is no longer daydreaming. If he has been asking himself questions about David, he has now forgotten them. He does not attempt to avoid his gaze: he allows himself to be invaded by the mystery created for him by David's admiring attitude.

William did not wait for the end of the meal before leaving and going to lie down in the meadow, beyond the orchard. It was not that Dieter had been disagreeable again. He had spoken only about plans with Quintarelli. Their discussion left the others free to chatter among themselves, and they seized the opportunity. Alberto was in a particularly lively mood. Mario had played the buffoon, telling silly jokes that made it difficult to keep a straight face. Renato also had taken part, more at ease now that he had regained his place next to William. But William remained distant despite the encouragements he received, ignoring inducements to enter the conversation and seeming irritated when they became too pressing. David had felt some scruples about taking part in the general gaiety. He would have liked to show the young man that he was still paying him attention; he would even have liked to share his serious mood, to join him in that reserve that made him seem more endowed with the secrets of human existence. He had felt himself cast aside and covered with the same scorn as that accorded to the others when, in the midst of shouts and bursts of laughter, William had got up and with his indolent walk, his mask of discontent had left the room.

He was able to follow him with his eyes, saw him crossing the yard, moving into the shadows of the orchard where the foliage kept on shaking after his passage, scattered with luminous sparklings like flickering eyelids. The boy was able to shake off Mario's company, escape Renato's vigilance and reach the orchard by making a wide detour. Now he is crouched under the twisted boughs of the old pear trees, his back leaning against a black tree trunk. He is watching the young man through tangles of grass stalks like the cames of a stained-glass window, and he has the feeling of being present at the advent of a body beginning to take shape, hoisting itself out of the primeval clay, irradiated with its own glory, like a dream of created matter. It is not someone stranded, marked with a secret wound, taking refuge in the unconsciousness of dreams or of self-destruction, but a being arisen from the grasses, the wild flowers, intent upon the forces at work fashioning him, absorbed in his unfoldment, in that fulfilling demanded of him in order that he may offer himself and be taken.

The body is floating above David's line of vision: he is afraid to move, for he wants to go on contemplating all those things he can never have enough of – that torso and that face laid among the grasses, so tender in repose, so calm, so attractive that even the insects are drawn to them, swarm above him, one or two unable to resist alighting on him, producing on his skin tiny moving patches that become trapped in the fine layer of his sweat.

At the same time, William's immobility makes him impatient. He longs for no less than he fears the moment when the young man will open his eyes, sit up, get to his feet. From the full height of his frame increased by the situation he occupies half-way up the orchard slope, will his gaze descend to where the boy is crouching? Will he walk down to him and stop right beside him, illuminating his loneliness with a smile? Will he give him the courage simply through the expression on his face, by a little tap on the cheek, perhaps, to accept unafraid his emotion, to restrain no longer the urge within him? The young man for the moment is still lying there in the grass, absorbed in his own thoughts or dreaming of something quite different. He is still all gentleness, he is stretched out there in the full bloom of his youth among the intertwining branches, the festoons of foliage, among the blue centaureas and the purple inflorescence of carnations.

With what appears to be a reflex reaction freeing William from some unpleasant thought, he raises his head into line with the rest of his body. As soon as he opens his eyes he blinks them rapidly under the intensity of the sunlight. He shades them with his hands, their palms turned towards the sun, and remains a moment thus, in that posture that displays the breadth of his chest. Using his abdominals, he sits up, draws up his legs, rests his fore-arms on his knees while his hands hang between them.

This could be the chance David has been waiting for to come out of the shade, not trying to hide that he had been watching him, that he had been waiting for this moment to manifest his presence in order, quite simply, to offer it to him, if it might happen to amuse him. William has pulled up a long grass stalk, bending it until it breaks between his fingers. However, he continues to pursue thoughts of some impulsive act of vengeance that contract his jaw muscles. There is nothing left of the grass stalk but a mutilated sprig that he throws away. He jumps to his feet. He lets himself be carried away by the slope whose steepness causes him to lengthen his stride.

David extricates himself from the orchard's tangled branches and is about to run towards him when William suddenly changes his course, giving him a shock that keeps him riveted to the spot. William approaches the bushes where a trickle of water overflowing from the pump basin helps to form there a quagmire where bramble bushes flourish. He straddles his legs, swiftly unzips the fly of his dungarees, hauls out his cock and calmly pisses, gazing all the while at the bright yellow, twisting jet that he shoots as far as he can. In that sturdy pose, he is radiant with a strangely majestic nonchalance, princely in its self-assurance. The little shakes he gives the docile appendix followed by a brief shudder and the rocking motion of his pelvis when he stows it away all evidence the same sovereign insouciance.

Bending now over the pump, William holds his hands under the stream of water. He rubs them together then cups them and splashes his face, neck and chest. He sprinkles all round him drops of spray that, against the black screen of the lilacs, glitter like crystal beads before vanishing. Refreshed, with gleaming skin, he walks round the pump, crosses the yard and reaches the stable.

There is no need now for David to keep back in the orchard shadows. He makes straight for the door through which William has disappeared. He does not want to lose another opportunity, so he hurries, running at top speed: but a few steps from the door he sees Renato who looks him scornfully up and down.

'Piss off!' he says in a low voice. 'And there's no point in hanging around, either!'

At once he turns on his heel and goes back inside where his voice can be heard, gentler now, because he is speaking to William. From chance words he catches, David guesses that he must be asking him what he's busy doing to his motorbike, beside which he is probably kneeling. Renato adopts the tone of a connoisseur and goes so far as to offer advice, launching out into long explanations that take on the tempo of some personal anecdote that requires him to employ onomatopoeias imitating reckless accelerations, corners taken at full speed, peto-maniac backfirings, more or less well-controlled screaming skids. Then David hears him ask the young man if he is thinking of going to town that evening.

The reply is long in coming, and its sense is lost in the guttural sounds of a gruff murmur. David cannot make head nor tail of it. He draws nearer. Renato's voice is heard again, but only the Christian names it is listing catch David's ear, as if the voice were trying to articulate these words more clearly. He gathers the talk is about a certain Stéphane whom William often meets and who is also working in the woods: together they keep company with common friends, girls whose names resemble a kind of litany or counting-out rhyme: Françoise, Tina, Janina, Isabelle. Renato is laughing about some boy nicknamed 'Fifteen Centimetres' and comments on the jokes of a certain 'Fag End'.

David moves away from the wall and shows himself in the opening of the door. Why would William want to share Renato's animosity towards him? David steps inside, guided in the dimness by the golden gleam of William's hair, whose face he sees on a level with the motorbike's broad tank. Leaping out from behind the bike, Renato comes and gives him two blows on the chest, screaming:

'What did I tell you! I warned you! Don't you understand French?'

His voice is toneless, as if his mouth was dry. He

does not give David time to answer:
'We don't want little queers like you here, got it?'
David steps aside. He is about to take the young man to witness. But Renato bursts out with:
'You have to watch out with that kind. Fucking plague they are. I don't know what he's up to, but he's spying on you. He hid himself in the orchard to spy on you. He was watching you pissing, there, right there! And now he's snooping around here!'
William stands up, brushes aside his forelock and looks at David who does not know how to protest his innocence. Renato goes up to him, and shouts at him even louder, almost spitting in his face:
'Fucking pervert! You bloody sneak! Get out!'
'Who d'you think you are?' David counters.
'One more step and I'll let you have it!'
Resolutely, calmly, experiencing a certain relish in his rashness, David takes a step towards William. Renato hurls himself upon David and throws him to the ground. His precise, nervous movements, their energy unleashed all the more by anger, take David by surprise: he's on his back, his legs pinioned between Renato's gripping knees, his arms pinned to the floor by the other boy's hands that press on his wrists with all his weight.
'So come on, out with it!' he growls, in a voice distorted by rage. 'I dare you to deny you were in the orchard! It was no accident, was it? Out picking apples, eh? Well? What you waiting for? Spit it out! What you doing here sneaking and snooping everywhere? If it's because you never seen a man's prick, what for you don't ask Dieter to show you his, eh? Not big enough for you, is it, Dieter's? Not to your taste, Dieter's little knob? Doesn't he have one? Come on, spit it out!'
Having witnessed this confrontation until now without really understanding what it's all about, William now tries to intervene, but all he does is tap

Renato's shoulder to make him let go of David, and then jerks his head in the direction of the yard, but Renato does not leave.

Furious at not having received any answer from David, not having made him give a single cry, not even a grimace, Renato doesn't want to abandon his prey. But he gradually releases his grip, then jumps to his feet. But he doesn't wait for David to stand up straight again before he throws himself upon him once more, seizes his wrist and twists it behind his back.

He forces him forward. David writhes with pain, the hurt makes him cry out. They reach the bottom of the stairs leading to the upper floor.

'I hope you got my message,' Renato says. 'We don't want any of your sort here, you poof!'

He gives him a violent shove, and David is flung against the steps where he collapses. He holds his hurt arm, rocking to calm its pain. He squeezes his eyes, his lips reveal teeth gritted in an effort to block the groans he cannot quite suppress. He sees his knuckles are skinned badly. A sharp burning sensation makes him feel his cheek where he had scratched himself against the steps as he fell.

From the yard come the sounds of voices, steps, car doors banging. He gets to his feet but does not feel strong enough to face the sunlight, the eyes, the questions. But the noise of the truck revving up again acts as a goad. He quickly brushes away bits of earth, dust, straw clinging to his clothes, stuffs his shirt back into his shorts, wipes his dirty hands and goes outside. He just has time to see in the back of the truck disappearing round a corner of the farmhouse the jostling faces of Mario, Renato and William. But Dieter is still there, waiting for him with his hands on his hips and asking him what he had been up to.

'I slipped and scratched myself against a tree trunk.'

Under the eyes of his mother who had frowned as soon as he appeared in the kitchen's mercilessly bright light, David passes his fingers over the scratches across his cheek, as if the anxiety she displays reveals their gravity, but also trying to conceal them as if they were shameful signs.

The young woman turns towards the foreman. She gives him a questioning look. Obeying what has now become an evening ritual, she is about to go and fetch a glass and a bottle of wine, but her glance again falls upon David, and she cannot help taking a closer look at his wounds.

'Let me have a look,' she cries when the boy tries to dodge away. 'It may need disinfecting.'

Already her hands are tilting his head, but David frees himself and gives her a sulky look.

'It's all in a day's work,' Dieter comments. 'No cause for alarm.'

'All the same – one never knows,' she protests.

The anxiety expressed in her voice's veiled tone provokes the foreman's merriment. He flops right back in his chair, his lips stretched wide on his white teeth as he laughs up at the ceiling, the Adam's apple bobs up and down between the tendons of his neck, the little warty lump of a nipple peeps round the edge of the bib of his dungarees, exposing itself at the centre of the stretched brown patch of the areola.

The young woman stands taken aback by this frank display of a body whose presence emits waves that seem to daze her. The solid volume of his body, its weight, the quality of its flesh are all expressed in the reverberating vibrations of his laughter that reorganize the space in the room, provoke distortions in its lines, enliven it in a disturbing manner.

She places the glass in front of the man, prepared to fill it, trying to concentrate on the gesture that requires her to hold the neck of the bottle steady above the glass. She is so painstaking, she bends to one side, gives the impression that she is hanging over Dieter as if to lend a willing ear to his unspoken declarations, or as if she is about to yield to the dizzy excitement he awakens in her.

The wine gurgles in the neck of the bottle, the brightness of the formica draws attention to the arm which is struggling to hold its strained position. The indirect lighting coming from the table top glazes her throat, her shoulders, her face, with a glow betraying an unease indistinguishable from some intense emotion. When she has finished pouring, she straightens up, her hand lingering on the bottle she sets next to the glass while she hesitates a second or two before looking deep into the foreman's eyes. He is smiling, giving the impression of making a vow in the broad movement of his lifted arm as he holds the liquid up to let the light shine through it.

As if regretting for a moment her too revealing neckline, the young woman folds her arms across her chest, pressing her hands on her shoulders. As she turns away, her eyes meet David's.

'Did you work hard today?' she asks him.

David nods his head.

'He's getting quite expert,' Dieter declares. 'He deserves a wage.'

'Really, are you sure he isn't bothering you? I'm so afraid he'll be a nuisance on the team.'

'Not at all, I can assure you. The lads are very pleased with him. I don't need to butt in at all. Isn't that so, David?'

The boy lowers his eyes. This can be taken as assent.

'I know nothing of what goes on among them,

they keep me at a distance. As soon as I poke my nose in, they shut up like clams. It's me who is the intruder.'

Perhaps he was attempting, with this apparently harmless remark, to encourage David to confide more in him.

'What about if we change places,' Dieter goes on. 'He'll work in the forest while I stay here with you, for a vacation.'

Once more his laugh re-echoes in the room, he stretches out an arm and places his hand on the young woman's shoulder where its pressure is prolonged, making the gesture more significant. She lowers her eyes, then slides them towards his. At this imploring look, he takes his hand away. The young woman sits down. She reminds Dieter that tomorrow, having as last week to take the wages to them, she will be bringing David herself in the car, so it will not be necessary for the foreman to come and pick him up. She talks to him about new information she has heard in the firm's office.

The conversation takes on a more spontaneous note. Nevertheless, the young woman's hands, laid before her on the table, are trembling. Within reach of them, already well thrust forward towards them, standing out upon the whiteness and smoothness of the formica that makes it seem bigger and picks out the various details of its callosities or pads of dark hair, there lies Dieter's hand, an obsessive yet peaceable image, whose fingers only slightly bent give a hint of the gentle imposition of hands that is prefigured in the way they are disposed.

David's eyes move from Dieter's hand to his mother's. He is aching to unite them, impatient to see them grow closer, imagining the way they would hold each other, even though he is doubtless considering them as independent of their owners and is hoping for the performance of another kind of union. He is thinking of the harmony that a replacement of the male protagonist would effectively establish in the room. His face gleams with the hint of a smile which, despite its tenuousness, his mother's curiosity disperses when she asks him what he is dreaming about.

VI

How can we modify the image that circumstances have given of us to others when we ourselves are not sure that it is altogether false, when the reactions of others impute to actions in which we see no harm an unhealthy, reprehensible origin? The entire world then rejects us as an aberration, a foreign body not tolerated by the social organism. It has become obvious to David that William definitely has been taken out of his reach.

This is the last day. The young man has ignored him. Renato has played the part of the unsurmountable barrier. Fate itself has entered into it: under the pretext that unloading is dangerous for someone inexperienced, Dieter has put Mario in charge of the boy, and they have stayed behind at the farm after the midday meal in order to do repairs to the pump. The long afternoon drags on. Time is standing still. The chatter of the lumberjack, not much inclined for hard work, does not amuse the boy.

'You know,' Mario begins, leaning against the pump after having interrupted the job to smoke a cigarette, 'you mustn't hold it against Renato. He's not a bad bugger.'

'Do you stay here on Saturdays and Sundays?'

'Me?' the lumberjack asks, pointing his thumb at

his chest. 'Yes, I suppose so, fairly often anyhow. I always have something to do . . . Sometimes they come and ask me to join a hand of cards. And there has to be someone here to hold the fort!'

'You stay here alone?'

'Sometimes Alberto stays too. When he's had a tiff with his fiancée. But as he has several, there's always one available. I don't know how he manages to work it, but his system seems to be foolproof, so he's not often at a loose end.'

The cigarette smoke scribbles arabesques on the dark backdrop of foliage; it seems to sketch ironic graffiti that are blown away by the breeze. Looking down at his cigarette that he keeps turning between his fingers, Mario returns to the subject that seems to be occupying his mind:

'You coming back here Monday?'

He doesn't leave David time to reply.

'You've not got into the way of things yet, we still don't rightly know you.'

From the wad of rag with which he has stopped the mouth of the pump in order to stop the dripping there fall at long intervals drops of water whose chiming notes on the flat surface in front take on an obsessive sharpness. Mario goes on:

'Even Renato'd be glad to see you back.'

The shrinking of the cigarette to the state of a fag-end compels Mario to hold it delicately between thumb and forefinger, leaving nothing but a flattened, yellowed stump, barely long enough to put between his lips.

'He's a funny lad, William is,' he says, giving the impression that he has guessed the thoughts in David's mind. 'One day he's all smiles, the next he has a face as long as a fiddle.'

Mario has managed to give David a warning. He drags in vain on his fag-end, so he finally decides to throw it away. He leaves the pump and stuffs his hands in his pockets, which, distended, exaggerate the arc of his bow legs.

'He's certainly somebody with an education but it's not easy to get him to talk. Always clean, always well-dressed ... It's because of him we have to repair this bloody trickle. He says it's getting impossible to wash with his feet in the clarts. He should've done the job himself, eh? And you wouldn't have refused to help him, would you? You'd have been better off than with me!'

He is watching David, giving little jerks of his chin. Then he spreads his arms in a despairing gesture.

'I never went to school. I was born here but then the war came, my folks was already getting on, I wanted to be in the open air ...'

He stretches, drops his gaze to the trickle of water at his feet, then wipes the back of his neck with his hand.

'Oh, well, let's try to get it done. I'll be needing some planks. Will you go and fetch me two or three?'

He picks up his trowel and starts mixing the rest of the mortar in the trough. David goes off to the shed. The afternoon light turns the stones the colour of honey. The boy gazes towards the fir plantations that are changing to blue at the end of the clearing. He stops, thinking he has heard the sound of a motor running but, in the piercing stridulations of the crickets, the silence and the immobility of the woods are all the reward of his waiting.

He is still waiting in the yard, even after the lumberjacks have returned and are eating in the dining room, all except William who has come down from his room naked to the waist, a towel round his neck, his toilet bag in his hand, going to the pump where now the hedge of brambles and lilacs hides him from sight.

Before his mother is due to arrive, David is tempted to go and join him once more, for the last time, but Renato is keeping an eye on him from the doorway against whose jamb he is leaning while he eats a sandwich. His father finally had to call him inside before David could feel the coast was clear. But he really doesn't know why he is so persistent: what has he to say to the young man?

He does not dare approach him directly. He goes round the back of the farmhouse, along the blind wall. He keeps stumbling on debris from the embankment, skins his elbow against boulders he has to squeeze past in places because the passage is so narrow, then finds his way blocked by nettles which force him to slow down and which he cannot help being stung by despite his efforts to stamp them down.

Having reached the other end of the wall, he peeps round the corner, examining the bushes that mark the limits of the farm as far as the lilac hedge where bright bursts of light moving among the leaves confirm that William is still washing at the pump. The feeling of being about to reach his goal and fear of letting the opportunity slip from his grasp make him so nervous that he cannot control himself: he begins shaking all over, and has to lean against the wall for a while to recover some semblance of calm.

Then he makes his way, crouching low, towards the screen of bushes that will be his cover. As soon as he is only a few steps away from it, he takes off as swift as an arrow for the bushes. There, bending his head, taking care not to brush against branches, not to make twigs crack, he slowly progresses until a break in the cover reveals a view of the pump and its basin. In fact, the screen of bushes has broken so unexpectedly that David, intent on making good progress, almost left himself unprotected. Startled to find the young man's figure so close, he withdraws behind the branches and crouches down. His neck is throbbing like a lizard's throat, his panting breath ruffles the leaves that cling to his face, the shadow accentuates the brilliance of his eyes.

The young man's naked body, standing against the light, is half in shadow, silhouetted against the halo of the setting sun. Where it strikes his skin, the golden radiance intensifies its tones as through an orange filter, bronzing his whole body. William is busy drying himself and is vigorously scrubbing his torso. He now takes hold of either end of his towel to rub his back dry.

In his desire to get a better view, David moves away from the cover of the branches. The light on his face as he looks out, perhaps some premonition makes the young man turn his head and catch sight of him. He stands stock still, his towel held on his hair, his features a picture of stupefaction and fury.

David does not attempt to run away. He straightens up slowly. William throws aside the towel and rushes on the boy. Three long strides are enough to reach him, but that is sufficient for David, through the clarity of the perceptions his keen gaze allows him of the jolting tremors and twists of this body hurled against him, to feel the reserves of violence necessary to his movements, the weight of this living mass, all symbolized by the shock wave that runs right through him with every jolt of a heel against the ground.

He feels, tightening on his arm, the brutal grip of the young man who drags him out of the bushes, brings him into the sunlight. He struggles with a swivelling motion that threatens to throw him off balance: his earth is no longer turning in the right direction. William increases the pressure of his fingers on his arm and while David keeps his head lowered yanks him from side to side with vigorous shakings. In the midst of this utter disarray that makes his head swim he clings to the image of the bare feet contracting in contact with the grass and the slippery earth, the fine phalanges of the toes, the arching sole with its paler, wrinkled skin, the taut tendon of the heel garlanded with a blue artery and its network of veins marbling the smooth skin.

William straightens his back. On the point of letting his indignation be felt to the full, he is restrained by the boy's submissive attitude. It intrigues him, it disconcerts him. It has the effect of a trap from which he does not see how he can free himself. He gives David another shake, but does not let him go, demanding an explanation, forcing him to look into his eyes.

Finally raising his head, David confronts a face that looks severe but unthreatening, abstracted as if concerned to avoid some kind of contamination, staying on the defensive. The parting on the left side now exists only in the natural fall of the hair, whose locks are ruffled here and there into spikes inflamed by the sunset. The blue of the iris, the crystalline enamel of the cornea owe their brilliance, in the back-lighting, only to the rigidity of that clear-sighted look penetrating to the depths of David's soul with the same interrogations, the same will to know the truth, the same obstinate urge to understand completely. His full lips, just compressed enough to wrinkle them a little, express a settled conviction and William, without taking his eyes off David, nods his head several times: 'So –' he seems to be saying, 'Renato was right after all!'

William cannot read anything in the dark waters of those wide-open eyes; he is sending down a sounding-line that never reaches bottom, he is descending into an abyss whose walls rise without end: he has to resign himself to this hangdog look, this imploring gaze, limpid, open to everything. The irritated expression that had racked his cat-like features begins to soften. He still looks stern but this severity is somewhat milder than his usual lofty impassibility, so little given to smiles. His eyebrows that anger had drawn moodily together have now been smoothed out in an almost serene level line. His compressed lips that trembled with the urge to curse the boy are now relaxing and assuming their natural, softer fullness. The tension is disappearing from the face, allowing the skin to wed the bone structure without deepening the hollows in the cheeks nor over-accenting the jut of the high cheekbones and the jaw. Only the eyes, because of their slanted shape and the luminosity – strangely bright in the shadows – of the pale irises, reveal a sort of ferocity; but the more generous masking of the thick-fringed upper lids is already keeping it in check, allowing a rush of indulgent generosity, of pity, even of tenderness in the gaze.

William releases David's arm. He once more tries to look deep into his eyes. He would like to enter into some kind of agreement with him, inspire self-confidence in him, lift his spirits. He looks up again, his hands loosely hanging on either side of his hips still betraying hesitation: then he raises them, and lays them firmly on the boy's shoulders, holding him thus, at arm's length, under the warm pressure of the broad palms. David leans with all his weight against these buttresses in a confused attempt to overthrow his adversary mixed with a desire to fling himself upon his breast. William is nonplussed by this awkward pressure that David is exerting on his arms. They are united in a motionless combat.

'Go back to the others now,' the young man says

at last in his grave voice – a voice so warm, encouraging, and a little disquieted.

His mother keeps turning from one lumberjack to the other in the group at the bottom of the ramp. Her frock seems dusted with light and contributes to the impression of a disembodied apparition that its fluttering suggests against the banked-up gravel. The three men stand apart, at a respectful distance, bending at the hips as if observing some rare phenomenon. Not far away, the black mass of the 203 looms like the incongruous carapace of a monstrous cockroach. Its front wheels are already turned for departure, giving it an impatient look.

David is unwilling to leave the refuge he has found under the branches in the orchard. He is sitting cross-legged on a low wall. His face and his bare knees make three pale patches of light in the russet shade. His fingers are playing listlessly with his shoelaces: he is still suffering from the shock of what has just been happening.

The young woman is voluble, carefree, sprightly, full of chatter. David hasn't entered her head, he does not belong to her life, she is given up to herself entirely, dazzled by the compliment she has been receiving. She who at home David remembers as taciturn, often lost in thought and rather sad, can be seen here convulsed with laughter that reveals a totally different person. She who – as he well knows – is seldom inclined to meet people and who never stops warning him to distrust others, is displaying herself now in a sociable, engaging light, gifted with astonishing conversational talents. He had thought her reserved, but the image she presents him with here seems frivolous, almost vulgar.

He jumps angrily from the wall and crosses the yard where his sudden appearance breaks up the group of lumberjacks, who are surprised to see him. Mario lifts welcoming arms and goes to meet him.

'Did Monsieur not hear Monsieur's car coming round?'

The expression on David's face stops any further talk of this kind.

'Are you sorry to be leaving us?'

He lays his hands on the boy's shoulder when David reaches him.

'That's going too far!' the young woman declares, accompanying her words with nods that show she is annoyed with David. 'These gentlemen have other things to do than to stand waiting here for your good grace!'

'You've become a real lumberjack,' Mario goes on, 'the forest won't let you go.'

The young woman gives a little laugh.

'It would surprise me very much if he were to distinguish himself in your profession,' she says. 'David's too much head-in-air.'

'Well, now,' Mario replies, 'that's not too bad if you want to fell trees. What d'you say to that, young man?'

David looks at his mother. There is defiance in the tone of his voice as he replies that he would not be averse to learning the craft.

'You see!' Mario cries.

The young woman goes up to David. She is about to make some affectionate gesture but he squirms away. She turns to Quintarelli, asking him about his family. Alberto too is not left out. He blushes as he replies. David is waiting on the fringe of the closed circle, kicking at pebbles with the toe of his shoe. He does not recognize immediately the figure that is attracting his attention at the other end of the building.

If it were not for his blond hair, William could appear like an intruder with those flannel slacks and that white sports shirt that give his burly build and his whole appearance such a different look. Although he knows about the young man's nocturnal expeditions, David had never imagined he could appear so alien as he does now in the lumberjacks' world. At once this discovery distresses him, for it effaces the image he had created, and that gave him possession of William: it diminishes that image, dissipates and disperses it.

The young man comes forward, sure of himself, determined, in an attitude that even portrays a certain arrogance. Could he have changed himself to fit this encounter in which he appears to want to show himself to his best advantage? Or was it simply to demonstrate his difference? Was he intending to ask for a lift in the car? Had it all been arranged that the young woman would drive him into town?

He was no more than a dozen paces from the group when, as he reached the door of the common living room, he started to enter it. As he put one foot over the threshold, he was stopped by David's movement in running towards him, but something in his look interrupts David's impulse. The boy realizes he does not know what he had intended to do, and so has lost the purpose of the action he had begun. William withdraws his foot from the threshold, lowers his head and approaches them.

Like the rapid flicker of a bird's eye, a brief flash in the young woman's look shows that she has seen the figure advancing, but her face betrays no curiosity. She stands listening attentively to the anecdote Mario has started, nodding her head encouragingly. It is not until Mario himself as well as the others, noticing the young man, break the circle for him and introduce him to her that she grants him a closer scrutiny. She shakes hands with him, she is claiming to be glad to make his acquaintance because until then he was just another name to her.

William observes the young woman's face. Whether because of the fiery twilight that tints his face with gold, or the skin braced by the vigorous bath, or the shirt collar opened like a fan or a corolla, or some force illuminating him from within, a touch of sublime handsomeness exalts the bold lines of his face, accentuates the contrast between his slanted eyes and their deep-set mystery under the eyebrows, the full-blocked lips in their softness at variance with the square, jutting, wilful jawline.

David turns towards his mother. He feels annoyed that she should still be talking to Mario, he cannot wait for her to look again at William; he has no doubt that she must have fallen under his spell or at least that she must want to have a better look at him. But her eyes include all four men in her attention, not singling out any one of them. She now makes signs of wanting to get away, and she asks David to get into the car towards which she herself is moving.

The boy casts a worried, despairing look at the young man, but the latter's eyes as they look at him contain no sign of hostility. His glance is insistent, but without bitterness, and displays so little curiosity that it seems to want to reassure, to promise something.

The young woman, whom the three others accompany, again tells David, in a tone of voice not devoid of irritation, to get into the car.

'Ah! He's got a liking for the open-air life now . . .' Mario declares.

'He never takes any notice of what one says,' she explains. 'At home, I always have to repeat things twenty times.'

'That's because the air of the town does not suit

him,' Mario says. 'When he's here, he understands everything double quick.'

'I'd like to see it!'

'We didn't have the time to lick him into shape proper. Another few days with us and you wouldn't recognize him!'

As David approaches, he gives him a little pat on the back.

'Don't forget what I told you. And bring us something to read. Give us a bit of education.'

The young woman has taken her place at the wheel. The motor soon starts humming. The boy sits in the back seat. Through the window when Mario slams the door he sees the lumberjacks silhouetted against the dying light. Hands in pockets, they smile their goodbyes: they are already far away in thought. The car's slow turn lengthens the distance between them and David can just make out, keeping back from the others, the young man whose elegance and beauty stand out against the farmhouse's rusty boardings. William's eyes, now just two narrow slits, shine as they follow the 203 until, having reached the top of the ramp, it vanishes out of sight behind the curving embankment of the road.

VII

If from a subjective point of view I am not altogether able to see myself in the figure of David, he brings back to me, along with the climate of the times he lives in, the general impression I had of the world at his age, one imbued with all the anxiety spread by the radio's alarming news broadcasts. The terms 'cold war', 'iron curtain', 'atomic power'; words like *casbah*, Maquis, *djebel*, *douar*, *fellagha*; the names of Massu, Mostaganem, Krim-Belkacem, René Pléven, Abdel Kader, Maurice Bourgès-Manoury, Pflimlin, Blida, Fehrat-Abbas were burned on my memory, independently, of course, of the beings and things they stood for and which for me only represented a constellation of baneful syllables. They impaired the serenity of summer, changed the colours in rays of light, gave the town and even the mountains a certain vulnerability. I would forget them and then, now and then, cloud shadows gliding across the alpine fields, the damp coolness of a corner of the garden, the whiteness of a façade would reawaken that lugubrious resonance their utterance on the radio had had in my mind ... Mingling with my little universe, limited indeed, but nevertheless composed of sunshine, flowers, sarabands of laundry clacking on washing-lines, the hot tar of roads, the murmur of streams, those radio voices brought me not the exterior world that I imagined to be little different from my own, but that disembodied, exclusively conceptual one of the Word: they revealed to me the terrorist force of language, always ready to propagate in a household's peaceful atmosphere, the calm of a district, these unsubstantial germs that were nevertheless sufficiently powerful to awaken uneasiness, suspend a threat over our heads, provide obsessive images of fire and blood.

David, at home with his mother who is listening to the news while she does the washing-up, brings back that climate of apocalypse in which, especially on Sunday afternoons, the echoes of radio voices used to plunge our district, reverberating from one façade to another in the deserted streets and suggesting – while the light perpetuated the immobility of things on the mournful emptiness of the roads, the cars stranded like wrecks along the pavements – images of those very apartments from which they were emanating being plunged into an asphyxiating silence.

Going up to the young woman, he asks if war is about to break out.

'But David,' she replies, 'there's war already! Battles are going on at this very moment. Men are shooting at each other. Bombs are exploding in towns killing passers-by. Helpless innocents are being killed or mutilated because they are caught by accident between two rival groups. It's horrifying!'

She finally switches off the radio and returns to the sink where noises of cupboard doors slamming open and shut and clashes of crockery sound like the echoes of some internal tumult. Afraid that his presence might annoy her, David only very hesitantly approaches her to help with the glasses already standing on the draining board.

Soon the young woman's gestures become calmer, as if the warm water in which her hands are working has some soothing virtues; perhaps, too, the kind attentions of her son are succeeding in easing her nerves by putting the subject in perspective against the much deeper worry of their own relationship.

'I hope you never know what war is,' she tells him. 'I saw what my brothers suffered, who were barely older than you. They had to scour the countryside for miles around in order to obtain half a dozen eggs or bits of cheese that had about as much taste as dry plaster. And often farmhouse doors were shut in their faces. Everything was lacking. And I won't mention those who profited from the situation, or the shameful things people were prepared to do because they were frightened or hungry.'

The sound of a two-stroke changing gear at a street corner then dying away with a sudden acceleration emphasizes the unfathomable emptiness in which the town is suspended, absorbed by the expectation of some undefined calamity.

Now bent over his desk in his room, David is busy doing a drawing. The refraction of light from the paper combined with the radiance of his face leaning over it lends his skin a subdued glow in which his features appear transfigured. From time to time, the fluttering of his eyelids presses the long eyelashes together, giving his face a sharper look that contrasts with the round cheeks and the plump lips.

Absorbed in the forms that his pencil strokes show him capable of creating, he does not hear his mother in the next room knocking repeatedly against the skirting-board with her carpet brush, although the dull knockings give the impression of deliberate violence, suggesting the obstination one might put into some desperate call for help.

The pencil's soft lead keep stroking the curves of a naked body. Each time it adds a little to parts of the features in a movement that imposes on the wrist a contorsion it seems to take pleasure in submitting to; other parts are retraced with movements that fail to produce this pleasing suppleness, requiring a less evanescent touch more suited to the subject. The clustered fingers pressed together near the pencil point contract on touching the surface of the paper. It would seem that even reproduced in an approximative way the shapes of the body engender a music through the mediation of the pencil and his hand that David is able to enjoy to such an extent, he cannot help smiling.

He has reached this point when a ring at the door makes him jump. Looking at his drawing, he obeys a reflex and hides it. He can sense his mother standing motionless, alarmed, annoyed, undecided. Finally, the bang of the brush against a piece of furniture indicates that she has resigned herself to go and open the door. Her footsteps make the floor shake as she rushes into the corridor, the heels of her slippers making little clacking noises that express the haste of her movements, almost her panic flight. The bolt clicks back, and at the same time David hears the squeal of hinges and the young woman's exclamation followed by phrases expressing in a suddenly lowered voice, as if she were blushing, her surprise, her confusion. The deep voice replying can only be that of the foreman.

There is a pause, a vibrant silence, then Dieter is speaking again, he cannot lower his tone to a murmur. The young woman's voice, clear and engaging, is inviting him to come in. The man's footsteps are more discreet, more hesitant than the habitual image of his walk would lead one to expect; the creaking leather of town shoes is disconcerting, the elegant silhouette they suggest do not correspond to the image David has of Dieter. The young woman starts talking again with a volubility that conceals her inflexions, gives her delivery a constricted character, as if she were finding difficulty in breathing. David is afraid she might come and ask him to join them, but, preceding the creaking, slower footsteps of Dieter – from whom come a few borborygmic sounds, curiously embarrassed brief phrases – the clacking of mules goes past his room in the direction of the living room which the familiar sound of the glass door opening indicates that the foreman is being invited to enter. It closes behind him: David hears the slight click of the handle.

It is still possible, thanks to sounds of creaking parquet, to identify various moves, sitting down, adopting attitudes. Indistinct echoes of Dieter's voice which has apparently regained its usual fluency reach David's ears, as well as bursts of laughter. The boy cannot bring himself to return to his drawing. The presence of the foreman and, even distant, peripheral, the continual buzz of conversation create a disturbance that takes away his concentration. He stands up, is about to open the door of his room, hesitates, returns to sit on the edge of his bed.

But he is distracted by the metallic sound of the Micheline re-echoing suddenly from the valley slopes like running sniper fire. He rushes to the window. Just coming out of the tunnel before the station, the train with its red and yellow carriages is still gliding behind houses that allow it to be seen only in sections; then, shaking off their hold, it finally runs completely free and begins tracing its dead-straight trajectory along the side of the valley, a congenial and sprightly salamander that stands out against the sombre green of the slopes and whose advance brings a livelier note to the alternate embankments and retaining walls in a vague undulation that encounters no obstacle, speeds at its even and debonair pace, passing isolated houses and the branches of spinneys whose inertia, at its passage, is striking enough to imagine them as dumbfounded. The throbbing of its entrails, the clanging of its wheels on the track, carried by the echo that amplifies these sounds, reaches David from time to time with a clarity as precise as if he were standing beside the railway line. The Micheline skirts the extreme edge of the ravine, travels along ridges that allow him to see the coupled wheels of the bogies. It bends round curves that wind along bluffs, it disappears a moment behind one of them then reappears, a little further on, diminished, inclined on a slope, is engulfed by a tunnel that deadens its throbbing but which, throwing its echoes again and letting a final reverberation be heard, indicates that it has emerged into the open ... But it does not reappear, leaving the valley bereft of its colours and its brief animation.

His mother has asked him to stay with her for a while in the living room. She has found an old pair of army fatigues: she has patched them and is now sewing on the buttons. The thimble encasing the tip of her index finger traces a faint flash of light in the semi-darkness each time she lifts her hand to draw her needle in a brisk movement that she makes emphatic when the thread is taut. The warmth gleams on her lowered face, her shoulders, her throat.

David, installed in an armchair, one leg hung over an arm serving as a reading-desk for the magazine he is leafing through, gives her a look in which resentment that narrows their beam is diffused gradually to become a dreamy contemplation. Only the interruption of the regular movement of the young woman's arm breaks the spell as he watches her twine the thread round the button, knot it and snap it in her teeth. She sighs, spreads the fatigues on her knees, holds them up by the arms, draws her head back to consider her handiwork.

'There,' she says, 'they'll protect you a bit better if you slip again.'

Raising her eyebrows, she gives a sigh of resignation that fails to obliterate any of her grievances against David's stubborn intention to return to the forest. She folds the fatigues, lays them down beside her, and then looks into the boy's eyes with a scrutinizing directness. As he supports her gaze without blinking, and indeed by hardening the expression on his own face, she gives up, and digs her hand into the basket of clothes for repair. She takes a pair of ankle socks, slips one on like a glove and inspects it by turning it this way and that.

'It's lucky for you that Dieter should want to take you on,' she continues. 'It's a big responsibility for him, not to mention the trouble. You should behave a little more pleasantly towards him. He doesn't like your attitude.'

David lowers his eyes, goes on leafing through the magazine. The ticking of the clock on the chimney piece makes itself heard in a moment of silence but is lost in the rustlings of the young woman's frock as she suddenly sinks back with her nape against the back of the sofa. Her eyes gleam with the light from outside that she stares at through the french window. She has that haggard look that David sees in her in moments of discouragement. Is she reliving some past episode? Has some event suddenly returning to her memory impelled her to remember others that could possibly explain something that still remains a painful enigma? Is she realizing too late the steps she should have taken? She sometimes grows tense in this way under the stress of some sudden thought, trembling like a sleeper whose dreams betray her actions in twitching hands.

Conscious that he would obtain no reply if he questioned her, and that once delivered from her visions she could no more talk about them than a somnambulist could talk of her sleepwalking; considering even that the person of his mother is something forbidden, secret, too serious and too intimate a part of her consciousness, as is the subject of her dreams, David has always refrained from questioning her about it. Not long ago, perhaps, he might have approached the young woman, sat down beside her; he might have taken her arm and passed it round his shoulders, and waited, close beside her, for her return to life. Today he is all the more able to measure the distance that separates them, and his own inexistence, his complete powerlessness in the face of whatever it is haunting his mother. He feels almost embarrassed to see her abandoned to such an intimate ecstasy.

'How hot is is,' she murmurs.

She smiles at her son, smiles to herself, as at some imagined face. She gets up, goes towards the mirror above the chimney piece. She gathers up her ponytail in one hand, turns her head this way and that, sucking in her cheeks, pouting her lips. She swings her hips, moving her weight from one leg to the other. She is playing for herself, all alone, the part of an affected young miss. Then she lets her hair fall, stops her simpering: it is as if she is thinking of someone, as if she is wondering what effect her face would have on him, without her mask. Her eyes slide away from the mirror, she tilts her head and goes swinging her hands in the folds of her frock on to the balcony. She bends over the plants, pulling off faded flowers. Again she seems to turn dreamy and looks down at the street as if she wanted to escape from some strange influence. She returns to the living room.

'Shall we have a snack?'

A deep note of exasperation contracts her voice, and it barely softens as she asks the boy what he would like.

While she is busy in the kitchen, David lays aside the magazine and takes his leg off the arm of the chair, intending to get up. But he stays there, resting against the back. The room's decoration, its furnishings, the rigidity of its shape occupy his field of vision as so many irritating restrictions. His body, now accustomed to evolving in open spaces, with wide-ranging views, everywhere free to enjoy breezes and sunshine, makes him feel the walls are too close, the room overcrowded, the atmosphere affectedly dainty. The air too has no bracing quality, lacks that feeling of strength and menace he has developed a liking for, and whose absence from his life makes his spirits droop.

He joins his mother in the kitchen. Soon they are facing each other at the table. They watch each other through the wreaths of steam rising from their bowls of hot chocolate. She is smiling. She tells him they could go to the cinema that evening. A quiver passes over her face, altering the smoothness of her mask-like features. It seems as if her whole life depends upon her son's reply. She slowly shakes her head from side to side.

'I love you,' she tells him. 'You don't realize how much I love you.'

VIII

He was probably not expecting that the real would offer such a tenacious resistance to his enthusiasm when they met again. William is sitting there, a few steps away, alone at the table that the others have already left. He is just finishing his breakfast and is still only half awake. David realizes he does not know how to approach him.

As long as the others were in the room, he had been unable to renew their relationship. David's appearance beside Dieter had caused some surprise, and with all eyes upon him, the affectionate comments his return provoked and Mario's enthusiastic demonstrations of joy provided a background of animation that isolated him so much, he was only able to glimpse the young man. The absence of hostility on the part of Renato, impressed by his perseverance, even brought David closer to him than to William.

Now the empty room lends itself at last to the possibility of more personal greetings, but the motionless air seems to hold them apart, accenting the distance that separates them. As if he had followed his course here in a dream's fluid motion, David suddenly is brought up short against that inflexibility of the real; his eyes meet the barrier of a person whose solid flesh and the form of whose body are retracted into a too-confined space. The enthusiasm that brought him here like a flash of lightning now deposits him, spent, without having reached his target. Here he is now encumbered with the weight of his joy as with a useless offering.

Dieter's voice, in discussion with Quintarelli a few steps from the door, can be heard fitfully, carried on the gusts of cool morning air. In the peaceful atmosphere of the room there hangs an aroma of Nescafé and warm rolls. The long table is scattered with breadcrumbs, the bowls have just been piled at a corner, along with the pots of jam and the tin of condensed milk with two openings punched in the top. William is sitting right at the end, in his place, back rounded, the spikes of his badly-combed hair sticking up in all directions against the black hearth. He has exchanged his dungarees for a checked shirt and a sweater. What his hanging lock shows of his face reveals bags under his eyes still puffy with sleep, haggard features, lips looking almost tumefied.

Perhaps it was because he was conscious of not looking at his best that he paid no attention to David. It might be said that he looked embarrassed, wanting to be left alone to mull things over. David does not know where to look to avoid disturbing anything by his attentions. He would like to go away, he is trapped in the toils of his own presence in this place, and does not know how to extricate himself without making a fuss. But perhaps also he has not entirely given up all hope, so he does not want to let such a favourable opportunity pass by.

Beyond the sonorous veil of voices coming from Dieter and Quintarelli, dull thuds are coming from the bed of the lorry on which tools are being loaded. A ray of sunshine enters the room, caressing the beams and joists of the ceiling. In contrast to the touch of coolness outside, the inside air feels almost warm.

The chink of a spoon makes David turn round. William is lifting his bowl to his lips and throwing back his head to drink from it. He is holding it with one hand, a forefinger hooked over the edge. After laying it down, he wipes his lips with his napkin taken up from his lap, and that he carefully folds. He sits up and seems about to stand – but remains seated, his chest against the edge of the table on which he had already placed his hands before rising, elbows pointing behind him, giving the impression of someone pursuing a certain line of thought or trying to recollect an idea that eludes him. With the end of his rolled-up napkin he starts drumming on the edge of the table, wagging his head to the rhythm, as if to keep at bay an attack of nerves or a burst of irritation. Finally he gets up, steps over the bench and proceeds with his rolling gait towards the cupboard in which, after having opened the squeaky door, he casts his napkin with a disdainful gesture.

When he turns round, he looks David straight in the eyes and, standing at ease, he looks at him from the end of the room, a long, fixed, resolute look. He returns to his place. As if he wants to show his dexterity or to impress David with it, he seizes his bowl in passing, and tosses it like a ball from hand to hand as he walks down the room to pile it on top of the others at the end of the table. Now he is almost next to David. The latter, worried about the initiative he senses William is about to take, can wait no longer: he prefers to forestall him by taking from inside his shirt a review that catches on the material. Only after having held it out is he able to articulate a few words as he advances towards the young man abruptly, taking him by surprise that in a reflex reaction makes him take a step back.

'I brought you this. Do you know it?'

William frowns. The gesture and the distraught

expression on the boy's face make him wonder if this is not some trick. He refuses to give way to the tender feeling the action inspires in him. At the sight of the cover, however, he smiles, and as he takes it nods his head in a knowing way.

'*Motorevue*, yes, of course, I've seen it.'

He leafs through the magazine; the glossy paper lighting his face rejuvenates it, sets an incandescent dot in the convex mirror of his eyes.

'You didn't buy it specially for me?'

'The newsagent had just received it. He still hadn't undone the packet.'

William leans against the edge of the table. He is not really looking at the photographs nor reading their captions: he is obviously wanting to give an impression of lively interest in the magazine. He is really seeking a formula to neutralize the emotion David's gesture has aroused and which holds them both in its grip, threatening them.

'You interested in bikes?'

'I don't know much about them. I tried to read some articles but they're too complicated for me.'

Again William gives him a long look. The rather pronounced wrinklings at the root of his nose express incredulity, his troubled eyes indicate perplexity, reticence. The memory of what happened round the pump returns and casts a shadow over the freedom of their meeting, introduces an uneasiness into their exchanges. William looks again at the review.

'I'm no specialist either,' he says.

Head bent over the magazine, his features are softened into a dreamy expression. David scrutinizes them: the tension and immobility of the boy's forehead make him look as if he is confronted with a sheet of plate glass making it impossible for him to make the leap into William's thought, into his garden, into all the images that keep haunting him.

The rustlings of the turned pages under William's fingers blend into an irritatingly regular rhythm that finally alerts the boy to the silence in which they have been forgotten. The young man nods his head. He waves the revue under David's eyes.

'I'd have to read it carefully – I couldn't return it to you so soon.'

'You can have it. It's for you.'

They jump at the sound of the truck's horn. They rush outside and see that the truck is no longer there. How on earth could they not have heard it leaving? They run round the corner of the farmhouse and catch sight of the yellow outlines of the Latil on the road at the top of the ramp, throbbing with the vibrations of the motor that Dieter is revving noisily.

David starts running at top speed, sufficiently in front of the young man to try to explain to the foreman, across the deafening noise of the tractor, that it is he who delayed William, that he alone is responsible for their being late. Dieter doesn't seem to take it badly, he's in a hurry, so he tells them to hop on. The boy is about to leave the seat to William but Dieter will not allow it. Thinking of safety, he guesses that William has the extra weight to keep him balanced at the back. William climbs on the platform and stands there between the chairs, holding on with one hand to the gin pole.

Dieter doesn't wait for him to get a proper grip, but sets off at a spanking pace. The embankments rush by. William's figure, knocked from side to side, seems about to be snatched away by the rough road whose verges are like jaws ready to close on him at any moment. He staggers at the turns, that Dieter takes a pleasure in negotiating without slowing down.

Soon the embankments are succeeded by black cliffs of firs. The speed plasters the shirt on

William's chest to outline it under the fabric. It blows his hair violently back, the blond locks rage above his bared brow, sometimes flutter round his cheekbones, like flames. As they enter deeper and deeper into the woods, low branches oblige him to get out of their way or to duck suddenly but it becomes less and less easy to avoid being struck by them. David is alarmed by every reckless bound of the tractor that Dieter deliberately causes to skid in the ruts. Bits of mud compressed by the tyre treads spurt out from beneath the wheels. Some spatter William's sweater, others cling like flies to his face, but throughout it all his eyes continue staring with their brilliant fixity.

Half hidden in the waves of ferns, the faces of the lumberjacks who are sitting down at the moment form isolated patches, enclosed in a blueish light that emphasizes the curve of their backs or sets off a shoulder, a nape, a profile. They have stopped for a snack. They exchange a few words, but so spaced-out, so much part of their mastication that they barely trouble the silence, which at once covers them with little sounds caused by little movements: the squeak of a cork, the clatter of a knife, the rustling of a piece of paper, the sigh of the ground under the weight of their boots. Even when they are suddenly amplified, these noises do not perturb the somnolence to which the forest is forever abandoned.
 Renato sitting with them has lost sight of William and David seated some way off on a rock; they are silent, patient, with a look of being just visitors, learners. They are not eating. In order to give himself something to do, so that he won't be bothered by anyone, William is carving a hazel wand. David sitting behind him takes refuge in his presence, hiding himself in the chaste friendship of

his broad back; he refuses to make the slightest movement that could disrupt the fragile harmony of their separateness. His eyes widen at the sight of the dimensions of the young man's frame as he moves them up the long flanks spreading from the narrow waist. Moulded in the close-fitting fabric of the shirt that the curve of the spine stretches to a point where it seems about to tear, his flanks swell, are animated by movements like echoes of the painstaking activities of his fingers, hidden from David's gaze. When he turns his face up to the trees the boy is still luxuriating in William's proximity, intoxicated by his odour mingling with the heavy scent of leaves, mosses, soil.

The figures of the lumberjacks remain drowned in the nocturnal vapours that surge from the foliage, veiling them in blueish light as faint as daybreak. From Dieter's talk there emerge words that speak of bomb attacks, ambushes, putsch, punitive expeditions. There is also something concerning the FLN, guerrillas, Ben Bella, Bab-el-Oued. The tones of his voice, re-echoed by the rocks that break here and there out of the soft earth, send sinister reverberations through the clearing, though they are confined to the narrow circle in which the men are sitting.

Renato is showing signs of impatience. He is not affected by the torpor weighing on the others as they listen to Dieter's talk. Raising his eyes, he catches sight of William and gives him a wink. He indicates the foreman with a slight movement of his head, seeming to make fun of him, then waves his sandwich, and, lifting his chin in disbelief, shows astonishment that the young man is not eating. When his invitation to share his sandwich elicits no response from William, he stands up and goes over to him after having fished something out of the haversack containing the men's food. He offers a portion to William who refuses it: after a few seconds of embarrassed silence, the young man remarks that David too has eaten nothing. Renato objects that the team is not provided with nursery pap, but with a smile, and saying there is still something left to eat, invites David to go and ask for some. David says thank you, but he is not hungry.

William throws away the hazel wand, slides off the rock, seizes the slice of bread Renato offers again, moves away to take a bite: it is almost as if he were hiding. With one hand in his pocket, the other holding the sandwich, he walks a few steps, loosely swaying. Renato does the same beside him, asks him if he would like something to drink, he can go and get it.

'It's all right,' William replies. 'But what I'd really like is a cigarette. I must have lost mine. Perhaps the packet fell while I was riding on the tractor.'

David offers to go and look for it, but Renato beats him to it. He runs away, plunging up to his chest in the thickets of ferns; he is hidden by a bush, then reappears a little further off, grabbing at branches to help him climb the combe that rises above the clearing. Only the moving bright shapes of his hands and his bare legs show where he has got to, then the outcrop of a big overhanging rock hides him again. There is one final glimpse of him as he reaches the level where he disappears among the fir trunks.

William forces David to accept half the sandwich Renato has given him, claiming that the boy would otherwise never hold out until the midday meal. Then he shoves his hands in his pockets, and starts scraping at mosses and lichens with the tip of his shoe. It is only when he feels the boy's insistent gaze moving over his hair, the arcs of his lowered lids, the curve of his lips, the contours of his body appearing here and there under the folds of his shirt and trousers as the tissues tighten, that he raises his head with a sudden movement sweeping aside his lock of hair and plunges his eyes into David's, less annoyed than ashamed to be encouraging an attachment he knows is directed only at an image in the boy's mind.

David bites the piece of bread, exaltation widening his gaze to take in the whole of the clearing, the play of shadows and half-lights between the trunks, between the branches, on the pale radiances that enamel the backs of leaves and gives them the appearance of a suspended shower of medallions. He luxuriates in this assurance, communicated by the way William looks at him, by the sense of his attention encircling him, by the security of his wisdom that is opening him immeasurably to the world.

The bumps and potholes of the road make the light truck jump and jolt. The more he tries to control himself, the more the rattle of the burning metal has a euphoric effect upon David: the puppet he has become presents, to his mind, a comic spectacle, and the sensation engendered by the inability to control himself arouses in him unexpected pleasure, not far from drunkenness. On either side of his legs he sees the boots and jeans of Mario and William who, bracing themselves against the sides, are better able to withstand the force of the joltings. He does not dare lift his eyes to their faces, whose amused expression he can only guess. The engine's deafening sound accompanied by a tumult of clankings and clinkings would in any case make conversation impossible.

While it gives protection from the sun, the tarpaulin cover creates a noticeable humidity in the space it defines, and this feeling of stifling confinement is not without its effect on the nerves. In the promiscuity he finds himself with William and Mario, his euphoria has the poignant character – a little silly, too – of the laughter of children excited by some unexpected treat, and whom a present bigger than they had asked for leaves dumbfounded, hysterical, light-headed. At the same time, these conditions encourage an intimacy one can not only not avoid, but that one is already experiencing, having foreseen it, on the verge of immodesty. Despite himself, David is liberated from his defensiveness, and now he feels himself in close contact with William, swept away with the young man in a whirl of movement that presses them one against the other. Added to the bouncings of the vehicle and its stupefying racket, the half-darkness blots out the space between their bodies, and only the lighter tones of their skin and the flash of their eyes distinguishes them one from another. It gives their arms and hands a patina that emphasizes the straight lines of tendons and articulations. It passes over their faces a balm that polishes them, burnishes them like a suntan.

In this lighting, Mario's face emerges transfigured. The unsuspected purity of lesser traits dissipates the rather unpleasant aspects of his physiognomy. He is nothing more than a luminous smile, a little mischievous, flickering on David's left, a little further back, like the flame of a night-light. To his right, the more distant head, William's, is outlined on the greenish background of the tarpaulin, still preserving in its swayings responsive to the truck's jolts that reserve embodied in the rigidity of his neck and nape; but whenever his eyes, the iris pailletted with blue and green, turn the two dark circles of the pupils upon David, a fine mesh of laughter-lines pleats the corners of the eyelids, and that mature face, usually tense with some serious concern, is endowed with the mocking charm of a high-school boy.

This smile that seals their complicity may have its source, it is true, in the victory the three of them have won over Dieter. On the pretext that the section they had started clearing that morning presented too many dangers, Dieter wanted David kept away from the place, and had already suggested to Quintarelli that a job should be found for the boy that would occupy him at the farm in company with Renato. But he was very much put out when he saw that David was already seated in the light truck. He wanted to make him get out but the boy insisted on staying put. The foreman then criticized William for being irresponsible. Mario claimed that there was nothing to be afraid of. William assured Dieter that he would take good care of David.

'That's not what you're paid for!' Dieter had shouted at him. 'Forestry has no connection with a holiday camp!'

'Who brought David here in the first place?' William retorted. 'Not me!'

And Mario, to cut short the altercation, had tapped on the driver's cabin window, informing Quinatarelli that he could start. Dieter, fuming, was left behind. When he regained enough breath to shout threats and warnings, the truck was already far away.

Apart from the connection with Dieter's discomfiture, and apart from the gaiety provoked by the vehicle's joltings, the smile David and William exchanged expresses a deeper complicity. Their smile is witness to their having won another kind of victory, one that was incommunicable.

They watch the moving shapes that are projected on the opening at the back as on a cinema screen. The half-light in which they are plunged intensifies the luminosity outside, and it is all the more difficult to discern the various elements of the passing scene because the dust raised by the truck's wheels continually whirls up behind them. When a lucky cross-breeze blows the dust cloud away for a moment, they see the sharp outlines of the shuddering power crane on the yellow Latil driven all-out by Dieter. Mario taps David's arm to draw his attention to it. He shouts something about the boss must have some urgent personal business to attend to, and he throws his head back in unrestrained merriment. Dieter can be seen behind the vibrating reflections of his windscreen. The jolts shaking his body help to confirm the impression that he is boiling with rage, and the swirls of dust all round him seem the very emanations of his fury. The tractor's chassis pitches from side to side, uncovering its torsion bars and its axles as it twists and turns, while the whole framework sputters and splutters as if it is about to fall to pieces. The tyres too seem to be skidding, handicapped by their great size that gives the contraption the look of some clumsy flat-footed thing. At bends, it disappears behind the embankment or shows only, coughing and snorting, the tip of its snout afflicted with the surly upper lip of the projecting winch. Then the whirlwinds of dust envelop it again in impenetrable veils.

    The truck is approaching the edge of the forest. The trees, growing ever closer, now leave only a single shaft of light that gets narrower and narrower in the closing perspective. They are driving more slowly, but the deeper ruts here shake the truck more violently, and, not having anything to hold on to, David keeps being thrown against Mario or against William. The silence of the woods muffles the roar of the motor. All that can be heard in the wake of the truck crawling between the fir trunks is the grinding and squeaking of its frame and of its tortured springs, mingled with little bursts of laughter.

IX

Limbs benumbed by the morning's work give to the lumberjacks' gestures and to their walk the dreamy indolence of the punch-drunk. When work stops, the return of silence does not simply invest their bodies with this cottony carapace that blurs their outlines: it also sucks them dry, even emptying their heads, wiping out words and images, making of these sleepwalking figures exiles from language.

Is it only exhaustion that explains these closed faces, these slow-moving limbs? Could this sudden oppression not arise from the displeasure they feel at seeing David and William keeping to themselves, giving the others the cold shoulder as it were, since they are not following the rest back to the farm this noon, but, on the boy's initiative, simply staying to picnic in the clearing? The lumberjacks hang on, dragging out the time, reluctant to leave the place, at least in David's eyes who is not all that eager for his confrontation with William: for he cannot envisage it without anxiety, and he is impatient to get this critical moment over, heavy as it is with insidious uneasiness and possibly resentment.

'Don't get up to anything, lads!'

Hands in pockets, Dieter has stopped a few steps from them as the lumberjacks move away. He comes closer.

'I'd prefer it if you did not wander away from here. The place is treacherous in parts. I don't want to have to scoop you up with a soup spoon from the bottom of a ravine.'

The hint of a smile just lifts one side of his moustache. He lowers his head and hoists himself up on top of a rock sticking out of the ground, where he tries to keep his balance. He suddenly looks into William's eyes.

'You have the entire responsibility. You know what'll become of you if something should happen.'

The young man offers an impassive face in which the candour of the blue eyes is in itself a mute guarantee of vigilance. Dieter turns towards David. His gaze now becomes softer, dreamy: his eyes shift a little, just enough to awaken a sparkle between the lashes.

'I've got to take you home in one piece to your mother this evening. You won't do anything rash?'

With a jerk of his chin he indicates the haversack the boy is swinging in front of him at the end of a cord.

'What kind of idea is it, to come and picnic here?' Dieter asks him.

David is growing impatient.

'Just for a change!' he replies.

The foreman does not insist. He orders them to be there ready when the crew returns. Gradually he sinks into the dense shadows, fading slowly away until soon nothing is left of his figure but a faint movement disappearing into the distance. It seems to oscillate in one place, then suddenly vanishes.

As if Dieter's presence had until then been spinning and anchoring all round him, in the manner of a spider spinning the threads of its web, a labyrinth of invisible fibres, his disappearance at once sets free the whole clearing. The lighter air, unbridled, resounds from near and far with a new volubility accorded it by this sudden enhancement of existence. As if at last liberated from the long wait in which they were frozen, the leaves and branches relax, animated by an unfolding impulse that evokes a sigh. Perfumes are released as from a body taking its ease – the scent of armpits, fragrances of natural oils exhaled by lifted hair or limbs unlocked from an embrace. Faint susurrations are being borne from place to place in the undergrowth, wafted on a discreet emanation, still timorous, but gradually beginning to develop more volume, until its voice is establishing a universal and companionable murmuration of liberty.

The young man, levering himself up on his hands against the stone at his back throws out his chest, offers his face to the all-invading sunlight, and breathes in the air impregnated by these tonic scents. With effortless ease he hoists himself on to the rock's flat surface where he has space enough to lie down, one leg bent, the other stretched out, his upper body supported on an elbow. He takes out his packet of cigarettes and sticks one between his lips. His eyes lowered on the box of matches avoid the boy's gaze that tries in vain to pierce the lattice of eyelashes. After several attempts, the flare of the match deflowers the silence that is concentrated round the flame. After taking a long drag, William's lips release ribbons of smoke that curl round his flaring nostrils before drifting away to be lost in the blue-lit halo suspended in the clearing. Half reclining on the rock like an actor on a divan, like a bather on the beach, like a statue on its plinth, he abandons himself to the languor of the pose which, while distancing him in some other, inaccessible world, displays him with an almost indecent ostentation. It seems as if in some perverse or teasing manner he is only deciding not to ignore David's confused aspirations simply in order to bend him more completely to his will.

Shafts of sunlight are refracted among the tree trunks. All along the trunks lit from behind there runs a fine silvery border that picks out each one separately, emphasizing its straightness and the ruggedness of the bark. The rays of light make spreads of leaves stand out here and there, enhancing the transparent ruby of crimson berries hanging on bare stems. Midges are concentrated in damp corners that they stipple with their grey and feverish nebulosity. From all round come crackings, rushes of sap, the sounds of fertile swellings, of fibres stretching. From the bottom of some ravine comes a whispering accompanied by a hushed tinkling of pebbles indicating the proximity of a stream. The forest is awakening, rising from its dreams.

Stretched out on the rock, William keeps his eyes closed on some enigmatic happiness. The movement of his arm when he brings the cigarette to his lips takes on a breadth of almost theatrical emphasis. Independent of the raised torso, level with the shoulder, it describes an arc as if it were following the rhythm of a music or marking the entry of a theme that takes the audience's breath away. In the same fashion, before returning to rest with the cigarette on the raised knee, his hand hovers a moment beside his face, announcing by its thrown-back oracular pose the manifestation of the smoke that is to be released from his lips and that he expels in a long, measured exhalation.

He finally turns his head in the boy's direction, and, after a slight delay, raises his eyelids to consider him.

'Your idea was excellent. I don't know why they always insist on returning to the farm at noon.'

His lips retain the rounded shape they had when he removed the cigarette from his mouth. He takes the time to inhale before opening them again. Again he turns his eyes on David. One raised eyebrow gives him a questioning look.

'You didn't have too much trouble getting Dieter's permission?'

'At first he told me it was impossible,' David answers. 'But he thought I meant that I wanted the whole team to have a picnic.'

'And he made no objections when he learned that I was in favour?'

The boy simply shakes his head. It appears that William finds nothing to admire in his physiognomy, and that he is on the contrary irked by the delicacy of his immature features, by the pallor of his skin with only a hint of down, by the unruliness of his dark locks related to the incoherent energy of growth, by the curves of his eyelids that underline the intensity of his alarmed and imploring gaze. It might almost be said that William can barely resist giving way to a violence within him that could easily impel him to pounce on the boy without bothering to ask himself if he was seeking to satisfy thus some bestial instinct aroused by David's attitude, or to appease a lust for dominance for which the boy's slavish comportment demonstrates that he is not just ready but even inclined to submit himself to.

William controls this impulse by sitting up with a sudden thrust of his loins, and adopting a cross-legged position. He jerks his chin at the haversack David is carrying.

'Well, what did your mother put in it for you?'

On his invitation and with his help, the boy climbs up on the rock, sits down in front of him, opens the bag and sets out between them, lit by the moving leaf-reflections, the pale yellow sphere of a melon, a bottle of lemonade, half a loaf, slices of ham in aluminium foil his fingers peel open, a dish of vegetable salad, then portions of Comté cheese and rosy cherries mixed with mellow apricots.

They did not wait to finish their meal before trying to reach the stream. The silvery, insistent sounds mingled with their talk and finally moved from the periphery of their hearing to the centre of their attention, imposing the image of a paradise of joy and freshness which, if it did not actually summon them, at least aroused their curiosity, reawakening in them memories of other happy occasions.

David and William let themselves slide down the ravine from which rises, through a dense growth of trees, that silvery thread of tinkling sound, mingling silky rustlings with brilliant clatterings. The branches prevent them from seeing the bottom, and the tree tops below them only allow them to estimate the steepness of the slope. They cling to anything to stop sliding, dropping from trunk to trunk whenever the incline becomes too precipitous. Under their boots the rocks and pebbles and the rain-softened earth keep slipping away, forcing them to grab at weeds and ferns that their weight uproots.

William goes in front of David. When he gets too far ahead of him, he waits, holds out his hand for the boy to grasp. Whenever David is carried away by the slope, he catches him in his arms. Every time that happens, David is thrown into excited confusion by that strong grip, by the power of the arm he grasps, by this unshakable anchorage in a world where the ground drops away beneath his feet and where he himself, unbalanced, can find no foothold. Even closer than the acrid odour of earth, the mixture of sweat and wet leather that emanates from William adds considerably to the thrills of his swimming senses.

They clamber down the slope without speaking, producing no other sound than that of the leaves they brush aside, the pebbles they dislodge, the branches they bend and that spring back into their original positions with a whistling crash, and the panting breaths that their own stumblings and slitherings produce. The leaps and bounds as their bodies advance jerkily provoke disturbances like flutters of emotion in the semi-darkness. They enter a region in which conifers give way to deciduous trees with airier crowns. The black, frail trunks of beech, ash, hazel, at first growing perpendicular to the slope, soon correct their growth and reach up to the sky where their foliage is drowned in light. They create a space less dense than that in which the tall timber rises, growing in serried clumps and leaving fairly extensive open areas like pockets of light in the darker greenery.

Moving without difficulty in these spaces in which the only obstacles are low branches under which they have to bend their heads, or a fallen trunk they must step over, William and David go in the direction of the light where soon, through the network of leafy branches, they make out the water's silvery weave running between mossy rocks. They are met by a penetrating odour of slime and mud.

The absence of a river bank deprives them of a clear view, but a footpath worn by anglers and that the interlaced branches of the slope covers with a tunnel-like vault invites them to follow the course of the stream. When they emerge into the light, they find they are standing on a narrow shore of turf and sand almost level with the stream that smashes over the rocks scattered along its bed. Hardly wider than a country road, it rolls along in its course everything at the bottom of this ravine whose sides ascend vertically, covered with clumps of bushes that hide their tops.

A little upstream, rockfalls have opened up the

cliffs and created a barrage where the water cascades here and there in flashing falls. William and David follow the footpath, climbing round huge blocks of fallen stone, and reach a smooth, dark, tranquil stretch of water lying at the foot of the cliffs, and which does not allow them to go further upstream. The accumulation of branches and sand against the rockfalls forms a spit of land wide enough for them to lie full length. They sit down.

They sit entranced by the overwhelming stillness of the place, by its natural atmosphere that they feel they have neither the right nor the means to disturb. Spread evenly between the rocks that emerge from it, the water comes from everywhere and nowhere – it just keeps coming. Its surface is without a ripple, polished like a mirror, and preserves an absolute calm. The cliff reflects in its glass its greyish, lichen-mottled wall, with its tufts of bushes growing in clefts of the friable rock. Opposite, there is a ledge from which the foliage hangs like curls falling over a forehead. The light penetrates through a small opening in the topmost leaves, and is diffused by successive screens of branches whose colours run through the gamut of every shade of green. A dense shadow reigns over the level of the water, a shadowy chill, mysterious shade; but at the end of the stretch of water a shaft of sunlight reveals, like the beam of a projector, a bank of earth and pebbles that looks like a small beach.

David and William are absorbed in this spectacle that could hold their attention for hours while they are in this rather blissful, mysteriously contented state. And this bemusement in a life so still continues, transforming itself into a well-being that weighs on their limbs, sinking them in a delicious torpor. The blue of the sky in the gaps between the leaves, the distant sprays of foliage on high branches lit by the glory of the sun, the nearer bushes whose emerald green mass is inclined towards the lake, the bare rock of the towering walls, the bronze sheen on the smooth water all seem to them to require no overlay of words. They have left the world of language, and if a need to communicate should arise within them, it would not be in the nature of an inspiration wanting to be expressed in speech: they would simply find themselves impelled by an urge to take each other by the hand.

William stretches out, leaning on one elbow. David ventures to ask him if he has ever been here before.

William answers no. He keeps his face turned away, and the view David has of his nape rising freely out of the open neck of his shirt, crowned with that spike that distributes the hair in a spiral on top of his head, so blond on the shadowy background, might incline him to think that he is lost in some nostalgic or remorseful daydream, moved by a sadness that makes him retire into himself, unless it be a question of that kind of pose adopted in order to mystify, provoke questions, create disquiet.

'Why did you come here to work?' David goes on. 'Are you on a training scheme?'

'It would take too long to explain,' says the young man.

In his voice there is a trace of irony that suggests he does not consider David capable of understanding. Nevertheless the boy goes on:

'Is it to save some money? Are you following a course of studies?'

'Studies . . . yes, if you like . . . Studies of human nature . . .'

He stares at the tips of his boots that he taps one against the other.

'And it's no cause for rejoicing,' he adds.

David asks him if he is studying to be a doctor. William bursts out laughing. He turns towards the boy.

'It's no use asking. I don't know myself what I want to become. I'm just filling in time here. It's something I was offered. It was this or something else . . . I had no choice.'

His face becomes serious, his expression almost contrite.

'I don't deserve any kind of admiration, you know.'

He is about to add something else, but he suddenly gives up. He lets himself fall back, joins his hands under his nape, stretches, sighs.

'Have no thoughts,' he said. 'It is necessary to be able to have no thoughts at all, to have no words in one's head. Seeing, hearing, feeling – nothing more.'

The sparkling light in the leafy vault concentrates on the convexity of his wide-open eyes a sprinkling of little dancing points of brilliance.

'I'm wondering if Renato knows this place,' he goes on.

He raises himself on one elbow and looks at David, who looks amazingly young.

'Perhaps we could invite him to eat with us here tomorrow?'

'Would his father let him?'

'His father – yes. But him – it's not so sure. But I think I can persuade him. It's better if he's with us, you understand?'

William accompanies these words with a more significant look at David, prolonging it until the boy, coming to himself again, agrees with a nod of his head. Then William stretches out again, making a comfortable place for himself in the sand with languorous jerkings of his hips. He closes his eyes.

'Wake me up if I fall asleep.'

The filtered sunlight suspends above his head a reflected radiance that catches now his hair, now his eyelashes, and also strays to his lips from which it seems to borrow the smile and scatter it over the shadowy glade.

Sitting with his arms tightly pressed round his knees, David looks as if he is making room for this body stretched out next to him and whose closeness is imposed upon him in this intimate invasion. His eyes follow beneath the shirt's fan of pleats the outlines of the chest's structure. The shapes die away at the level of the belt beneath which the flat belly is lost. The boy contemplates this body, this face resting on the pillow of the arms. So much grace and power confer upon him a radiance, a privilege that David is frightened of being the only one to receive. He cannot imagine that the mysterious forces and causes that have breathed into this flesh, minutely measured, the rhythms necessary to create such a harmonious morphology should have been mobilized for nothing, through a sheer, gratuitous, capricious concern for perfection. At the same time as the pleasure he takes in this spectacle, he feels the frustration of those who are deprived of it. He feels it would be a scandal, a terrible loss, if William were to remain in the anonymity of these woods, afflicted with this useless beauty that is destroying itself by having to live only for itself.

He is watching her out of the corner of his eye while she is busy at the sink. He is waiting behind her back, with a towel in his hands, waiting for her to place the glasses on the draining board. Head bent, she is pensive: she seems about to stop what she is doing in order to follow a train of thought. Her ponytail curls on her nape and with a cat-like undulation comes and settles in the hollow of her shoulder, to release a flowering – like a self-caress –

of that touch of sensuality otherwise absent from her reserved appearance. David's eye lingers on this little coil, shifts slightly to the earlobe and the half profile.

'Today they didn't report any bomb attack. Perhaps the situation is going to clear up?'

The young woman starts again on the washing-up, more vigorously than before.

'But some soldiers have been killed. They were caught in an ambush during a route march. They arrived there only a week ago. I feel sorry for their parents. It must be horrible when you see the gendarmes arriving . . .'

David takes one of the glasses she has just placed on the draining board. As he is drying it he walks towards the table where he puts it down. He returns to the sink for the next one.

'Did you already know my father, during the war?' he asks, casually.

'I was too young to go out with boys,' she replies. 'And probably he wasn't thinking of girls yet. He was serving in the Maquis.'

'Do you really not have any photo of him?'

The young woman looks at David over her shoulder.

'It hurts me when you start on about that, you know!'

The boy lowers his head to the two plates he is wiping – back of one, front of the other, then vice versa after having changed them round, creating a delicate tinkling of porcelain.

'I'd like to know what he was like.'

The young woman wipes her hands on her apron.

'What use would that be to you? Do you suppose your schoolmates are interested in their father's faces?'

The boy goes and places the plates on the table,

beside the three piled glasses. When he turns back to his mother, she is still standing there motionless against the sink, trying to catch her son's eye, but he turns away.

'He also didn't know his father,' she goes on. 'That didn't prevent him from making his way in life. He didn't grow up like the others, of course. You cannot hold it against him, he didn't even have his mother. He can never stay in one place. He wouldn't have been any more present if he had stayed with us. Like the majority of fathers, you know.'

She frowns.

'Why are you talking to me about it now, this evening? Has someone been asking you questions? Have they been bothering you about it?'

'What I'd like to know is,' he mumbles, 'if I'd want to be like him.'

The young woman's gaze lingers on his face, moves up to his hair and seems to move over it like a caress. The boy raises his eyes.

'Do I look like him? Do you think I can become like him?'

She leans her hip against the sink, crosses her hands on her apron.

'You have some of his features, of course. But transformed – they belong only to you.'

'What do I have like him?'

'The shape of the face, something around the chin. His way of walking, a bit, too. You've certainly inherited his character but it's difficult to say anything definite. How can you tell?'

David is obviously offering himself up for examination. His immobility indicates that he is waiting for other details, that he demands them.

'I've already told you,' the young woman continues. 'He was rather fair, he had blue eyes. From that point of view you don't resemble him at all.'

He lowers his head, goes on with the drying that he had interrupted.

'How did you find him? Did he attract you immediately?'

She turns her back on him. This time she grabs the cutlery, throws it in the basin and rinses one piece after another under the hot tap.

'Things don't happen like that. The first time I saw him, he didn't look any different from the others. And then, gradually, I got to like the kind of person he was. It was a kind of pity I felt for him, really. Now I feel he was very clever.'

The boy places the plate on the table, holding it so that it doesn't make any noise.

'If he had had dark hair and dark eyes,' he says, 'would you have loved him in the same way?'

'Probably. Falling in love often depends on unaccountable things.'

'You had no special preference?'

She leaves the sink, seizes a towel in one hand, the cutlery in the other.

'When I was younger, yes, certainly,' she says. 'As you grow older, you no longer see people in that way.'

She opens the sideboard drawer, throws in the pieces of cutlery one by one as she dries them. Their noise cuts across the silence with a certain violence, as if it indicated nervous tension. David stays beside the table. Suddenly he asks:

'Did he remind you of my father – William?'

His mother turns around, frowning.

'William? But he's just a child!'

'He's about the same age as my father was when you first met him!'

She shuts the drawer. She seizes the plates on the table.

'Well, I didn't think of your father when I saw him. By the way, does he get on well with the others?'

'Why?'

'He had never worked with his hands, it seems. He was taken on for some private reason. They're very discreet about him.'

She arranges the plates in the lower section of the sideboard. When she stands up, she faces David, hands on her hips. He looks as if he's falling asleep on his feet, she says. She tells him not to bother making his lunch for tomorrow: she will do it for him.

X

As soon as he jumps off the Latil, David hears loud revving noises whose impetuous accelerations are re-echoed by the valley slopes. It is obviously the sound of a motorbike engine being warmed up, and though he cannot see the reason why, he guesses that William is getting ready to leave. He refrains from running, but all the same, he hastens his steps to reach the farmyard.

He has no time to form theories about this departure, for anxiety prevents him from seeking any explanations. He barely replies to Quintarelli's greeting. He would like to avoid Alberto and Mario busy loading the light trunk, which is blocking just that part of the yard where William is warming up his engine. But Mario intercepts him, not releasing the hand he shakes. He wants to know in detail what David has brought for his snack. He says he has prepared something pretty good, 'Just you wait and see.'

David manages to get away from him, goes round the truck and finds William on his bike, hands on the handlebars, his face expressing a scrupulous attention to the sound of the motor. Renato is standing beside him, his arms folded.

David goes up to them. He asks William where he is going.

'We're fed up here – we're leaving!' Renato shouts.

But he is smiling and the amused look on the young man's face confirms that it is only a joke on Renato's part.

'Come on, now, are you going to let me try her out?' Renato goes on, suddenly uncrossing his arms and taking up a defiant stance.

William gets off the bike on the side opposite the youth who makes haste to settle himself into the saddle. While he is making himself comfortable, the young man gives him some instructions. Under his mop of hair, Renato's face is radiant. The motor's vibrations make his shoulders shake in a way that seems to amplify the delight he cannot suppress. There is a striking contrast between the stained, shapeless, rough garments three sizes too big for him and the stripped elegance of the motorbike's forms that look as if they might slip from between his legs. He insists that he has already driven a bike. His eager nods betray his impatience to be off. He shoves out his elbows to push aside William who is holding on to him over the first few metres taken at reduced speed. When he releases him, the bike gives a lurch forward from a too sudden acceleration, but Renato keeps control. The bouncings of the wheels on the irregular surface of the ground shake his hips, and the slow speed doesn't allow him to follow a straight line, so he is zigzagging a little. Then he finds the suitable speed and, applauded by Mario who encourages him as if he were entering a championship rally, he crosses the yard and speeds up the ramp instead of making a half turn. William shakes his head, hissing between his teeth.

'I told him not to go as far as the road,' he sighs.

Going up to David, he takes the haversack he is holding, weighs it and hands it back, nodding his head. 'We won't starve with all that,' he says.

'I thought you were leaving for good,' David murmurs.

'I had a job convincing our young mate,' William admits. 'And he didn't accept unconditionally, as you see.'

The noise of the engine is heard again. Renato reappears round the corner of the farmhouse, and the deep, regular roar of the cylinders seems of itself to bring him back beside William.

Knees and cheeks reddened, hair blown back, Renato remains bent over the handlebars, his fingers blue with cold gripping the handles. On William's order, he relinquishes them and, without getting off, slides back into the rear seat. The young man cocks his leg over the bike and takes over the controls.

He looks at David, gives him a wink, turns the front wheel and suddenly drives off, throwing up a hail of gravel.

The light of the sun at its zenith weighs motionless upon the leafy boughs. Under its rays, the stones are burning hot. The relief of the rocky wall is invisible beneath the vibrant light it refracts. The whole of the lake trapped under this shadeless brilliance has taken on an unreal tonality in which nothing distinguishes stone from water. Everything that is rock remains fixed, bright, vertical. The mass of water carefully extending its grey surface into even the remotest, smallest recesses remains flat, limpid and sombre. Even at the edge, which is shallow, it hardly loses any power of reflection, revealing, under its surface tension and its amber warmth, the sandy bottom scattered with rust-red pebbles.

'Just great, this place!' Renato exclaims, tossing from one hand to another a flat stone that he forgets to skim across the calm water.

At once thinking it useless to make his way along by the bottom of the cliff where the spit of sand has taken a sickle shape and, right against the abrupt slope cluttered with dead trees brought down by the floods, offers no way out, he makes for the submerged barrage of fallen rocks, seeking a road through. He manages to go quite far. His figure, doubled by its inverted reflection, creates the illusion that he is gliding on the surface of the lake. The rocks he is using are sometimes so far apart and so narrow that he several times almost falls, and with his upper body bending sharply, tipping forward again and again, it is only by making violent contortions that he can regain his balance. Jumping from rock to rock, he succeeds in reaching one that is set fairly far out in the stretch of water. It is just above the surface, presenting an inclined plane that is prolonged under the water, but there is enough of it above the surface to be able to move about on. Renato waves wildly to the other two, and his shout is reduced to an echo.

'What about a swim?' he cries.

His hands are on his hips, his shoulders shaking with laughter. William takes a last drag on the cigarette he has only just lighted.

'Last one in's a chicken!' he shouts back.

'Chicken yourself!' Renato replies.

At once he scrambles back to them, only avoiding a bad fall by the impetus of his leaps from rock to rock. William turning to David gives him a tap on the shoulder.

'Hurry up!' he whispers, 'we've got to be in the water before him!'

He unbuttons his shirt, crouches down to unlace his boots, takes them off, stands up, undoes his leather belt and drops his work pants. David is struggling with his laces, all knots, when Renato appears, already bare to the waist, repeating gleefully that they'll 'never make me a chicken'. He gets out of his boots by sticking their heels between two rocks and pulling on them. He unbuttons his shorts that drop round his feet: they only have to be kicked away, and with a couple of jumps he is at the water's edge, his bronzed arms and legs seeming to emerge from a dead-white swimsuit. He sticks his tongue out at them: 'Yah! Cissies!'

William is hopping first on one leg then on the other to get his socks off, but he stops Renato from jumping in:

'In the buff or not at all when *we* go swimming,' he orders.

In front of the somewhat demoralized youth, William puts his hands to his hips, inserts his thumbs under the elastic of his briefs, and bends down to take them off. Standing up again, he rubs his chest and shakes his legs one in front of the other in an attempt to loosen his muscles, contracted by the prospect of entering the ice-cold water.

Renato shrugs his shoulders: he should have said so in the first place, but what the hell, he lowers his briefs and throws them away with a laugh. The little tube of wrinkled flesh, in a nest of black curls, jiggles at his crotch, and suddenly enlivens his pallor. A nervous musculature is already precisely outlined under his fine skin, as David glimpses out of the corner of his eye while struggling out of his shirt.

Some distance away from William, Renato too is shivering and is no less reluctant to get wet. Perhaps out of modesty he just turns his head to see what the young man is doing, and his hilarious look might be taken as timidity. They watch each other, distrustful, expecting some dirty trick on the part of one or the other. Suddenly Renato turns back, gives a great kick and makes a huge translucid water-splash that sprays into a brief rainbow and hits William smack in the middle. The young man gasps for breath, bends forward helplessly for a second, but soon pulls himself together and with a rush of genuine anger that mobilizes all his strength, he dashes forward. Great shimmering corollas of spray burst open round his splashing feet; he seizes Renato by the shoulders when he tries to escape, and with a leg-trip throws him into the water. The youth rolls over and gets up. Now he is splashing William with great armfuls of water, and William gives him as good as he gets. Their bodies are bending and rising, sparkling with pearly drops and trickles. Retreating under Renato's better-directed assaults, William finally slips. The youth is triumphant, but stops in the middle of his victory dance when he notices David still standing in his briefs on the bank.

'What's he think he's doing, standing there like a dying duck?' he cries indignantly.

William stands up. His drenched hair is clinging in curly points all round his face. Big drops are glittering on his shoulders. He goes up to David, and holds out a hand to him.

'Come on, you can get wet bit by bit.'

Renato runs up and tries to splash him, and David jumps as if waking from a dream. He drops his briefs and dashes into the water, under the protection of William who stands up for him despite the protests of the other boy.

'Wet your nape first,' the young man advises David. 'Come here, I'll help you.'

He takes some water in his hollowed hands and makes it run down David's neck. He continues this way several times, faster and faster. David has eyes only for those shoulder muscles rippling beneath the brown skin, for their tensions and twistings: he is overwhelmed to be the object of these attentions and his reactions are rather slow until William, interrupting his ministrations, assures him that there is nothing to be afraid of and enlists him on his side in the battle against Renato.

The latter has not ceased harassing them, and his vigour is redoubled when he sees them turning round and giving him a taste of his own medicine. For a while the silence of the gorges is shattered by a terrific noise of splashing water and echoing shouts, bursts of laughter. Under the combined attacks of William and David, Renato falls back. Finally he beats a retreat. He swims away.

William continues the game with David. He does not spare him. Using the palms of his hands he rakes the surface and subjects him to a crossfire of liquid salvoes that he aims precisely at his face. He draws nearer, too, little by little, hemming him in by a pincer movement with more and more violent jets of water, unwilling to stop until his adversary falls, all the time giving the impression of wanting to be as close as possible to him in order to keep him at bay. And doubtless he would have attained his ends if the yodelling cry from Renato, prolonged by its reverberating echo, had not attracted their attention.

He has reached a little beach on the opposite bank, and is signalling to them to come and join him. William makes sure that David knows how to swim but does not insist upon his following him. He dives in, and David dives in too. But he does not take the same direction: he swims towards the rock on which Renato had climbed for a moment.

On the little beach, William is following Renato who is pointing out things to him. His figure stands out while that of the youth, because of its whiteness, blends in with the refracted light on the stones. He appears to be inviting him to scramble up the water course, beyond the bend that takes it to the other side of the rocks, but William refuses, and dives back into the water. For a few seconds his body remains suspended, then his arms incline and he tilts, with back arched, plunging in without a splash, disappearing into a coronal of glass no sooner formed than smashed to smithereens, leaving on the surface only a gentle seething that disperses in concentric waves. William's head emerges quite a long way downstream, his hair parted on his temples in two smooth bands, lustrous, shining like gold, his mouth open, chin dripping: then the rounded joints of his shoulders, and finally an arm lifted as he cushions his cheek on the surface and hauls his body forward with the plunging arm while the other arm rises on the other side.

It needs only a few strong strokes for him to reach the rock on which David is perched. He approaches softly, impelled in a final glide, his arms along his body, legs together. He does not try to hoist himself on the rock, but simply holds on with one hand, looking at David. His body is floating, telescoped by the refraction, undulating and blond on green depths. The languid movements he gives his limbs in order to keep him afloat create a weak eddy whose reflections dance and crisscross on his skin. Sometimes he seems to grow lighter almost to the point of being lifted out of the water, and the muscles of his shoulders emerge, or the shining globes of his paler buttocks.

'Come on,' he says. 'I know a way to warm us up.'

He swims away, and lets David dive from the rock. They swim back to the shore, using the breast stroke. A few metres from the edge the water becomes shallow, and they regain the spit of sand walking over the slippery stones that twist their feet. On dry land, William places David in front of him then bends forward in the posture of a wrestler.

He explains that they must try to hit each other with the flat of the hand. They have a right to only one blow at a time, and the one who is supposed to receive it has to avoid it without shifting his feet. He gives David's back a pat and shows him how he could have avoided it by moving away. He invites David to give the first blow. The boy aims at his shoulder but William ducks and the hand travels through a void. Now it is the young man's turn. He pretends to be going to strike David on the side, and when his hand shoots out David bends sideways, but the hand slaps his thigh. As their exchanges continue he gains self-confidence and becomes more skilful. William encourages him and compliments him.

When Renato joins them again, he asks them what they're doing and calls them a pair of chilly mortals. For his part, he has discovered some fabulous places for fishing. He had seen enormous trout with their muzzles sticking out of their holes. He could have caught them if he'd had a prong. William and David are famished so they take the provisions out of their haversacks, lay them out on a flat stone and start to eat. Renato, still dripping wet, shivering, his lips blue with cold, never stops talking. He does not refuse the sandwich David offers him, and goes on talking as he eats it. William comes and goes, sits down, squats at the edge of the water, comes back to the improvised table, chooses his next snack, steps away, jumps on a stone, lies down, makes signs to David who has plenty of opportunity to observe in detail the supple mobility of his limbs, to discover new and always harmonious outlines that the body presents in all these postures. The slaps David has landed on it have left red marks in places.

As if the tangible existence, guaranteed by its nudity, of a man's body dispersed some anxiety in him, satisfied the need to feel strongly protected, David that day, at the edge of the lake, at the foot of those cliffs behind which the sun is already beginning to set, attains a sort of certitude, a sense of security.

Above and beyond the fatigue David feels from the afternoon's work, there now comes to overwhelm him the healthy lassitude derived from the swim, just as the young man's slaps and punches, and the soreness from the sun are all gradually beginning to burn and scorch his skin. The discomfort he feels gives him the impression of floating in an enlarged body whose rough resistance to his workclothes pleases him when he moves.

The motorbike has some difficulty in starting. Standing on straddled legs above the engine, William begins regulating the cylinders, then, putting his foot on the starter, he kicks it with a power stroke as he turns the handles. The engine sputters, the pedal jumps back with the spring of the ratchet. He tries again. The declining sun is shining through the woods where its rays illuminate the thickets, shine through the branches on the tall trunks. The motorbike is not standing in the sun, but the shadow contains enough luminosity to streak the mudguard and the chromium fittings with bands of light that accentuate the swellings and the rounded parts' organic forms.

These stripes shiver to the motor's vibrations: it has finally consented to come into gear, after a few throaty coughs, to settle down to a steady note. As William straddles the seat, the bike sinks slightly under his weight. David cannot make his mind up. The young man is about to invite him to jump on the rear saddle when Renato comes running up, alerted by the running engine. He pushes David out of the way: 'Thinking I was going to let you take my place, was you?'

William gives him a stern look but does not intervene. Renato instals himself on the rear saddle, and cannot help rocking the bike.

'You're not on a roundabout!' William reprimands him.

'What you waiting for? Let's go!' the youth answers.

William pretends not to hear. He looks at David. He seems to be reproaching him for not being more on the ball. He takes his hands off the handlebars, sits up straight and points to the tank's bulging top.

There's room for a little one here, if you like,' he tells him.

'The kid's seat!' Renato mocks.

'It'll not be very comfortable,' William continues, 'but we don't have to go very far.'

David follows his directions. He puts his hands on the centre of the handlebars, so that he won't interfere with the controls, clasps the tank between his thighs, and by bringing up his knees manages to prop his feet against the framework. Then William leans forward to grasp the handles, settles his chest against the boy's back, and presses his head down into the hollow of his shoulders. With a slight pressure from his chin, William invites the boy to move his head and presses his cheek against David's ear.

Renato is betting they won't make more than a hundred metres, that on the bumpy road they're going to come a proper cropper, but the roar of the motor puts paid to his forebodings, and when, after having let out the clutch, and tested the stability of the bike over a few metres, William puts his feet on the pedals, David must have the impression that the young man has enclosed him within his enveloping body.

He advances at a moderate speed along the road, the springs absorbing the irregularities, the bike rolling smoothly. The long perspective of fir trunks ahead of them rises like a guard of honour. The dense foliage on the branches stifles the roar of the motor that they swallow up in successive waves. The delicate clattering of pebbles under the tyres creates a discreet accompaniment that seems the very soul of complicity and lends a clandestine turn to their escapade. Under the curling lip of the mudguard, the lacy impressions made by the wheel leave a trail of grey embossings. William releases the clutch and accelerates. The bike's course becomes straighter. Speed gives the air a consistency that exerts a stubborn pressure on the chest and the face. It ruffles the tissue of sleeves in a way that makes it slap the skin with the violence of whip lashes. It drags the hair back by the roots, that tingle with the strength of the pull. The eyes narrowed to needle points are bathed in tears whose serpentings along the temples produce a burning sensation. Still unmoved a few metres in front, the pebbles on the road become underneath the bike nothing but a wavering web, striped like the beaded curtain of a sudden shower. The tips of the fir trees wave against a moving sky, then, suddenly swept away, they vanish behind the motorbike that is now racing over the billowy contours of field paths.

David feels he would like to swallow whole those long hedges of the flying fields, fill himself with those solitudes of green grass, hold in both arms those crests covered with the black fur of the fir forests, leap into those limitless spaces towards which William is carrying him off.

XI

There are dawns whose leaden light hangs like a warning. The day takes on a surly physiognomy, anticipating a fundamental frustration everywhere, the air lacks the breath of folly, the absence of sunlight deprives us of the will to smile. David is discovering this also.

This morning, William manifestly opposes the unapproachable barricade of his presence to the two boys by the care he devotes to his bike, by the seriousness he brings to the task in hand, by the painstaking nature of the job he has undertaken: opposes his whole body that has returned to the importantly occupied and slightly disdainful comportment of a real adult to the boys' immaturity. He has despatched them into the chimerical world of infancy, isolated them in the non-existence of childhood limbo. Disturbed perhaps by regret at having given way to their caprices and their wiles, at having rediscovered with them an insouciance and a joyfulness unsuited to his age, today he is choosing to accentuate his difference from them, for he has to recover a dignity he had altogether lost. He is again occupied by projects in comparison with which a forest picnic, a swim in a stream, an ambition to impress the two boys by his skill in handling a motorbike now seem derisory. The indifference he shows them has nothing hostile in it, and it is not at all high-handed: it simply advertises the reality of their incompatible situations. Between him and them there is this abyss by virtue of which Renato and David do not exist for William.

He stands up. Placing his hands on the handlebar grips, he gives the bike a push forward, kicking away the stand that with a click flips into place. The bike now rests on its wheels. He straddles it and tries, kicking the starter again and again, to get it moving. The motor, still cold, responds only with feeble splutterings. Renato takes advantage of a pause to ask, coming forward and putting a hand on the saddle, if he can get on. William's response snaps out at once, cutting:

'I'm not your chauffeur!'

William gives the starter an even stronger kick and the engine starts. He revs it up to a loud roar two or three times, then zooms off. The throb of the motor, re-echoed by the slopes of the blind valley, lasts no longer than a roll of thunder, and quickly dies away. Renato turns towards David and pulls a face.

'Did you two have a row?' David asks.

Renato gives a forced laugh, a little snort.

'You don't know William. He's often like that.'

'Did he go out yesterday evening?'

'Maybe. I heard nothing. I don't spy on him.'

Renato goes towards the light truck. David follows him.

'All the same, he seemed put out,' he insists.

'Sometimes he doesn't want to see anyone. It's a mystery.'

The day does not brighten. A stuffy feeling in the air dampens sounds, and the baggy clouds sag with a weight of pewter.

The rain finally started falling. The size of the drops made the rain heavy enough to pass through the foliage, after which, becoming finer, it kept falling persistently and hard enough to interrupt the work. Flashes of lightning and claps of thunder gave warning of a coming storm, always dangerous in forests, and it was decided that it would be better to return to the farm. Now Dieter is pacing backwards and forwards from the open door to the table where everyone, by habit or at a loose end, is just sitting in his usual place. The foreman's pacings, indicating an impatience that propels him back and forth and gives his turns an irritated abruptness, play against the bleary daylight entering the room.

Renato is looking intently at David sitting opposite him, and his narrowed eyes are gleaming maliciously. For some time now the anxious expressions on the boy's face have been a source of amusement to him, and he watches for the nervous starts David gives as he waits for William's return. It might be said that Renato is preparing to rob him of the instinctive movement he will have on hearing the sound of the motorbike, since William, detained by ignition troubles probably worsened by the bad weather, has not yet returned.

Draughts emphasize the icy touch, on the nape, on the temples, of soaking locks, of rain dripping from the hair and transforming the most sodden parts of clothing into clammy patches that dry out on the skin, imprisoning the body in an iron clamp. The humidity takes away all spirit of shelter from the room, and the damp condenses on everything in a sticky film: the wood of the table top is slimy.

Through the continual splashing of rain and the chiming of drops falling from the eaves on gravel and stones, a distant humming is heard. The first to notice it, David turns towards the window giving on the ramp but the embankment obstructs his view and he resists the temptation to get up and have a look.

'Our one-man rally fan is back,' Dieter says derisively. 'He must like cold showers, too! What an idea to go tree-felling on a motorbike. Does the floor of the truck give him piles or something?'

The coughing sound of the bike's engine turning on a reduced throttle, low yet clear, throbs through the wall, filtering between the stones. An indefinable shadow glides past the streaming window giving on the yard; framed by the open doorway, the image of a figure crouched in a zigzag lightning shape on its engine strikes the retina that freezes it like a snapshot – rain-plastered hair diminishing the volume of a head drawn down into the shoulders, the sodden shirt sticking like a sloughing skin to the vertebrae, the trousers clinging to the hips and thighs, the body at one with its bike, the whole suggesting, through a heavy drizzle, some half-fabulous creature, a sort of headstrong beast impelled forward by the blind force of its thrusting mass.

The image disappears. The sound of the engine has died away, and all that can be heard now is the lancinating hiss of the rain dredging through empty space. The orchard foliage can be recognized only through the shiverings of its clumps, shaken by gusts as if they were being uplifted by inhalations rising from their trunks' profoundest roots. Closer at hand, the raindrops never stop riddling the gravel in the yard: they displace the little stones, and their stubborn pattering is mingled with the dull shocks of pebbles knocking against each other, jumping about in the midst of this translucent carpet woven of water-spurts. As if it was abstracting them from their private thoughts and preoccupations, in order to have them all to itself, the rain immobilizes the men in its curtain of water.

Holding everything in suspense, it constitutes an event in itself that calls each one back to his deepest depths, conducts him beyond memory, plunges him again in his antecedents – molluscs and plankton. Even Dieter forgets the subject of his vengeances, his complaints. All his impatience, expressed in the tense face, the clenched fists, the angry gestures disappears in his softened aspect, so subdued, dumbfounded. It is Quintarelli who, the first to rouse himself from this torpor, breaks the silence. He declares that the storm has arrived just in time to save the gardens from drought.

'And the gutters, too,' Mario adds, putting an armful of glasses on the table, along with the tin of Nescafé. 'I can just see us with our pots and pans tonight, chasing the drips!'

Alberto, sitting in William's seat, is spreading some jam on a slice of bread.

'In Indo,' Dieter murmurs, 'during the monsoon season, the rain lasts for days and weeks. The steam rising from the ricefields is enough to make you think the earth is floating between water and sky. It's like breathing wet cotton, it chokes you so you can hardly speak.'

He seizes his chair and comes to the table with it. With a wave of the hand, he refuses the coffee Mario offers him. He sits down and once more contemplates the rain.

'They don't have this in Algeria,' he goes on. 'But they don't know why they're fighting either, not any more. Our conscripts are spineless drips. The other day again, I heard on the radio that a whole platoon of them had been wiped out by a handful of rebels during a simple training exercise.'

The atmosphere, already depressed, became even gloomier with the discomfort induced by these words. An exasperation similar to that caused in him by radio voices impels David to get up and free himself from the oppression created by all those eyes fixed upon Dieter.

In fact, it is something else that worries him and he makes straight for the door. He simply puts his head out, to check that beyond the shed, where the stable stands, William is not to be seen. For his own satisfaction, he feels the need to know if he is still feeling so stand-offish.

Dieter's voice seems to reassure him that the attention of all is absorbed in his monologue, so he feels he ought to be able to make off without being noticed. He already has one foot outside when out of the shadows in the room emerge the dancing patches that are the knees, the hands, the laughing face of Renato.

'I advise you not to go there,' he tells the boy. 'He's not at his best when he's like that.'

Nevertheless David crosses the threshold. With raindrops pearling his brow and his cheeks, he turns back towards Renato and gives him a defiant look. The latter simply leans against the door post. He shrugs his shoulders.

'Do as you please,' he sighs. 'It's your funeral.'

At the bottom of the steps that rise into denser shadow, David is sitting with his shoulder resting against the planks of the wall. The pallid light from the yard just reaches him and illumines the oval of his face that the wet hair seems to make more forlorn. He is the prisoner of his action. His only hope is that the rain will continue. He worries about the angle of the down-curving branches or the trembling of their leaves, the liveliness of the rivulets in the yard, the splashing of the raindrops dancing above the gravel in a faint cloud of vapour. He presses his knees together, squeezes his chest with his arms, participates with all his might in the violence of the rain. The least sign of its clearing up provokes in him another attack of nervous tension and causes him pain. The loud voices of Mario, Alberto and Renato busy in the barn with tidying and sharpening tools are kept at bay by the hissing of the rain: the space in which they are re-echoing belongs to another world.

At last, he hears the noises he was waiting for: the creaking of the beams supporting the ceiling under the weight of a body getting up, the tread of boots on the wooden floor, the scraping sound of dragging steps and almost immediately afterwards the grating of the door when William pulls it open then closes it just as carelessly, and the approaching tramp of his boots along the corridor, ever more distinct. The confusion of the boy's feelings about how the young man will behave towards him keeps David on the rack. He cannot bring himself to turn round except by struggling against some vague pressure that blocks all movement. Twisting his neck a little more, he raises his eyes. William is coming down the stairs, arms hanging, his figure ghost-like in the moving shadows and in the khaki dungarees as if he is moving through the swirling mists of a dream.

As he comes more into the light, its gleams touch his skin here and there in fine pale patches, spreading first over the deep chest in the open collar, then reaching the cheeks, invading the prominent features. In case he might prevent him from passing, David stands up and moves aside. William seems reluctant to stop beside him and walks over to the threshold of the door. He gazes out at the rain-blurred surroundings before turning back to the boy.

The candour of David's face defuses the stream of invective he seemed about to direct against him. He comes and goes, irritably, sits down at the bottom of the stairs and inspects the base of his fingernails, raising them to his lips to bite off the little spurs of skin around them. This does not occupy him for long. He lifts his head, his features are tense, the corners of his eyelids, half closed, slant up towards the temples. He leans against the wall, rests his shoulder and his forehead there. David watches him out of the corner of his eye. He notices the hands between his knees, hanging down as if broken. The light picks out on them the torturous meandering of arteries, deepens the creases, strokes the delicate pads of the phalanges. He defies the building of the wall the young man is putting up in order to exclude him, and wills himself not to give in to the temptation to run away that William's attitude inspires in him.

The rain now seems to be no more than a silent mist that drips from mass to mass of foliage, exposing the foreground branchings against an ever-paler background of the bushes enrobed in its gauze. The lilac leaves bend under the weight of the drops that hang their pearls on their varnished backs, roll towards the point and shiver those on which they finally fall. The clouds catch on the dark brush of the firs, leaving on them long cottonwool mufflers. The noise of the rain is reduced to a crepitation in which can be distinguished, at intervals, the pecking of nearer raindrops. The voices and the chiming of tools coming from the barn carry better now.

William, still leaning against the wall, is lost in dreams, as can be observed from the minuscule contractions pleating his eyelids, the movements of his lips as he bites them, the feverish play of his fingers whose nails he clicks against his thumb nail. He suddenly relaxes, stretches out his legs, his arms, and sighs. Arms again propped on his knees, he considers David, whose obstinate presence there, right in front of him, now intrigues rather than annoys him. Without taking his eyes off him, he nods his head, slowly, giving the impression that he is expressing thus, with a hint of irony, the admiration the boy's performance arouses in him.

'You want to save me, I know, but there can be no question of that.'

The blue of his eyes gives a cruel glint to the black dots of his pupils.

'You're too late, the harm's already done.'

He shakes his head, barely opening his lips:

'I can't explain to you, you can never understand.'

He lowers his face into his hands, pressing his fingertips on his eyelids.

'Pictures, pictures,' he murmurs, with a strangled cry. 'How I wish I could turn off the picture-show in my head!'

He takes away his hands, lifts his face, mouth open like a diver surfacing.

'There! Now I'd like to be alone. In any case you're not the one I might need, I don't give a fuck for what your eyes express, and yet you manage to make me put up with you. You're really tough! I'm going to miss you!'

He is shaken by silent laughter. He clenches his fists, rushes to the door, ready to make off into the rain or to howl his despair. He turns back. His features are shadowy against the light from outside. The light glides over the outlines of his head, vaguely suggests a relaxing of his features, a sign of tender contrition, the hint of a smile. His shoulders rise, indicating that he has been inspired to make some gesture. He goes to the boy, and strokes with the tips of his fingers the faint down on his upper lip.

XII

The rain has turned the earth sodden. Each step threatens to become a glissade, the squared timbers have become all sticky, and precautions are needed when loading them. Even Renato has been ordered to keep out of the way. Standing beside the Latil parked at the edge of the escarpment that dominates the felling area, he watches operations impatiently. His conception of the way *he* would do things, and do them so much better than the others, prompts him to sketch the appropriate gestures, like a spectator hoping to provoke in the workers whose movements he is following those actions he would like to see them take. Although it is solidly attached to the earth by its yokes, the tractor tends to be dragged away by the weight of the unbarked logs on the derricking winch, and at times can even rise up at the back when the trunk catches on some projection.

The lumberjacks' figures swarm like flies in the sea of severed branches and the ribbons of bark. They gesticulate, shouting at one another, cursing, firing off volleys of oaths. Each log is a special case that demands careful inspection and causes disagreements about how it should be handled. Much less experienced than the others, William remains silent but has to pull his weight. Under pretext of his youth and his agility, he even seems to be landed with the most unpleasant tasks. It is most often he who is called upon to clamber up the steep rise when a trunk is being lifted there. While the others are able to take a breather, he has to pull out the wedges, free the cable, haul it back for the next log. Grabbing it by the hoisting ring, and passing the cable over his shoulder, he has to lean on it with all his weight to unroll it, and, in the manner of a mountaineer roping down, he braces himself against it in order to descend the slope. Stones come loose under the pressure of his boots, he slithers on patches of moss and tufts of grass. His hands are red with rust, the veins and tendons of his neck stand out, his face is begrimed with greasy streaks where he has been wiping away the sweat. He doesn't argue. He carries out orders as soon as he receives them.

Dieter, on the Latil, keeps on giving them. Renato, pointing, makes fun of him to David whom he approaches now. He thinks the boss's methods are stupid and cannot understand why he stops him from joining the logging crew. Of course, he thinks he has done far more loads than Dieter, and in much more difficult conditions. There is no fear of *him* having an accident, and even less of his provoking one. His father could direct operations on his own: then they would have fewer problems, and finish quicker. The youth raises his head defiantly. On his face directed towards Dieter all expression is concentrated in the lips, curling up in a grimace of disgust. The locks of his hair, both wavy and straight, hang down to his nose, creating a helmet through which only occasional flashes can be seen indicating the fury in his gaze.

Despite the brutal tone he tries to give the question, it is not without some embarrassment that he asks David if William had talked to him yesterday, had hinted at anything. David enjoys delaying his reply. Yes, William had spoken to him. What did he say? He confesses that it was mostly beyond him.

'I'm not surprised,' Renato exclaims. 'He tried that on with me as well, but I put him in his place double quick, I can tell you.'

He moves away a few paces, as if he doesn't need to hear anything else. But he soon turns back.

'Ever noticed he adores playing the star?'

'He wasn't putting on an act at all,' David retorts.

'Naturally he would take advantage of a ninny like you!'

'It doesn't mean that just because you don't understand him what he says has no meaning.'

'That kind doesn't belong in a place like this,' Renato declares. 'All the same, he has no right to complain. It wasn't us went and took him on. It's all his own fault if he's stuck here with us.'

'What do you mean?'

The youth assures David that he knows what he knows, but, not being a tittle-tattle, he won't say anything more. However he does go so far as to say that the young man is more accustomed to partying than to working with his hands. He is acquainted with some of William's friends – young loafers who like getting up to all kinds of pranks like parading around stark naked in the convent gardens, picking up chicks and even chickens then letting them go after having stripped them and slathered them with sump oil, organizing at their homes parties of a very special kind at which they hold contests whose nature cannot be explained to a lad of David's sensitive character. According to Renato, the boy would do well to keep away from those young men. And William, too, is not the kind of person to be seen with. The very fact that he is obliged to go into hiding here in the woods should be enough to make him think twice about associating with him . . .

Renato gives a block of wood a furious kick and leaves David standing there, incredulous but disturbed, reluctant now to turn eyes on William in whom he expects to see confirmed the portrait that has just been painted of him. He cannot repress that sense of fear that wells up inside him every time he seeks him out, and which prevents him from seeing him as he really is, thus creating that abyss that at once yawns open, grows ever deeper, becomes unbridgeable.

William is lying under a beech tree. David is seated at some distance from him. He does not wonder at William's detached attitude, which he cannot believe to be either capricious or assumed. He really feels that it springs from a profounder source, that it is rooted in a life force, that it testifies to a sensitivity and a wisdom that are inaccessible to him but to which William is indebted for his enviable impenetrability. It is the index to events the nature of which he does not deem himself worthy enough to understand, to sentiments he will never have the capacity to experience, to sorrows having no common measure with his own, sorrows as mysterious and significant as the rotation of the earth or the immutability of the sun. That is what William is the possessor of behind his closed lids, under the noble severity of his features, in the divine burden of his abandoned limbs – all of which invests his person with magnificence. His silence is like a sacrament, elevated and ennobling, escaping from all common earthly measure and from all triviality. David withdraws within himself in order to receive his grace, fearing to lose even the smallest part of it.

His breathing stirs the sides of the shirt flung open on the ribs, it stretches the pliant flesh of the trunk and moulds beneath the skin the structure of the thoracic cage. His breathing imbues William with a fragility that suggests he too is vulnerable, ephemeral. This alarms David as much as the young man's submissiveness at work, which reduces him to a nobody, at everyone's beck and call, without an existence of his own. Though he might be the first to suffer from it, David would have preferred to see a moody disobedience that would accord more with the dignity of the personage and give more weight to his participation in the work. There is here something like a breach in the armour, something that, perilously close to resignation or stupidity, damages his integrity and makes his presence less dependable.

The pleasure of looking at him, the privilege of being present at the intimate ceremony of his siesta do not suffice to explain the anxious fascination in which David finds himself snared. He tries to explain to himself the power William exercises over him, and that he presumes is contained in whatever it is he is hiding from him, in what Dieter and Renato know about him but cannot reveal. He would like to be able to come to a better understanding of the personage, the better to define the scope of whatever it is that authorizes him to be what he has to be.

The young man is no longer sleeping. Raising himself on one elbow, he keeps his eyes lowered, but the expression on his face, even when looking down, shows he is on the alert, perhaps ill at ease. He is catching ants with the help of a grass stalk along which he makes them climb, teasingly turning it upside down when they reach the top and prepare to descend. David contemplates this face whose features have always seemed to him to display a cruelty that now is intensified. He studies the elegantly bunched fingers holding the stalk, the tensions of the muscles in the forearm, the folds and swellings of the trunk revealed by the open shirt and accentuated by the constricting pose. He no longer knows what to think about a being so reserved and at the same time so present, so secret and ambiguous. But it is precisely the fear that this sense of helplessness engenders, almost as if each time he approaches him his very life is at stake, that makes William so precious to him.

As he waits for the young woman who has gone into the farmhouse where the lumberjacks have invited her to have coffee, David is leaning against the 203 which she has allowed him to move to the road. He had made a bet with Renato that he knew how to drive, so he did not waste the opportunity to prove it to him. Nor does he fail to glow with pride when William follows him.
 They are now overlooking the open space that is the theatre of their daily life. Having it spread out before their eyes like this, they are able to see it in uncompromising long shot, like a domain they cannot bring themselves to believe they are familiar with. David asks William what he knows about cars, what experience he has had of driving, what are his favourite models. William replies in a tone without conviction, in an allusive but sufficiently evocative manner for the boy to want to know in more detail his opinions on Buicks, Pontiacs, Frigates, Jeeps, Triumphs – the names he threw out at random. But he sees he is not very keen to talk on the subject and has to content himself with imagining the responses.
 His mother's figure at last appears on top of the ramp. The diaphanous material of her frock floats around the opaque nucleus of her thighs. As if corroded by the light, her legs taper finely to the ankles, almost creating the illusion that they do not

touch the ground. The young woman is advancing towards them, placing one foot in front of the other, as if walking along a railway line. David goes slowly to meet her. William, his hands in his back pockets, saunters along behind him. The young woman does not give her son time to begin what he had to say to her: she comments that he could have parked the car a bit closer to the farm, then without a pause she addresses herself to the young man:

'My son often talks about you, so I hope he doesn't bother you too much?'

William seems confused and merely shakes his head. He has nothing to say: he stares at the young woman, and for a second the intensity of his gaze surprises her.

'It's very good of you to look after him,' she goes on. 'You yourself, I think, are not altogether accustomed to life in the woods?'

William mutters something about soon getting used to it, and the contrast between the gravity of his voice and the mediocrity of his answer creates a certain chill, as if he had spoken ironically.

David watches him anxiously. He had obviously hoped for a different approach. In his heart of hearts he blames his mother, in whom he does not know how to instil a little sensitivity, to induce a little vulnerability in order to make her more receptive. Turning back to William, he clenches his fists. He is expecting him to take a firm, assured attitude: he is in despair over the blush that tints his cheekbones and his temples; he feels embarrassed for him because of the awkwardness he displays and that detracts from his presence, softens his features, lends a feverish touch to the brilliance of his eyes.

The young woman rattles on in the ladylike manner she has adopted and which she accentuates by having recourse to high-toned generalities. In her opinion, it is good to vary one's experience of life, to have several strings to one's bow, and not to put all one's eggs in one basket ... At his age, William has plenty of time before him, he can take his time, the future lies all ahead. William is not listening to her. At most, he is amused by the efforts she is making to furnish the silences. Perhaps he is taking pleasure in seeing her put out of countenance by his reserve, by his gaze, so that she has to put up this smokescreen of words in self-protection. His eyes wander over the young woman's body, resting on her shoulders, appraising the slenderness of her waist, the curve of the hips, the globes of her breasts. They return to her face, to her eyes. From her figure, hip elegantly displaced, emanates an aura that seems to invest the space in front of her, filling it with the spectral gestures she finds herself performing.

Beside his mother, David is moved at the sight of this metamorphosis. He no longer exists for William, who, captivated, forgets to repress the smile that makes him flower, spreads over his breast, his arms, and tempers his virility with a delicate restraint, lending his manhood a surprising gentleness. The boy turns towards his mother. He becomes annoyed when he sees her obstinately asking William questions revealing a purely formal interest in him, a housewife's prattle, almost unkind in its triviality. Indeed, she remains completely unmoved before the fervour manifested in the young man's eyes. She cannot but notice it but all it does is to make her more talkative, in the kind of intoxication caused by the knowledge that she is admired. This attitude is rather that of a mother amused by the remarks of her son's classmates who take her for a big sister, and not the nervous exaltation that the presence and the piercing gaze of the foreman give her.

Discouraged by the evasive replies William gives her, she is bereft of further inspiration and turns towards David. She tells him they must be thinking of getting home: she seems as if she wants the boy to be a witness to her goodwill, never suspecting that she has not behaved as he would wish. So she shows astonishment when he looks away from her with an irritated, worried face.

'You weren't intending to stay the night, were you?' she asks him, all at once supposing that William and he had arranged something of the kind.

Without waiting for an answer, she thanks William for the care he is taking of David, hopes he will have a good weekend, and proceeds to the car, the stuff of her dress fluttering around her. David gives William a worried look. William's eyes are following his mother until, slamming the car door, she is hidden from his sight. Then he turns to the boy a transfigured face. His gaze, as his expression gradually changes, expresses a new enthusiasm, gentle, penetrating, full of gratitude – a look of supplication.

XIII

Installed on the sofa next to the young woman, whose proximity, in the presence of David, makes him feel rather restive, Dieter reclines against the back, and in this slumped position that favours his indolence, he is thinking, eyes alert, passing a finger over his lips. His arm raised horizontally and laid along the top of the supporting cushions brings his hand to the level of the young woman's neck in what looks a strategic position. His sunburn is so strikingly emphasized by the dead whiteness of his shirt that it almost obliterates his features. In a slow, easy movement he swings with a rhythmical regularity the leg he has crossed over his left knee and which, lifting the flannel trouser turnup from the bony ankle joint, displays a leather shoe with black quarters and a white, pointed vamp.* He is carefully shaved, his cheeks gleam in the half-light; they are plumped by the smile that curves his lips and cocks the two hyphens that are his moustache right under his nose. His eyes, fixed on David, are shining.

In conflict with his mother, the boy, slouched in an armchair, adopts a sullen attitude. The support

---

* These are what are known as 'co-respondent shoes' in the USA. (*Translator's note*)

he knows the foreman prepared to give him does not improve his temper. As the days go by, Dieter is gradually making a place for himself here, and his conciliatory role accords him familiarities that he often mistakes for rights. He is making himself very much at home, and the apartment is already stamped with his presence, for it has become his territory. He is becoming the indispensable intermediary between David and his mother – or at least sufficiently importunate to be able to short-circuit their relationship. David sees his mother becoming incapable of trusting her own judgement in any decision regarding him, as if, obliged to put herself in the foreman's hands, she had contracted a habit of dependence. Dieter enjoys keeping up the suspense which allows him to savour the extent of his domination. He finally uncrosses his legs, sits up from the sofa back and bends forward, his elbows on his knees.

'If that's really what he wants . . .' he begins, lifting his hands, palms in air. 'I'll have to discuss it with Quintarelli, but there's no risk of him making any objections – on the contrary.'

As she stares deep into David's eyes, she gives the feeling that she is making a final appeal to everything that binds them, even to his pity, as if she felt herself threatened.

'Let me ask you again,' she says with a certain urgency of tone, 'what advantage would you have sleeping at the farm? I'd be very much surprised if the men keep late hours and in any case you yourself are too tired at the day's end to be able to get anything from their company. You'll simply be giving them extra bother, that's all.'

The boy runs a finger along the piping on the arm of his chair.

'As for being bothered by him,' Dieter breaks in, 'I can assure you that they won't see it like that.

They'll be very happy to have him.'

'He might give a thought to me, too,' she complains.

'Are you afraid of being left alone?'

The question has been put slowly, slyly, and the young woman does not reply. Dieter pauses a moment before continuing:

'These trips back and forth by tractor are tiresome: I can understand him wanting to give them up. I myself would save time,' he adds.

Weary of resistance, she in her turn flops against the back of the sofa. Dieter casts a glance at David, looks back to the young woman, brings his hand close to hers and then covers it. She gently draws her hand away, checks the hem of her skirt, and sighs:

'Then all I can do is submit,' she says.

The shadow of the plane trees around the square dapples the pavement inundated with the saffron glow of evening. The absence of traffic at this hour delivers the town to pedestrians who have dined early, their distant, slow silhouettes in front of David and his mother brighten and fade, brighten again after a few steps in the patchy illumination of the setting sun's rays. The atmosphere is peaceful, relaxed, with just the right amount of lively coolness to make it possible to appreciate the rustling of the leaves responding to a dandling breeze. However, from the open windows can sometimes be heard, borne on the breeze, the nasal rhetoric of the radio, aureoled by the petrified religious silence of the listeners.

The even rhythm of the young woman's clacking high heels on the pavement produce a tranquil, carefree, even euphoric state of mind that finds in the pleasure of the perambulation an excuse to prolong it. The young woman has put on a yellow organdie frock whose pleats and flying panels take on subtly graduated tones in the brighter light between the trees, yet stand out against the trunks in the shade of which the fabric appears to be more of a lemon colour. Having to carry her handbag obliges her to keep one of her arms bent but the other, swinging freely and supple, accompanies the nonchalant cadence of her steps; her fingers, ruffling the pleats and making the skirt bell out, give her walk a slightly dancing appearance, almost as if she is humming a popular hit. She is happy, there is within her a self-confidence whose vibrations pulsing round her body envelop her in a kind of dream; she is in harmony with the insouciant fluidity of life: her heightened senses allow her to touch the materiality of things, the earth is firm beneath her steps.

David keeps expecting her to catch up with him but once he starts out with her he immediately forges ahead. He points out that at this pace they will never arrive in time or that they'll find no seats left. She assures him that they have plenty of time, that it is pointless to arrive long before the starting time, when the cinema might not even be open yet.

They plunge into the denser pedestrian animation of the main street. Young men in summer clothes mill around in noisy groups. As for the girls, they allow themselves facetious remarks that make them burst into giggles, or sometimes even deliberately accost the youths as if accidentally and then sail away from them with their noses in the air, arm in arm, shoulder to shoulder. Couples walking behind little boys in white shirts or little girls with beribboned topknots are apparently bound for the same destination as David and his mother; and there are the elderly, and solitary workmen.

Some men turn back to stare at the young woman, their malicious eyes shamelessly revealing the frank pleasure they take in looking her up and down. As she takes no notice or even accepts such homage good-naturedly, they take it as an encouragement to go up and speak to her. David cannot understand the complaisant manner in which his mother lends herself to these flirtations. The obsequious modesty of these men makes him fear them as if they had the plague. He draws near his mother and pulls her arm discreetly to keep her out of contact with them.

The further they go down the street, the more these manifestations of lust are multiplied: he feels converging upon them a battery of exasperating stares. Even the cars whose numbers are gradually increasing seem to him to adopt a suspicious crawl as they reach their level. Their carriage-work, their windows and their chromium fittings zigzagged with moving reflections suggest an ambush of eager voyeurs. The purring of tyres on the asphalt; the hiss of air upon the radiator grilles and around the hubcaps overrides the sound of the engines reduced to a low hum under their bonnets.

It so happens that a sudden acceleration or an exhaust in bad condition rends the peaceful atmosphere with a more powerful series of bangs. This is how David caught a still-distant sound, a deep buzzing that suggested a motorbike engine. He jumped out into the road to make sure. And he does indeed see a motorbike approaching. He thinks he can recognize William on it. He tries to wave to him. Behind the helmeted rider is another helmet tucked into the shoulder. The bike is going too fast for him to be able to identify for certain the young man. Left imprinted on his retina is the image of a gaze fixed straight ahead and the fierce flash of a smile.

The suitcase, sharply defined against the bed

covering, lit by the pallid gleam from the window, is animated, in the very immobility of its openness, with persistence, patience: it regulates the volume of the room around it. David's figure in a corner is confused with the outlines of the furniture shadowy against the walls. This preparation of his luggage acquires a solemnity lending his decision a dimension he had not foreseen. Of course his mother is responsible for that; but her reaction is thrusting David back upon himself, on a consideration of the unconsidered motives that have impelled them, on the uprooting he has set his heart upon, on the sense of strangeness he now receives from the apartment, from his own familiar room. The selection of things he will take away from it must not contaminate the other place. He keeps in the background hoping to immunize himself against powers not so much invested in the underclothes filling the suitcase as bestowed on them by the hands that have chosen them, folded, arranged, piled them; that have charged them with the somewhat stifling affection which his mother still persists in surrounding him with – all the more so when she sees that he can no longer find what he will be needing. This tenderness illuminates the underclothes, it swells their fabrics, it gives their arrangement a poignant character.

A breeze blowing through the window carries with it a breath of fresh air, odd sounds, progressively identifiable: the yapping of a dog far away in the countryside, the roaring of a car engine, the sound distorted as it ascends the zigzag mountain road, the rustlings of the river deep in the valley.

The door opens casting a parallelepiped of yellow light in which the young woman is silhouetted. She is astonished to find David sitting in the dark and switches on the light. She goes over to him, and lays before him a small bag tied with a piece of cord.

'Isn't it lucky, I've just found it. It's not exactly what you need, but all the same it's better than nothing.'

She opens it on the desk, revealing an interior divided into compartments filled with tiny toilet articles. David notices a comb, a nail file, a pair of scissors, a safety razor with spare blades, a shaving brush and even a stick of shaving soap.

'You won't be needing all this but I've been able to get all the essentials in this compartment.'

A third section does indeed contain, underneath a little mirror, an expanding compartment supplied with a flap that can be made secure by a press-stud. She takes out a box in which she has placed a cake of soap, a small bottle she has filled with eau-de-Cologne, a toothbrush, a tube of toothpaste.

'Take care of it,' she tells him. 'This toilet kit belonged to your father.'

He gives her a questioning look. She explains that he had used it in the army. A *maquisard* had given it to him in exchange for something or other. She adds that perhaps he had simply given it to him as a present – no one could refuse your father anything.

While the boy examines the bag of khaki oilcloth whose glazed fabric is cracking at certain well-worn points, the young woman recapitulates the contents of the suitcase, wondering if what she has put in will be enough. Won't he be needing some warm clothes? Is it wise of him not to take any blankets? And has he remembered to lay in a stock of books? And writing materials? Can she expect a letter from him? If he hands it to Dieter, she would have it the same evening.

She realizes she may have left an impression of having given herself away. She turns her head to one side, folds her arms across her chest as if she felt cold: she glimpses her reflection in the wardrobe mirror, and behind her image David's gaze following her movements. A rebellious impulse runs through her, she is almost on the point of losing her temper. She turns on her heel and goes to the window whose shutters she closes. When she turns round, she seems depressed again: she goes and sits on the bed, beside the suitcase, and from that vantage point she finally confronts the boy's gaze.

'For some time now, you haven't been your usual self, David. What's the matter?'

She goes on to confess that he worries her, she doesn't know any longer what to do for the best for him. She would at least like to know that he is not unhappy because of her. David's face clouds over, he shrugs his shoulders and looks down again at the toilet kit whose contents he ventures to handle carefully one by one. She asks him how he feels about the foreman. She mentions the goodwill he always shows towards him, and tries to prove to David, by recalling his gestures, his behaviour the evening before, the extent of the affection the foreman feels for him. She is surprised that he is not more grateful towards him, that he even acts in a hostile manner towards him.

David remains silent. Pressing his fingertips on the glazed surface of the oilcloth, he becomes absorbed in the intriguing sensation produced by the soft, firm consistency of the material, smooth as skin. The young woman imagines that he prefers William. Because of affinity of character and belonging as they do to the same age group, he must in fact feel himself closer to the young man. The boy raises his head. He hangs on his mother's lips. She goes on to say she does not know the young man well enough. He had made a good impression upon her, and she has no doubt he is very nice. But

David must not neglect the duties he has towards others. Standing up, she makes him promise to see to it.

'And you'll write to me, won't you?' she concludes, giving him a kiss.

XIV

Every separation, even when it is a willing one, even temporary, has in it the violence of an uprooting that does us harm and also tortures us with remorse: seeing a cherished person go away gives us, at the same time as an awareness of his solitude and his distress, a consciousness of the inexorable helplessness that destines us to treachery and cruelty. David has that consciousness as he watches the 203 departing in the direction of the high screen of firs, where it is swallowed up, disappearing with a final flash of its rear window.

But Mario is soon there beside him: he takes his suitcase and accompanies him to the farmhouse. Excitement makes him give little bursts of laughter that are all the welcome he can show the boy. The pebbles crunch under his hobnailed boots. When they reach the bottom of the ramp, Alberto comes to meet them, timidly, his hands in his pockets, preceded by his shadow immensely elongated on the gravel reddened by the rising sun. He shakes hands with David. At the back of the light truck parked near the shed, Renato, interrupted in the middle of some repairs, is silhouetted against the gold of the first rays of sun. Mario calls to him, asks him why he doesn't come and welcome his workmate. The youth waves his hand in David's direction.

Then comes the meeting, always so moving, with William. The young man appears in the doorway just as David is about to enter it. He has been to the barber's who has let him keep his forelock but has given him a short back and sides. It makes his face look more square, wilful, cleansed of the sombre thoughts that clouded it only two days ago, imposing the true features, the hard eyes, the fleshy lips. Nothing happens between them except an exchange of absolute silences giving way to an astonishment at finding themselves face to face, so different, such strangers, without knowing why.

'He's a regular member of the crew from now on,' Mario says.

The young man just nods and moves away. Without giving him a moment to greet Quintarelli at table who asks if he has had his *colazione*, Mario invites David to leave his bag in the other room, to which he conducts him. They will think later about where to instal his bed. William is walking backwards and forwards alongside the table. His unoccupied air hardly disguises the embarrassment he appears to feel in having to approach David.

'You've come at the right moment,' Mario tells the young man. 'Show him where the things are, I've a job to do.'

The young man hesitates slightly then goes with his languid gait towards the cupboard, seeming reluctant to take on this chore. In his deep voice, rather sulky, he shows the boy where the bowls, glasses and cutlery are kept. A spicy aroma overlaid by the yeasty smell of new-baked bread envelops them. William runs his eyes over the shelves in order not to have to turn them on David: a certain stiffness in his demeanour betrays his irritation with the insistent way the boy is observing him. He tells him just to help himself but David declares he has already breakfasted. Quintarelli beckons to them. He is holding out a bowl that he gives to understand is to be sampled by the boy.

'You can't refuse,' William whispers to him.

He pushes him towards the lumberjack, who invites him to sit down. With little pats on the shoulder and an engaging smile, he persuades him to taste what he has prepared.

He waits for David to raise the first spoonful to his mouth. The dunked bread on the palate has a rich consistency that enhances its sweetness and the taste of the milk. The boy shows his appreciation, smiles at the lumberjack who, putting on the cap he had until then been twisting in his fingers, sets it straight and leaves.

William sits down beside David. His arms and hands contrast with the dark tones of the table. With his middle finger, the young man rounds up the scattered crumbs that stick to the pad, and this activity would seem to require all his attention if his profile had not shown him to be preoccupied with the effort to formulate a question he cannot bring himself to ask. The growing exasperation he feels accelerates the rhythm of his breathing, as if he is in the grip of rising anger. He is about to give up the struggle and places both hands on the table edge preparatory to standing up: but David resolves to ask if it was he whom he had caught sight of on the bike the other evening in town.

'Did you recognize me?'

'With the helmet and the leather *blouson*, I might have been mistaken.'

William looks deep into his eyes. This sustained look sets the seal on some kind of complicity.

'Forgive me for not having responded to your wave,' William says. 'The fact is, I am not supposed to go into town. It could cause trouble.'

'I won't say anything about it,' says David.

'Didn't your mother stay to see you settled?'

David explains that, having borrowed the car without permission, she was afraid it might be needed at the office.

'I'm going to ask her to invite you to stay with us,' he adds.

There is a certain provocation in the way he says it. William is silent. Then he stands up, saying it is time to join the others.

They are all waiting beside the truck, commenting on Dieter's non-arrival. Renato exchanges a sly grin with Alberto, but in his father's presence, he has to hold his tongue. Mario proposes that they should not wait for the foreman.

David has never before seen such an expression on William's face. A smile slants his deep-set eyes towards his temples, as if pulled by invisible fingers; his lips part broadly on the perfect whiteness of his teeth. Waving his hand and crouching to leap over the backboard of the truck, he is responding to the greeting of a young man in sweater and shorts standing on top of a load of unbarked logs he is making secure. Dieter is there also, next to the driver's cabin, discussing something with the truck driver, a man about thirty. The articulated semi-trailer is parked on the open space where the trunks transported from the logging areas are stocked.

Except for Renato who is feeling famished and for whom this unscheduled stop constitutes an unwelcome delay, they all crowd round the semi-trailer. After exchanging a few playful slaps on the shoulders, William and the other young man draw away from the rest in order to talk. The young man from the trailer can't seem to keep still: he advances, retreats, throws out his arms, bends double, straightens up. Patches of sunlight dapple his skin daubed with blobs of resin and engine grease.

William responds to his gestures and actions. He does not appear embarrassed at all when the other lays an arm round his shoulders to whisper in his ear, then points to his own chest and suddenly is bent double with uncontrollable laughter. Without exactly adopting the same comportment, William appears to be so much in tune with the other's antics that he tolerates all his excesses, anticipates them, goes along with them. Their animated movements shimmer against the open space separating them from a flutterby of butterflies: their movements suggest a comic double act, a ballet *pas de deux*, and the connivance, the intimate acquaintanceship, the fundamental affinity such reciprocity presupposes lends their complicity the enchantment of a stage performance. The added grace this common accord brings to their physical charm and the radiance their comradeship diffuses on their transfigured features situate them in some other existence where, ignoring all else, they renew their sacred vows of friendship. This virile conviviality, at once crude and subtle, unrestrained and pregnant with unspoken loyalties, reveals to David a possible ideal, a fulfilment of all his buried longings and that he himself, on his own, could never have endowed with this kind of expression – if, at that very moment, it had not been demonstrated to him.

It is only when the two friends begin responding to the farewells shouted by the lumberjacks that he realizes the moment has arrived for him to return to the light truck. Dieter rushes to the Latil parked a little further off. Mario is arguing with Quintarelli and does not appear to be bothering about David who is in no hurry to rejoin them. A shrill whistle followed by his shouted name make him jump. William and his friend are inviting him to join them and the truck driver whose driving cab they are standing beside. All three of them are looking at him with amusement. William comes to meet him.

'They've offered to take us back in their truck,' he says.

He introduces him to the other two: he is surprised when they ask him to remember them to his mother. William's friend shakes his hand vigorously and calmly looks him over, and the frankness of his laughing gaze is a guarantee that he is very well disposed towards the boy. However, he transfers his gaze fairly soon to William, to whom he gives a light punch on the shoulder: he doesn't want to bring to an end the pleasure they are taking in this meeting, but the truck driver is revving up, and they can't dawdle any longer.

Soon they are all installed in the driver's cab, with David sandwiched between the two young men. The height at which they are perched above the road, and the feeling of being propelled forward by the bounds and rebounds of the truck, protected only by the thin membrane of the windscreen, makes him quite dizzy. The importunate close contact of the muscular bodies of William and the other young man crushing him between them not only impregnates his whole being with their male vigour: also, the jerks of the cab that keep throwing them against him involve David directly in their secret intimity, as in some great adventure.

Dazed, light-headed, he cannot follow the conversation the two friends keep up across him. Nevertheless he gathers that the other young man is insisting on William's being present that evening at some reunion. He assures him that there is nothing to fear, and chaffs him about his cowardice. William remains doubtful. He says he will decide later.

The roof of the farmhouse appears all too soon round a bend in the road.

So David was able to participate in the enjoyment of those hours of repose he had so far never experienced here, and was amazed at the lumberjacks' inertia, curious about the dreams that held them in prolonged spells. And now, from the camp bed belonging to Alberto who, to make room for him, had made no bones about dossing in the barn on a few forgotten bundles of hay, David discovers the peace of mind accorded by the closed space in which they are gathered, the weight and the enraptured presence of sleeping bodies. This discovery keeps him awake: he himself cannot let himself sink into that enviable unconsciousness. He does not dare move, for the rustlings and creakings he would produce would brand him as a nuisance. On the ceiling he makes out shapes that become faces; sometimes he can no longer recover the real element that was his point of departure underneath the image he has invented. His eyes are often drawn to the window, attracted by the radiance the moon casts on the recess, that is partioned by the oblique, distorted shadow of the frames. The sleepers' breathing grows louder, but even though he continues to be lulled by its hypnotic rhythms, he cannot keep his sleepless mind from wandering to other things.

The nearby persistent hooting of an owl suddenly lays its menace over the house, or at least recalls its insecurity, the fragility of its walls, the illusory protection of its roof. Only William's image can present itself to David as a safe refuge, where – without feeling himself in total security, knowing the young man's equal vulnerability – he would feel able to confront all dangers. Doubtless it is his absence from the farm this evening that is at the root of this fear. Perhaps it is in order to bring him to an awareness of this absence that an insidious worry has kept him awake, reminding him of

William's precarious situation: this obscure disquiet has been slowly ripening within him, and has found its flowering in the cry of the owl.

He rises on one elbow. The brilliance of the moon is reflected on his face, whose smooth oval is isolated by it in the shadows. He listens. He is waiting for an echo from the night announcing William's return. He stretches his nerves to breaking point so as to make his hearing carry as far as possible, beyond the screen of fir plantations and the rolling heights from the top of which his familiarity with the road allows his imagination to lie in wait. He wears himself out by this watchfulness, that only makes his anguish worse. The silence he runs his head against is like the slightly mocking wall of indifference encountered in people entrusted with a secret, and it gives him the growing conviction that some misadventure has befallen the young man.

He lies back on his pillow. The attention of all the world is focused on the distant town, on an incident that David, knowing nothing of the dangers that threaten William, feels furious at not being able to even guess at. On the simplest level, going on the confidences offered this morning and the veiled allusions of his irregular situation he had overheard coming from the young man and his friend, David envisions him arrested by the gendarmes, hauled off to the police station, slumped on a bench in a bare room, legs spread, head in hands or leaning against a shining dark green wall in the attitude he had the other day at the bottom of the stairs leading to his room, as he waited for the rain to stop.

David does not know the reason why William has to keep in hiding, and he does not seek to know. It is enough for him to know that the young man is an undesirable, an outcast, a man on the run. The vulnerability that informs his personality not only makes him more precious: it lends his presence a character of immediacy, something radical. His gaze glides over the wan blue walls, over the shapeless masses of the sleepers. Their breathing, more and more sonorous, dilates their being: their breath seems to be accumulating all the emanations of their flesh, and despite the spaces between the beds, this gives an impression of promiscuity. The boy turns to face the wall, hoping to insulate himself against this encroachment: he wants to make sure of having a space to himself in which to entertain his chimeras, to devote himself to those preoccupations that are important to him, to try to pursue his vigil.

He cannot check the time, but it is perhaps too early to expect William's return. Yet it seems to him as if the night, so long in coming in summer, had fallen long, long ago. He remains watchful, sitting up as soon as he hears a noise, but he finds it so difficult to hear anything in the room's atmosphere to which the breathings and tossings and turnings of the sleepers give a consistency of cottonwool. He gets up stealthily, carrying his shoes; he has no difficulty in finding his way through the shadows lit by the moon's rays. He goes out into the yard, whose wide stretch of gravel looks almost phosphorescent, and tries to make out forms in the mysterious vagueness investing the elements of a decor he knows only by day.

The rugged relief of the mountains, so steep, has taken on an almost flattened appearance. High, small and brilliant, the full moon makes the crests diaphanous and fills the depths with some snowy substance. The flanks of the blind valley whose daytime images and odours fill David's memory, the spread of the fir plantations all along the skyline ridges, the undulations of the fields, the bramble thickets, the orchard and the hedges – all this universe, at this hour of the night appearing so evanescent, is suspended upon the crystalline tinkling of water trickling from the tank. Underscoring this sound, to which no source can be attributed because it seems to be born of the space it has completely taken over, he can still make out the creak of a door or a shutter stirred by a breath of wind. Such insubstantial plaints distract his attention from time to time, when he would rather direct it further off, to some lost otherwhere. In the end he becomes convinced that it is not the wind at the origin of these faint callings that begin to obsess him like the howlings of a dog shivering with fear, all alone in some abandoned building, behind a locked door, and that fill one with helpless despair at not being able to rescue him.

XV

When I recall the feelings I formerly nourished in my heart towards classmates and also towards strangers, I see that the fascination they exerted upon me is nothing less than that of William upon David; and first and foremost those feelings can be summed up in the yearning I had, not to embrace them or to be embraced by them, but to sleep in their company, to have common cause with them in negotiating the passage of the night.

All at once, he cannot believe the reality of the situation that now confronts him: he is not in his room, nor is he in the room the lumberjacks use as a dormitory, and the bed he is lying on is not Alberto's. The light in the room is still only a vague, faint luminosity, but it is enough for him to be able to make out the shelves on which William's things, bathed in the haloes of time that cling to and immobilize their forms, are crystallized in patient, infinite expectation. At the same time, he sees, among other clothes, William's dungarees hanging on a nail beside the shelves: they not only assert themselves as the young man's – they seem to be his temporarily abandoned integument, waiting to be reincarnated with him as soon as he is good and ready.

He has awakened in William's room: he has been

sleeping there, no doubt about that, and his emotion is reinforced by the shock of not having been aware of it; by regret, too, that this obliviousness has deprived him of the occasion to enjoy it. The walls are turning a pale mauve; the door, the dungarees, the things on the shelves are starting to reveal their true colours. Turning on his side, David discovers, right next to him, the opaque mass rolled in a blanket that resolves itself as the figure of the young man lying on the floor. He can hardly be distinguished from the shadows still engulfing the floor.

The dawn light brightens and expands its field, just touches him. It describes the contours of a border that sets him apart but also accentuates his immobility, the impenetrable aspect of his back. David puts out a hand, suspends it a moment above his shoulder before touching it. The contact is enough to make William stir, shoving away whatever it is above him. He grumbles, stretches his arms, contorting his features violently. He turns his head towards David, and only a faint gleam between the lids reveals that he is looking at the boy. He asks him if he has slept well: his thick voice is still a prisoner in the depths of his body. He rises on one elbow, runs a hand through his hair, and the blanket falls away from his naked torso.

'You mustn't wait for me when I go out,' he says. 'You had fallen asleep on the stairs. I hope you haven't caught cold.'

He yawns. He goes on:

'You're a sound sleeper, I couldn't wake you, I had a job carrying you up here.'

He gives David a little punch on the arm, tells him to get up and get dressed, as he doesn't have anything to fit him. He falls back, his hands behind his nape. In the armpits there is a rough parting between the tufts of rusty hair glowing like torches on either side of his face. David offers to bring him his breakfast but he says no thank you: he just wants him to come and give him a call if he still hasn't come downstairs when the others are ready to start for the felling area.

The slam of a car door shatters the dawn silence. The room slowly fills with rosy light. William pulls the blanket back up to his eyes, turns on his side, disappears under the stiff folds.

Still only a little slowed-down maybe, as if under the effects of a drug that is loading his feet with lead and is lending certain of his gestures an exaggerated amplitude, William shows no loss of strength. As in a slow-motion film, it still manifests itself all the more so as he is lacking the agility and the precision that would keep it in check or consume it in the fires of action. William is impressive in his strength and endurance, at least in the eyes of the one who knows he had little sleep.

His face is reddened by his efforts. The splinters sticking in his hair, the grease stains mingling with trickles of sweat, the stubble of beard shading his jaw underline the tired features, but beneath his somewhat haggard appearance he seems determined, he never tries to take a breather, he launches out in a fresh assault upon the trimmed branches, pulling great handfuls out of their tangled mass, moving in a sort of drunken dream.

Besides, for a wonder at this hour in the morning, the whole crew would appear to be in a state of grace. Fulfilled desires have quietened their hearts, and prospects of further happiness are calming their impatience. Close at hand, the blows of Renato's bill-hook and their sharp, clean echoes indicate a tranquil mood. Further off, but with a carrying quality, the sonorous axe strokes keep up their regular cadence; the rare words exchanged when they stop for a moment are spoken by peaceable, conciliatory voices. Their world here is bounded by the confines these familiar sounds give to space, by this muffled atmosphere, by these shafts of powdery sunlight set aslant in the tall, sombre colonnade of the virgin forest.

As David is panting hard, pulling out a particularly difficult branch that keeps catching all the time on stunted growths, William who happens to be passing by notices his struggles and lends him a hand. He tells the boy he doesn't have to feel obliged to work so hard, it's not necessary to clear everything away, all that's needed is to thin out the brakes in order to facilitate the lopping of branches from the felled timber. David says he wants to help him, conscious as he is of being responsible for the young man's bad night, and adds that he takes pleasure in this sort of work. William smiles and assures him that he never needs much sleep.

They return towards the branches that Renato is piling up. The dialogue they had started causes them to keep together. The two of them do the work that until now they had performed separately. William asks David if his first night at the farm had passed off all right. David ventures a few questions about the meeting William had gone to. He confesses that for a moment he had been afraid he had got into trouble.

A strident whistle interrupts these confidences. The fir tree is about to fall, and they have been warned to keep out of the way. The young man shows the boy a patch of sunshine among the shadows where they sit down on a stump, volatile freckles of light dancing on their faces. The silence that has fallen intensifies the awesome immobility of the woods, dramatized and heightened by expectancy. The rustlings of branches stacked nearby and quietly settling, the endless fizzing of insects emphasizes even further this monstrous paralysis. William, bending down, is picking from his boots the hard slugs of mud incrusted in the soles. David is watching the bright lights the sun's rays are scattering among his hair where it is cropped round the ears and on the temples, the fine platinum threads in the gold of the forelock falling over his nose, the illuminated contour of his face against the shadows.

The young man asks him in what part of the town he lives. When David has told him, he replies that he had thought as much, for he had glimpsed the boy's mother there: the café where he had the meeting with his friends was near there. Further remarks, kept to himself, lend his face a pensive look.

The absence of noise concentrates the atmosphere surrounding their camaraderie even more intensely than on the day beside the river. It confronts them with an intimity in which they are still groping their way. William asks how the problem of the sleeping arrangements had been resolved. He supposes that David cannot be much at ease among those snorers. He proposes that the boy should move in with him. Then Alberto can have his own bed back. He himself has scruples about occupying a room all to himself.

The sledgehammer blows on the wedges have been rhythming his words: now they stop. Cracking sounds, at first faint and hesitant then grinding and confused, alert them to the tree's imminent fall. Through the screen of trunks, David and William can make out a vague stirring among the crowns, something begins swooning and almost at once they see the long black shape of the fir tree lean and sink, with almost no other sound than a sigh.

The enlarged and elongated image of the window

that the moonlight casts right into the room, into the corner formed by the wall and the door, is imperceptibly shifting. It reaches the right hand that during his sleep the young man allows to hang from his bed. The brilliant spotlight of the moon seems to cut it off from the rest of the body for the purpose of some sketch entitled 'Study of a Hand' or for an operation or a manicure, focusing its beam on the wrist delicately embossed by veins flowing down the back towards the slackened fingers with an attentive, scrupulous lighting that, for all its neutrality, is almost crude: it is in harmony with the fine texture of the skin exhibiting the traces of slight folds at the knuckles; with the minutiae of the lines like pencil strokes that present a peculiar definition of touch; with the energy his flesh never ceases to radiate. The faint reverberation from the illumined part of the wall is sufficient to model, beyond this frame of light bathing the hand, the hanks of muscle in the arm outside the sleeping bag, the satin-smooth roundness of the shoulder, the arch of the chest, the head laid on the other arm, bent, whose contact prints lines across the cheek.

Even though veiled in the mists of moondark, the outlines of that torso and that face are highlighted by the luminescences of moist skin. The young man is sleeping. His astonished eyebrows, his eyelids taut in a kind of blank stare give him the look of someone in a swoon, a look accentuated by the pulpy firmness of his full lips, parted on his regular, faintly hissing breath. Lying head thrown back in a sort of seizure, one might think him spellbound by some stupefying spectacle.

Night has fallen a good while ago, but David is still not asleep. On the bed he has set up alongside William's, he lies turned towards him, unable to relinquish the sight of him, avid of his presence that sleep places abundantly at his disposition, never tiring of this inexhaustible pleasure. Even more than the boy had been able to do in observing the pageantry of his movements, of his very nakedness, he now takes measure of the force possessing the body of this man from the colossal amplitude of his breathing, that dilates every fibre of his flesh, and hints at the presence, at the hidden heart of its organs, of a machinery capable of crushing one to death.

At the same time, one cannot help feeling that it is a delicate engine, easily broken, with no guarantee of permanence, threatened constantly with failure: and after each exhalation David remains suspended until the next is released, as if it was not absolutely sure that it would come. He has to overcome this recurrent anxiety in order to feel again, as he listens to that breathing, the overwhelming sensations of power and health the sleeper dispenses. His calm imposes itself on the air of the room, his breath rhythms its space that he inundates with his presence, with his odour, with his warmth. David feels on his own face the intermittent caress of that breathing, and it seems to him that out of the depths of his sleep William is exerting himself to communicate to him through his exhalations a fluid that will make him grow and permit him to be reunited with him.

Those gleams caused by sweat on the lip, along the bridge of the nose, beneath the orbital arch and at the inner corners of the eyelids confirm this impression of effort, of concentration and almost of prayer. Elsewhere, the folds that his posture provokes in his relaxed flesh lead the eye to a body all sensitivity, embodying everything in its gentle, warm emanation. And, dropping almost sharply from the shoulder, raised like a sail above the voyaging body, the arm floats free, crosses the softness of the sleeping bag, lets its hand hang between the two beds, inactive. The candour of the moonlight exhibits him, presents his inertia as a sign, emphasizing in it an expectancy.

XVI

He feels on his shoulder the pressure of the hand shaking him. He makes out the arc of the arm thrown over him, drawn by a thin thread of refracted light as if painted on the skin by the milky luminescence of the early morning.

'What's up with you?'

William keeps his hand on David's shoulder, shaking it again. From the boy's face, his eyes slide down his body entangled in its nightclothes and part of the sleeping bag.

'Do you put to sea every night like that?'

David struggles to keep awake. William slaps his cheek, tells him it's time to get up. He himself is gathering his strength to extricate himself at last from his sleeping bag. Once he is sitting up, however, he forgets to get out, but just sits there with rounded back, legs pulled up against his chest. He yawns and rubs his face with his hands.

David half sits up, his torso supported behind by his arms. For a moment, it feels as if the vapours of sleep are returning, or rather reconstituting themselves from their fragments floating in the light. The boy and the young man are rapt in the remains of dreams.

William is drawn in upon himself, his forehead laid on his knees. At last he lifts his head, stretches.

With a powerful thrust of his legs he stands up on the bed. His hands on his hips, chest out, head back against the ceiling, he looks down on David, taking advantage of this elevated position the mattress gives him in guise of a pedestal, and, embodying the cliché of a tyrant dominating his slave, he extends a foot above the boy's chest, rises it to his chin that he lifts up with the tip of his big toe. Then he clambers across him and goes to the window which he opens wide on the pink and blue light outside. Arms spread between the two window frames he is still holding, he offers himself to the cool air that he inhales deeply, throwing his head back. Almost at once he turns back to David whose sluggishness he greets with a reproving shake of the head.

'Get yourself over here!' he shouts. 'Otherwise I'm coming to haul you out!'

The promptness with which the boy obeys lets us suppose that he was fully expecting this invitation. As he goes over to him he contemplates William's naked figure that the light it is penetrated by absorbs, giving to the relief of his form still in shadow, to the curving expanses of the back on either side of the spine's supple furrow, to the moons of the buttocks gently hollowing on the haunches, to the tapering bevelled thighs and the muscular calves – giving to all this a shaded modelling under the downy bloom that softens it with the effect of a lingering caress. David moves up to his side in front of the window, lightly brushing against this body toughened by the cold. William does not move away, does not try to withdraw himself from this contact: he is looking at the sky, the horizon of the wooded crests now sparkling in the rising sun. He tightens his arms, crossed, hands on shoulders, over his chest.

With a hard nudge of his hip, he shoves the boy

away, asks him if he is awake now, tells him they must hurry. With that firm step that makes the walls resound to the vibrations and throbbings of his body, he dashes to the back of the room but stands perplexed when faced with the confusion David has sown among their clothes. He seizes the boy's pants, decides to put them on, does the same with his shirt.

'What if I go to work like this?'

'Shall we exchange clothes?' David suggests.

Slipping out of his pyjamas, he puts on William's shirt and work pants. They look at one another for a moment, feeling an emotion that takes the edge off the joke, deprives them of the fun they had counted on.

'They wouldn't find us funny,' William says. 'Can you imagine Dieter's face?'

Suddenly, he is in a great hurry. Rubbing his hands over his face, he makes his stubble crackle: he will have to shave again! At this remark, David runs to his things and brings back his father's toilet kit, unrolling it after undoing the cord. He takes out the razor, the packet of blades. The young man examines them.

'There is even some shaving soap,' David adds.

'English blades,' William comments. 'They're the best. Where did you find these?'

David shrugs his shoulders. The toilet things had been lying at home in the corner of a cupboard. He explains how his mother had come to give it to him.

David has entered into a different relationship with William. From now on, he cannot but receive – almost as a self-inflicted punishment – what he had been seeking to take and that now is offered to him with simple directness: the friendship of William; his story, too. The young man has talked to him about it. During the pause following the meal, he carries the boy off, unknown to the others, to unveil an ultimate secret to him. They climb up into the meadow above the farm. They push their way through the tall grasses that plunge all round them like waves shackled to the seabed, glossy with silken shimmerings similar to the sunny vibrations on the spinning spokes of a bicycle wheel. They release the harsh reek of forage. Grasshoppers and crickets scatter before their feet sheaves of springheeled trajectories. The rustling of the vegetation they crush underfoot, the rasping of seed-heads against their clothes encloses them in the bubble of their own reverberation chamber which they transport with them amid the crackling stridulations of insects. The slope is becoming steeper and brings almost level with their faces the field's undulating surface. Their only landmark is the black streak of the crest against the sky. William's pensive profile stands out clearly against the azure. From time to time the breezes ruffle his locks, flap his unbuttoned shirt drenched with light and fluttering on his bare brown flanks. As they draw closer to the fir plantations, the air brings them gusts of their fresh scent. From there, the field drops from sight, and their gaze plunges straight down into the valley. The diminished farm shows how surprisingly high they are now, at so short a distance. The absence of movement, the vacuum surrounding its buildings and stifling all life make it look like an empty, discarded hermit shell abandoned on the ocean's sandy deeps. Suddenly William points out to David a little hollow ensconced in an outcrop of grey rocks.

'That's it,' he says.

He moves forward into what appears to be his private domain.

'What do you think of my little nook?'

He is about twenty steps away, and his voice, full

of excitement, only reaches David with a time-lag in which it sounds muffled. The severe, haunting presence of the firs that rear their sombre, looming ramparts establishes a vigilant threat that robs the place of absolute exclusivity.

'Well? What do you think of my eyrie?' he wants to know.

David finds the spot somewhat too primitive. William invites him to take a look at the view from its edge. The whole length of the blind valley stretches beneath their eyes, with its deep-down golden meadows furrowed by the capricious serpentings of the foresters' path, the thickly-wooded flanks slashed with long white rides.

'It reminds me of other landscapes,' William says. 'I come here in order to dream I am back there again, in conditions different from those in which I saw them. I come here to forget what stopped me from seeing them.'

David watches his flashing eyes. William turns away, sits a little further off.

'If ever the police come to the farm for me,' he goes on, 'I'll come here. You're the only one who knows.'

'I'll hide your bike,' David says. 'They'll think you've skedaddled.'

Going to sit beside William, he continues:

'I'll come and let you know when they've cleared off.'

William sits with hanging head. He has picked a little violet flower that he keeps turning in his fingers. With a jerk of his head he throws back the forelock hanging over his brow.

'You might be accused of being my accomplice. Doesn't that scare you?'

His blue eyes piercing his own, trying to visualize in him some unimaginable other, disconcert David, make him conscious once more of his powerlessness. He swallows nervously before muttering that it is William he is scared for.

These words stymie their conversation. They don't have enough material available in their minds to continue it, and this inability to speak, this sudden annihilation of thought leaves them perplexed, overcome by the total indifference of everything around them. William leans back on one elbow, his open shirt revealing his supple waist and broad chest.

'There's not much fear of the police turning up. If they ever get me, it will be simply in the course of some routine control. Or if someone denounces me.'

'What'll happen if they nab you?'

'Nothing, really. A few months in detention. And of course the obligation to return to the army.'

He strokes his lips with the flower.

'I could ask my mother to help you cross the frontier,' the boy suggests.

'Whatever you do, don't say a word about this to her! I've ways of doing it on my own. I just haven't finally decided, that's all.'

The expression on his face is anxious, nervous.

'She hasn't been talking to you about me? She doesn't know anything, does she?'

'In any case, she would never denounce you.'

Straying from the forest where it must have distractedly ventured, a butterfly gambols around them with agitated flutterings, then flies upwards, breaking the blue expanse of sky. William had lain down to watch its ascent. Now he is crossing his hands under his head, closing his eyes to say:

'She's beautiful, your mother.'

I see them now with the others, at twilight, seated side by side next to Mario on the bench which he has carried outside. They are on one side of the door, while on the other side Quintarelli occupies the chair, the only one available at the farm and that the foreman monopolizes at the midday break. Renato and Alberto are sitting on the threshold. That is where the crew spends its brief evenings. They are there under the eaves of the dwelling whose stones compose a background of even mosaic for their faces, watching the yard, the weary foliage of the orchard and the hedges, the mountain's immutability on the eternity of the sky. Their inaction keeps them on the look-out for any entertainment, always lacking; so they are all the more sensitive to echoes of distant events resounding on the air's partitions, caressing them with their dying waves, injecting them with intuitions they do not know the source of.

Silently nestling between William and Mario, David manages to disperse the spectre of anxiety that has not ceased to haunt him since the young man had informed him of the nature of his present situation. The connivance he feels the lumberjacks are a party to relegates his worries to the level of illusions. It instils in him a confidence that sets his mind sufficiently at rest to allow him to appreciate the peacefulness of the occasion, to bring him, in the bliss of fatigue and the relaxation of tensions, the disorienting sense of a mysterious certainty. The thought of William's irregular situation still hovers around in his consciousness but no longer causes him to feel in the other's presence that embarrassed concern one feels for a condemned man or an invalid; it does not obsess him to the point of forcing him to face events in a last extremity. Supported in this by the attitude of the young man sitting next to him, he is led to believe him unassailable.

The others let their uninsistent presences be felt in their quiet voices, their bemused attention. It seems as if each one, absorbed by the evening's fugitive impressions, intervenes only in obedience to instinctive rules, in order to prevent the silence from seizing up and permanently paralysing the fragile waves that ensure the continuance of their easy exchanges of words. Without following a strict rotation but conforming to a sort of pre-established coherence, to a cast-list imposed as much by the rhythm of their elocution as by an implicit hierarchy, Alberto, Mario, Quintarelli throw out a remark, evoke a memory, express an opinion, reply to a question already asked some time ago. What they have to say is of no importance: they are fulfilling the role of concert artistes which is like the duty the birds feel to occupy with their trills the still-luminous air of nightfall.

Sometimes a flight of oratory alerts the attention to a face isolated by its expression on the blurred background of listeners. A hand is lifted, immobilizing in the air its flambeau of fingers. In the form an attitude imposes upon an arm, a torso, or the legs, language unveils its most intimate fibres or stimulates them in such a manner that it impels the speaker almost to the verge of a dance, reducing his features, in the blue afterglow, to the mask of one pure emotion. The collection of listening faces gathered round the narrator reflects the same emotion, and the oblique lighting, emphasizing in the same way the wrinkled skins and the granulation of the stones, tends to assimilate their substances one with the other. Then the hand is dropped, the expression fades away from the face that returns to its former fluid, undifferentiated structure. The eyes once more are turned away, gazing into the distance, sliding over the surface of the yard, losing themselves in the masses of foliage now turning opaque; or they cloud over as they rise towards the abrupt barrier of the heights brought nearer by the gathering dark. It is then, perhaps, that they pursue other images emerging from the memory or printed on their retinas by a calmer flow of words in the depths of their being.

Mario is the main soloist in the movements of this concerto. The Italian language raises its voice in a series of *vocalises* that pinpoint its voluble inflexions. It inscribes on air a continuous arabesque of supple downstrokes and upstrokes, it brushes the gravel, it rockets suddenly higher than the farmhouse roof, it descends by stages in the fashion of an ornamental fountain, leaping up again, falling back, throbbing, halting on a sudden dip.

At one moment, Alberto, leaning round the doorpost, questions William about some girl. With an impassibility that astonishes David, the young man replies in his even, deep voice. The boy feels in the marrow of his bones its vibrant timbre transmitted by the wood of the bench: he concentrates all his senses on this invisible gift he receives from William, curling himself round this sonorous presence deep within him.

With the evening cool, and the almost total darkness, the sky opens itself to the infinite. The first rare stars blink, here and there, through mists on the point of vanishing. The grilling of a cigarette concentrates the darkness round its glowing red dot and sketches in front of black silhouettes stencilled on blackness a sequence of unspoken words. Involvement of the body demanded by his deep-voiced response has brought William in closer contact with David. He has no intention of breaking this contact whose immobility now can be ascribed only to deliberate intention, to the expression of an exclusive tenderness.

XVII

This morning, when they see Dieter storming into the room and disturbing the powdery luminosity of the shaft of sunlight, those lumberjacks still at table display their customary mutism. Dieter is all indignation caused by the news he has heard on the radio. He talks about insidious propaganda coming to the aid of a foreign power. Intellectuals are spreading the rumour that the army is resorting to torture in order to dismantle the network of insurgents in the bombing offensive.

'Even if it's true,' he claims, 'who are they to talk of morality, and who gives them the right to preach? How can they judge, so far from the conflict, at ease in their period armchairs?'

He stops, rises on his toes, pretends to adjust the knot of a cravat and to pull on the lapels of a jacket.

'By virtue of the Declaration of the Rights of Man . . .' he intones.

But what do they know of the conditions in which things are happening? Would they talk like that, and would they say the same things if they had to do the dirty work?

'Salan* is just beginning to get the better of the

---

* French general under de Gaulle in Algeria, later imprisoned for opposition to his policies and for founding the OAS (Secret Army Organization). *(Translator's note)*

National Liberation Army. The SAS officers responsible for the *mechtas** are so well respected that they can walk about unarmed in the *bled*,† at the back of beyond, among the natives who become their friends.'

According to him, the army is carrying out a remarkable campaign of pacification: it's obvious they're trying to put a spoke in the wheels, to sabotage Salan's efforts, undermine the army's morale.

'The FLN‡ itself is obliged to employ force to intimidate Algerians supporting our lads,' he exclaims. 'And do you know how they go about their dirty business, the FLN? They encircle the *douars*,§ drive the men out of the *gourbis*¶ and massacre them with picks, knives and axes. They transform the houses and the lanes into slaughter-houses!'

Mario cannot suppress a movement of impatience, and he bangs his bowl down on the table. His irritation disconcerts the foreman who is looking at the others as if asking them in what way his words could have offended them. The lumberjack leaves the table, goes to take up the kitchen utensils which he proceeds to manipulate with no other intention, it would seem, than to demonstrate, through the clatterings he is provoking, his disagreement: then he decides to leave, barrelling towards the door so unswervingly that Dieter, watching him in bewilderment, only just has the presence of mind to step out of his way. Alberto in his turn leaves the table. The foreman then turns to

---

* Arab word: hamlet.
† Arab word: remote countryside.
‡ Front de Libération Nationale: National Liberation Army (of Algeria)
§ Arab word: rural administrative district.
¶ Arab word: shack. (*Translator's notes*)

Quintarelli, who is finishing off a bowl of soup laced with wine.

'After all,' Dieter continues, 'under the pretexts of philosophy or morality, people are sowing doubt in others' minds, going for courageous young lads, calling upon them to rebel, supporting a generation of shirkers!'

His voice lingers on the air with vibrations of an ugly insinuation that David is now better able to comprehend. Seated next to William, he tries not to betray his feelings, but he finds it hard to swallow and his slice of bread and butter trembles in his hand when he lifts it to his lips. He gives the young man looks that are as discreet as possible; he suffers for him because of the hatred with which Dieter pursues him but from which he cannot protect William without compromising him.

He imperceptibly slides his arm along the edge of the table until his elbow is touching William's elbow, and he presses his arm against his. The young man gives him a wink, then folds his napkin and gets up. David joins him at the cupboard. They then prepare to leave, ostensibly ignoring Dieter who addresses the boy:

'Doesn't anybody say good morning now?'

David starts. The foreman smiles: it is impossible to tell if the smile is one of amusement or flattery.

'You're not learning very good habits here,' he goes on. 'Your mother isn't very happy about you, and she's still waiting for the letter you were going to write to her.'

'I didn't promise anything,' the boy protests.

'Just a few words would have given her pleasure. You still have time. I'll pass it on to her this evening.'

David shrugs his shoulders. He will be seeing her tomorrow. He takes advantage of Dieter's silence to get away. He hurries to rejoin the others, nearly bumping into William who is waiting for him outside the door.

With his elbows on the edge of the tank, David is watching William soaping his chest and under his arms. He is soon lost in admiration of the play of shifting planes that the rapid gestures animate in the young man's anatomy: he still feels the same overwhelming emotion at the sight. The liberties now accorded him have not dulled its intensity, which, when it attains a certain degree, seems to be beyond his power to control and causes him to withdraw from its spell, like a sleeper awakened by the too insistent hold of a dream. As if he is now becoming conscious of transgressing his privileges, of taking improper possession of this naked body's unstinted beauty, he lowers his eyes. And another worry takes the place of these scruples.

'But what if we are stopped by the gendarmes?'

William leans towards the trickle of water under which he is rinsing his washcloth. He turns to David impatiently.

'Anyhow, the police are not on my trail,' he cries. 'They've other things to see to. And the gendarmes are like everyone else. When it gets late, they piss off home.'

The boy doesn't seem so sure. He runs his fingers round the edge of the tank. His gaze, attracted by the gleam of the water, glides over its surface. In it, the sky is reflecting its cloudless infinity, of an intense blue. The ripples caused by the trickle of water are stretching and twisting its inherent flatness, thus flexibly but unceasingly distorted, shattered under the wavelets' sparkling crescents.

William's inverted image also is fragmented into moving parts. Flattened, undulating, it is fluttering like an oriflame endlessly discomposed and re-composed. Nevertheless, the eye, instinctively adapting itself, manages to make allowances for this wavering mosaic, or to adapt itself sufficiently to its syncopations to be able to discount the distortion effect: the young man's body appears as if through the reflections of a loosely shaken, elastic film, as infrangible as the impalpable frontier of a radar screen. Under this glaze, he rears up into a firmament more blue than any paradisal beyond, his body more golden and more precise, washed clear of the dust haze in which a body is obscured on contact with air and light. He seems like some young god venturing to break the surface of the real, a faun impelled by curiosity to the verges of the visible, shaking free of its mists the world's frail membrane of illusions that he ruffles with his breath, his aura.

The contemplation of this image induces a kind of vertigo. Its lack of consistency forgotten, one at once loses sight of the landmarks of the real: it would seem as if, in a vague state of weightlessness, one were seeing the world from below, from the bottom of a well or a waterhole, through a filter that both sharpens and distorts one's view of material existence. From the zenith he has reached at the frontier of his aerial domain, William's trunk is drawn out in a bird's eye perspective, his distant face is lost at an inaccessible altitude, and suddenly David realizes that for the last few moments the young man has been standing quite still: he too is watching through the tank's reflecting pool, watching him, as he is watching William.

Those eyes in the shadow of the arching eyebrows leave no doubt about what they are seeing in him: he senses that they are reading him down to the uttermost depths of his being, discovering things that even he himself does not know the existence of. In the tilted face, with its attentive, penetrating expression, he finds a sweetness that confuses him. He does not know how to interpret it; he does not know the answer it is asking him to give.

He drags his gaze away, and turns it again upon the real figure of William standing there with his hand on the back of his neck. His inclined profile outlined on the sulphur-yellow background of the sun's rays emphasizes the curve of his full, pouting lips. While his hand slowly resumes its to-and-fro on his chest to wipe away the soap, he appears to be doing more than just daydream: he seems annoyed, doubtful.

'You don't have to feel you must keep your promise if you realize that there are risks involved,' David says.

William turns towards him, his expression still a little haggard, and he rinses his body off with more vigour.

'In fact,' he finally declares, 'you're not too happy about me driving you back to your mother?'

The boy lowers his head.

'I thought she was dying to see you,' William goes on. 'But if you think our visit won't be to her liking, we can go somewhere else.'

David sees him looking for his towel, which is lying behind him on the grass. He hastens to pick it up and hand it to him.

'If she's taken by surprise,' he explains, 'she may not be all that pleased to see us.'

'Well, make up your mind. If we're not going, I'll not bother tidying myself up.'

And he waits there, hands on hips, the towel round his neck.

'Let's give it a try,' David says. 'If she doesn't treat you right, I'll give her a piece of my mind!'

'In that case,' says William, 'I still have to get shaved.'

He unrolls the toilet kit on the edge of the tank, takes out the shaving brush that he wets and covers with foam by rubbing it on the shaving stick. Approaching his face to the pocket mirror, he spreads the foam over his cheeks, his chin, around his lips whose dark petals curl out under the mask of snow. David follows these ritual preparations with some emotion. Like the rest of his face, uncovered, the eyes are revealed to him as those of an unknown being, fragile yet tough, concentrated in that cruel glitter, those diamond fires.

As William starts using the razor and finds some difficulty in following its course in the narrow confines of the mirror, David offers to hold it up to his face. The young man indicates the degree of incline needed to hold it at so that he won't have to bend down to look in it. David can imagine no closer link with him than to be his looking-glass, no more exalted role that that of bringing him his own reflected face as it now appears, emerging gradually, so smooth and so clear, from the scrapings of the beard. The care the young man takes of his appearance delights the boy. It is the symbol of an impulse strong enough to carry David away with him on the back of the motorbike, to the conquest of promised domains.

'Why don't you let your moustache grow?'

William pauses, lifting the razor from his face. His eyes fathom David's in wide surprise.

'Do you want me to look like Dieter?'

David wants to deny it but William does not give him time:

'I never thought about it,' he says, applying the razor again to his face.

But he does not start shaving at once: he studies his face a while, adding that maybe it's worth considering.

Nothing makes one feel more inferior than having to wait in front of a door whose bell one has just rung. Even when one knows the apartment it protects, and even when one is familiar with the person or the family occupying it, it only needs a few seconds in front of that massive, flat panel, encased in its doorframe, where one stands, memory a blank, in suspended hope of a still-uncertain response, to start fantasizing a mythical image of the interior and of the person within, whom one no longer imagines as possessing a face and a body, but rather as some enormous, awesome, all-pervading corporeity.

The situation in which, accompanied by William, he finds himself confronted by the door that is no longer his but his mother's exclusively, leads David to consider it for the first time in this manner. It is this very expectative uncertainty that links him to William, whose nervous, irresolute present attitude he understands all too well. Under the crude lighting the door lamp casts over him, the young man can hide nothing of the unease he is feeling, that alters his features, stretches the skin on his temples, elongates his eyelids, makes the bridge of his nose stand out, hollows his cheeks, brings into subjection his entire frame through a contraction that lifts it as if on a long intake of breath and makes him imperceptibly vibrate. Under David's gaze he attempts to disguise his nervousness, but the nonchalance he assumes still makes him no less tense. He works his fingers in his pockets, his eyes wander round the walls, he puts his weight on one foot, then the other. The meanness of the scene, the discouraging character of this place offers him no distraction; he moves to the handrail, leans on his elbow on it in an attitude of someone resigned to wait in patience, torso inclined, legs crossed, one hand gripping the other's wrist.

Leaning against the doorframe, David examines him. How could his mother remain insensible to the magnetism flowing from William's person? How could she not be touched by that gracefulness and not offer herself entirely to everything the young man brings her in his radiant beauty, the fire of his eyes, his subdued violence even?

William raises his head, a questioning look in his eyes. The apartment's silence begins to intrigue them. David rings again. Almost immediately this time a door banging and the muffled sounds of footsteps approaching reassure him and at the same time revive his initial apprehensions.

The young woman cannot conceal her astonishment. Lost in the shadowy corridor whose light she has not switched on, her face is no more than a pale aura. William has abandoned the handrail and now oscillates at the centre of a ballet of shadows turning all round him, as if in withdrawing they wanted to introduce him, shove him forward. It is he the young woman looks at first, and David tries to make out, from the way her eyes flash, what emotion this vision awakens in her. But, opening the door wider, she turns her eyes on her son, frowns, imagining some catastrophe, waiting for an explanation. As David tells her of William's plan to substitute the promised letter with a surprise visit, she again looks at the young man.

'We should have let you know,' he says.

'Well,' she answers, 'I never thought . . .'

Feeling at home again, David takes the initiative and pushes the door right open, inviting William to come in.

'As you can see,' the young woman excuses herself, 'I am already in my dressing gown. It's not suitable for receiving guests.'

'We won't be staying long,' William answers, bored already.

Once the door is closed behind them they are plunged into the unease one feels too vividly on seeing the uneasiness of others: for a moment that seems to them an eternity, in the subdued lighting of the corridor where David has switched on the lamp, they reveal all the simplicity, even the half-wittedness that astonishment causes in them.

The young woman is holding her collar tightly across her chest, even though it is already correctly closed. Next to William, she looks quite tiny, and is diminished even more by this protective gesture. But the young man is radiant. His height, the breadth of his shoulders, his well-muscled blond flesh emphasize the density of his presence, but he is hampered by it as by some unsuitable accessory, he is embarrassed by his commanding appearance as much as if he were stark naked.

Again she expresses her astonishment, admits her confusion. David, his back pressed to the wall, loses nothing of their exchanges, stands aside to let them enter the living room.

'I suppose you made the trip on your motorbike,' she says with a hint of amusement in her voice. 'Coming to see me was a good excuse for that . . .' she adds, turning to the boy.

'He didn't ask me to do anything,' William assures her. 'It was me suggested it to him.'

Sitting on the edge of the sofa, she is once more examining the young man seated beside her. David tries to be as unobtrusive as possible: he devours them with his eyes.

XVIII

Up above the farm, David is again trying to get to the bottom of William's attitude towards his mother. He is waiting for them on the road where the lumberjacks are accompanying the young woman back to her car; each time their conversation seems on the point of ending, they find some way to keep it going, and thus climb the ramp, all the way from the yard, stopping to talk again and again, like a swarm of bees buzzing round their queen.

He has spent the whole day impatiently waiting for this moment. He has been living in the expectation of this fresh encounter in order to confirm what he senses is a new state of mind in his mother. He is hoping to discover again in her attitude that deference she showed, that consideration accorded William, even more noticeable in daylight, and enriched by the thoughts, the reflections she must have weighed. He feels annoyed that present conditions do not allow her to reveal her intentions. As on all her visits to the farm, the lumberjacks monopolize her company and think it is their duty to entertain her: they have an inexhaustible reserve of questions, stories, jokes that make her laugh.

Today, moreover, Dieter is there. As if alerted by some premonition, he has not cut short his presence at the farm: he has preferred to wait for her there rather than meet her on the road. Under the pretext of feeling thirsty, he had installed himself in the room: inquisitorial, domineering: his bulky figure seemed to make the room overcrowded. And now he is not taking part in the discussion led, as usual, by Mario, but keeps behind the young woman, following in her footsteps, confining himself to occupying what he considers to be his rightful place, in a manner both self-important and admonitory.

David, furious, moves a few metres away from the group. Hands in pockets, sulking, grumbling, he kicks at the pebbles. Mario's arias, rising and falling endlessly on the breeze, become as exasperating as the piercing shriek of a mechanical saw. When he lifts his face, when he is once more able to appreciate the light gilding the fields, when his eyes follow the long shadow shapes spreading out over the wooded slopes, when he raises his eyes towards the crests that imprison this luminous corner of the landscape in their sombre ramparts, a sudden intuition chills him, his brow is furrowed with care, and a wrinkle appears at the root of his nose as he tries to understand its cause – for he cannot comprehend this sadness mixed with happiness.

His mother's voice calling to him puts an end to his torment. They are all watching him, waiting.

'It's time we were leaving!'

Turning then to William, giving him a significant look and a smile that a trembling of the lips, a slight withdrawal of the head, a certain feverishness in the eyes cloud with disquiet, and which also seems to be a sort of act of defiance, she reminds David that they have a guest this evening, and that he ought to make himself ready to receive him.

She does not notice the reaction her revelation provokes. The lumberjacks, it is true, are now behind her back, and it is only their reaction William sees as they look at him: it is a condescending surprise, only slightly ironical or jealous. She has already turned her gaze back to David. Why doesn't he run and get his things? The boy goes up to her, looks her up and down:

'You know very well,' he tells her, trying to keep his voice down so that the others cannot hear, 'I'm coming back with William!'

She warns him not to forget anything, and follows him with her eyes when he goes to join the young man again. Her lively, hurried farewells to the lumberjacks belie the disarray that strikes her at the spectacle of the couple formed by William and her son.

Struck dumb until that moment, the foreman goes over to her, frowning. Still in a state of confusion, she begins to take her leave of him, but he makes a sign with his hand indicating that he wants to accompany her back home.

The lumberjacks are going back to the farm. They feel reluctant to speak to William and David who are following behind but who, in answer to a common preoccupation, turn to look back at the road. They see the young woman obviously distressed as she listens to Dieter lecturing her. She has still not given him any answer when she sits at the wheel, nonchalantly closing the door on which the foreman is leaning as he delivers his speech. He stands upright from time to time, but keeps one hand on the car. He raises the other level with his face, sticks out the index finger and wags it in the gesture used to threaten or warn.

The look David gives William expresses all his distress at the sight. The latter simply shrugs his shoulders, slaps him on the shoulder, and gives him a smile.

Even more than the reservations Dieter expressed, and the cautious, worried attitude they have led the young woman to adopt, it is the weighty tone she has chosen to give her invitation that most embarrasses William. Because of his apprehensive adoration of the young man, David does not find it easy to play the role of intermediary now incumbent upon him. The ruses he resorts to in his tentative efforts to break the ice, to extinguish these flashes of crystal, silverware and porcelain, to muffle those subtle and high-toned chimes they produce when knocking against each other, creating in the air above the damask tablecloth a refined but insulating sense of security – these ruses have no success.

What the young woman sees her son sharing with William is not unrelated, at its most trivial level, to the kind of *entente* (as fascinating as it is exasperating for a third party) that is perpetuated over the years between former college or army friends. The portraits David gives of the lumberjacks, the comical episodes related to their common experience of life in the forest awaken in William, despite his natural reserve, an echo strong enough to provoke him to laughter, and to make him enhance the boy's tales with his own contributions. However, even though it is at his instigation that they return time and time again to stories about the forest, their descriptions cannot hold her complete attention. Her questions encourage an exchange that, because of the intonations, the inflections, the flights of eloquence woven into it, is more evocative of persons celebrating thus the plighting of troths than of the actual experiences behind the words.

She often seems to be in the grip of a dilemma that insinuates itself into her lapses of attention, and soon takes it over completely: she seems to be thinking of what she herself has been experiencing in recent days, and to be recalling a face, an expression, a gesture whose image continues to torment her. As soon as William notices this he stops listening to David; but wonders about her lapses of attention, and does not doubt that Dieter's intervention is the cause. He lowers his eyes, but the impulse that immediately pulses through him, that straightens his back and makes him raise his face, giving his look a suppliant insistence, brings him to the verge of a confession: it is almost as if he is impatient to hear the question that would lead him to it, and is even almost on the point of provoking it.

David falls silent. As words die away, they are confronted with the one reality, that of their own bodies, that abandons them to the heady consciousness of their presences' essential vertigo. The noises of the cutlery on the plates, however discreet, underline the vague expectancy of their common suspense.

Finally, venturing to expose herself to the ambush William has prepared, the young woman raises her head, believing she can guess the meaning in his pathetic look, and gives him a somewhat strained, rather desolate smile. He feels encouraged, gets his tongue back, and, in his grave, rich, well-tempered voice, compliments her on the meal, saying she ought not to have taken so much trouble just for him. She for her part feels that it is very little compared with all the care he has taken of David.

The latter hastens to list the young man's merits. He explains to his mother the way William stood up for him against Renato and Dieter, how he had shown him the secrets of the woods and the river, and how he had offered to share his room so that he might be more comfortably accommodated. He alludes to his wisdom, his experience. He describes him as an accomplished sportsman, a matchless swimmer: 'You should just see him in the water. He moves like a flash – now you see him, now you don't.'

William's cheeks flush slightly; he tells the boy to stop exaggerating. The boy denies the charge, explaining that the young man could hardly judge by himself because he cannot see himself. Looking deep into one another's eyes, they give the impression that they are recognizing for the first time sentiments they had never admitted to, like a married couple in conversation with a stranger discovering an image of themselves they would never have ventured to apply to themselves without the mediation of a third person.

David turns again to his mother. He describes how William works, performing tasks that are feats of strength. He tells her how, for a bet, he had made Dieter lose face by managing to dislodge a felled tree that the latter, even with his tractor, had not been able to budge an inch.

'It was easy,' William protests. 'He was just going about it the wrong way.'

'Alberto couldn't shift it either,' the boy insists. 'Yet he's not lacking in experience and he looks much stronger than you.'

'I've already explained to you that they should have made play with the flexibility of the timber. You can make the flooring of a bridge give way simply by utilizing the vibrations produced when marching across it.'

This explanation only reinforces David's veneration. Turning to his mother, he defies her not to be impressed also by William. She lowers her eyes. Moving the handles of her knife and fork to the edge of her plate with precise, delicate gestures, the very image of the words she takes such care in choosing, she questions the young man about his tastes, his education, his origins, his family. David, who had never dared to ask him such direct questions, listens all the more eagerly to William's answers; he shows no hesitation in giving them other than as the result of a desire to be as exact as possible.

'And how did you come to take this job in the forest?' the young woman finally asks.

This time, he does hesitate, looking at David for advice as to whether it was an opportune moment or not to go on. In David's eyes he discovers an indecision similar to his own, and at the same time absolute confidence in him.

'It's a long story,' he sighs.

'I want you to tell me,' she says. 'But first of all, if I may, I'll clear the table.'

David stands up, begs her to remain seated, saying he can take care of the next course just as well as she. While he is collecting the dirty plates, gathering up the cutlery and taking it all to the kitchen, William is telling his mother what he had already revealed to David: his mobilization, his drafting into the parachute regiment, Algeria, the beauty of that country, the horrors of war, his leave, his decision not to return to his unit, his desertion.

Attentive to that voice invading the silence, and whose level murmur promises a lengthy tale, whose regular delivery seems as if it is going to make itself at home here, resounding throughout the apartment, making itself heard through walls and partitions, David cannot repress a rush of gratitude that demands instant expression, so he embraces the furniture, the doors, he even hugs the dessert dishes before reappearing in the dining room, as if he was certain of victory, as if, on this night of all nights, he had at last been granted the privilege of feeling himself at one with the world.

Neither his mother nor William notice him when

he returns. Moreover, he tries to make himself as inconspicuous as possible, and even hesitates a moment as to whether he should bring in the cake – perhaps he should wait until William has finished. He observes the young man's attitude, bent forward, elbows on the table, one hand playing with his glass, making it sparkle in the light. He watches the movements of those full, pale lips, the fold of his eyelids that he lowers and raises, casting anxious glances at the young woman from time to time, in a regular rhythm. She is hanging on his lips. Her attentiveness makes her frown; her crossed arms accentuate their pressure on her breasts as she tries to contain the emotion that almost makes her tremble. David knows her well enough to realize that she has been completely won over.

They have not noticed his leaving: they do not seem to be worried about it, or curious to know where he has gone; they are not waiting for him to return. He is watching them through the panes of the living-room door; his figure is lost in the darkness of the corridor, so he no longer needs to hide. He notices that they have not moved, that they have hardly changed their positions since he left them deep in conversation on the sofa.

They were talking about William's situation, worrying about Dieter's suspicions, seeking a way to counter them. David remained silent, for the finer points of the problem were beyond his comprehension. Above all, his presence might constitute an obstacle to the development of their dialogue, so he has moved away from the door.

But he comes back to it, urged on by a desire to be associated with their new understanding, to revel in the climate of hope and felicity born of the rejection of all fear from their words: but he is still unsure, unable to make out through the glass door if the calm and the immobility of the air around them, the attenuation of things swallowed up by their own plenitude are reflecting their state of mind or are simply due to the growing heaviness of such a late hour, to the peace of night.

Leaning forward and turned only very slightly towards the young woman, William sits in the patient, submissive, prayerful posture of someone who has talked himself out. He is shorn of all mystery, one no longer senses any violence within him, and the youthfulness of his face and figure is all that is left to him. He is waiting, producing an impression of naïvety and confusion, and when he turns his head towards the young woman, he has a look of supplication.

She, leaning against the sofa back, her legs crossed, affects a worried expression. One of her hands is playing with her necklace, and she turns her eyes away when the young man gives her that imploring look. She appears embarrassed by the acute self-consciousness of her body under that shifting gaze; it quite disconcerts her, and the pleasure she finds herself taking in it does so even more. But probably she is thinking it is all some childish game; she is slowly swinging her leg, crossed over the other one, for she must not accord too much importance to the beatings of her heart.

David makes up his mind to enter the room. Thankful for the diversion his entrance causes, his mother shakes her head in mock anger:

'And where did you get to?' she asks.

The boy looks at William who has not altered his position. He flops into the armchair opposite them. With one leg hanging over the arm of the chair, he pretends he is trying to guess the nature of the conversation they have had during his absence, and his eyes, half closed, let a mocking gleam filter through his eyelashes.

'What have you been up to?'

'Nothing! I did the washing-up, if you really want to know.'

'That could easily have waited. We'll have plenty of time tomorrow.'

'That's just it. I was thinking that tomorrow we could go and picnic beside the river. Wait till you see the place we discovered – it's fantastic.'

'But David, you know that's not possible!'

She turns to William, giving him a disconsolate look. The young man stiffens, and once more he has his usual wild, sullen look. The smile he forces himself to put on does not succeed in disguising the violence that is so intriguing in a being still so close to adolescence. David, at the sight of that severe face, feels frightened again, in spite of the reassurance in the limpidity and acuity of the gaze plunging deep into his own.

William stands up. He announces that it is time for him to be going.

'You can sleep here,' David says.

William explains that at weekends he visits people who are expecting to see him, who would be worried if he did not show up. He seizes the *blouson* he had thrown down on a low table. The young woman stands up, and they are both surprised to see how moved they are. She smiles, he blushes slightly, the paillettes in his eyes seem iridescent in their candid openness, his smiling lips form a good-natured pout.

'Will they still be expecting you?' David asks.

William reassures him with a pat on the shoulder, then makes his way into the corridor.

'Shall we be seeing you during the next two days?' the boy asks again.

His mother points out that he ought to leave William a little time to himself.

'That's no problem,' the latter remarks. 'Anyhow,

I'll be looking in.'

He opens the front door himself, steps out hurriedly on to the landing. He turns round and stands motionless for a few seconds under the livid lighting that enhances his blondness but blurs his face with shadow. All that can be seen of his features expresses devotion, gratitude, energy. Then a brief flash zigzags on the leather of the *blouson* that gives his back an improbable hunch, his silhouette runs down the stairs, his hurried steps making them re-echo as if he were a burglar in full flight.

XIX

Unlike nature and certain flawless creatures, imposing themselves by their strength as much as by their beauty, the world of men appears composed of bogus enigmas, of secrets impossible to keep, mysteries that leave no trace. Before we lend ourselves to such pretences, we spy upon them, unknown to the grown-ups. David gets a chance to do so once more with Dieter's Sunday visit to his mother, even though they have closed the living-room door.

Beyond the window of his room open to the fields above the town, the earth is laid in ecstasy under the radiance of summer's iridescent light, the depths of sky white as sunlit sails, the languid, spellbound clarity, the concentrated calm of the roof tiles, the whole realm of nature calling together and making its own those conditions in which thought willingly renounces all effort. In the corridor and in the rest of the apartment lying stunned around the living room, there is the same haunting silence, this atmosphere of intrigue, this knot of fibres and nerves laid bare, this burning pain. And then, among the rare words Dieter utters, David seems to recognize his own name. He listens a little more intently. His mother keeps up a mute reserve, stubbornly prolonged, as if she has been struck dumb. Dieter's voice takes charge of the silence, as it were, as he develops arguments under pressure of a hairspring that can no longer control the clockwork of his loquacity. He is also talking louder and David is no longer left in any doubt that he is reproaching his mother with not showing enough firmness.

As if the nature of such remarks had reached a limit of tolerance or revived in her faculties that had for a while been dormant, the young woman is inspired by a force that brings to her lips a harsh, rapid sequence of sharp, distinct words, on an aggressive undertow that makes them sound like machine-gun fire. She is asserting that after all she cannot impose upon a boy of her son's age conditions that only suit her own convenience. Dieter for his part retorts that David should not be allowed to impose his own caprices upon her, such as his infatuation for William!

Probably on a sign from the young woman, he lowers his voice. The contents of his speech are once more drowned in the muffled echoes of his grumbling tones. It is easy for David to guess that the young man is now being hauled over the coals: he is able to make out expressions like 'bad company', 'unhealthy influence', 'pernicious example', and, quite clearly, the word 'riff-raff'. His mother is probably casting doubt on these opinions. It must be difficult for her to recognize in them the well-mannered young man she had received. Muffled bursts of sarcastic laughter make the air shake with vibrations that seem to tighten a grip upon the temples. Dieter cannot control his voice when it is forced out by this laugh, and it brings to David's ears the qualification 'naïve'.

The young woman asks him if he has precise information. Has he heard rumours of something? Would the boss have taken on William if he had not had guarantees? – The boss? The only guarantees he got were those offered by his own son, and she knows as well as he does the kind of queer customer that son is!

Still lacking conviction, his mother's timid replies suggest to David that Dieter is determined to keep up his retaliations. She is trying to protest, putting forward arguments, but he does not relent: his firm tone of voice delivers peremptory retorts of stinging severity. Soon the boy makes out the rustling sounds of cushions relieved of the pressure of bodies standing up, the tap of heels on the parquet. He is about to close the door of his room but remains intrigued by the long pause Dieter and his mother allow themselves, and that is all the more enigmatic because their voices are silenced, and there is no sound to indicate the nature of their attitudes.

Then all at once the footsteps are heard again, accompanied by murmurs that the door's opening almost immediately allows to be heard in the corridor. David has retired out of sight into his room. The low, muffled voices hardly reach the door. He does not hear the front door opening, but the sharp slam when it closes makes him jump. For a moment the foreman's steps re-echoing in the stairwell form a counterpoint to the slower clatter of his mother's heels as she returns to the living room: then their motifs separate, disengage, and in their divergence gain an autonomy of soloists. The echo of Dieter's footsteps dies away without having first diminished in intensity, whereas the lighter ones of his mother leave an impression of wandering in a sort of confusion, allowing David to guess that she is far from happy.

She seemed startled by William's reappearance in her house, and the impression left in David by her timorous attitude, her averted eyes, that trace of reticence still sufficiently colour his emotions to prevent him – like some insidious headache – from giving himself completely to the pleasure now before him: William's proximity, the congenial presence of his truck-driver friend seated opposite them, the atmosphere of the small bar where they have met, surrounded by young people from the town who have chosen this retreat on the highway as their Sunday rendezvous.

Yes, without this ill-defined worry, he could have enjoyed the happiness the present situation offers him. Here, his close links with William are given official approval by the glances – not too insistent, just barely curious – that moving from one to the other continually bring them together. David receives a kind of baptism from them: the anonymous crowd gives him an identity as no single person could have done – himself even less – in his relationship with William. No one would dream of disputing the place he occupies next to the young man: everything conspires to establish the proof, which until then he had been unable to discover, of their intimate companionship.

So now he is savouring a sense of revenge: he sees opening up before him places his loneliness and his age had barred him from, or to which his mother's presence would not have been enough to introduce him to. He squeezes his hands together between his knees, not daring to look around him, his happiness is so great. He does not feel himself to be sufficiently integrated into this ambience – commonplace yet jovial, festive, euphoric; and can hardly believe he is just another of all these youths with their jigging knees, their restless hips, their bare necks' fullness thrown back in laughter, their muscular arms milling in the air above their heads – to be able to participate really in their bacchanalia in the midst of this arid, almost desolate plateau, and that resembles a rout of demons or fauns. He cannot bring himself to rise to the fullness of the enjoyment that nevertheless his immersion in a universe he had never dreamed of entering offers him, the joy of a novice exalted by the awe-inspiring spectacle of the wild moorlands, by the intoxication of a stinging wind, by the flashes of gold cast here and there by the radiance of the immense sky. And William, as he talks to Stéphane, continuously moves close to David, touching his shoulder, his waist, his thighs as if anxious to preserve their nearness to one another, as if he himself is experiencing the joy, and indeed the pride, in being able to show himself with the boy.

In front of them, Stéphane is almost unrecognizable with his dark glasses, his carefully coiffured hair, the elegance of his clothes – open-necked shirt and striped sports jacket. Everything about him speaks of his belonging to a well-off social class, but, after hearing what Dieter had said about him, David still wonders if this can really be the boss's son. He is less talkative, his face is less animated than when they had met in the forest. The frequent flashes from his sunglasses betray an anxious vigilance, he never says anything without first checking his neighbours: he leans right over the table towards William in order to reassure him that he has nothing to fear, advises him to stay put, that he could never find a better hideout, that Dieter after all knows nothing, and would have trouble transforming his suppositions into proofs. He sits up, leans back again in his chair, and resettles his jacket with a shrug of his shoulders.

William twists the stem of his glass between his fingers. He is thinking things over: he feels worried all the same, for there is no likelihood of being demobilized so soon. Stéphane looks at David, leans forward again and with a little jerk of his chin points the boy out to William:

'We'd have to wangle some way to prove that you have family responsibilities,' he says. 'Then they couldn't touch you.'

William and David look at one another.

'Couldn't you pass him off as a child out of wedlock?'

'I'd have to have sired him at a very early age!'

'Shit, that's right.'

But, chin on palm, he pursues his idea. Again he leans forward suddenly:

'As long as you're twenty-one. Then you have the right to adopt a child. I think that might be a way out.'

Taken aback, William hardly dares look at David.

'You wouldn't have anything against it, would you?' Stéphane asks David. 'We'd have to come to an arrangement with your mother. Would she be prepared to help us?'

Of course, David cannot answer that. Besides, friends of William and Stéphane have come up to say hallo. By inviting them to sit at their table, Stèphane puts an end to the discussion. The talk now turns to other acquaintances, Christian names are bandied about, names of places and families. They chat about the 14 July celebrations, open-air dances at the end of the week. They wonder which would be the best one to go to. The neon sign has been switched on, its letters running disjointedly along the bar's terrace like a silent message in the desolation of darkening moors that yet are still far from being completely swamped by night. The interior of the little shack is also lighted, its illuminated bay windows contrasting with the gilded radiance of the declining day. William and David look at one another, unable to resolve the mute interrogation in their eyes.

Their presence in the kitchen contracts its narrow space. The young woman, disconcerted, is indulging in useless gestures, almost scared. She gives the impression, in the way she is opening and shutting one after another the cupboard doors, forgetting what it was she was looking for, then moving somewhere else, looking no less flustered, bumping into the furniture – she gives the impression of a bird that feels threatened even inside its own cage. Her panic amuses David.

'Where's the fire?' he laughs.

She shrugs her shoulders, relaxes, raises a hand to her forehead, and gives them a rather weary smile.

'You must be hungry, so late.'

Her eyes linger on William. His blond hair, the amber tint of his skin, the supple outlines of his pose, one hip gracefully displaced, introduce such a sensational contrast into the blinding whiteness of the room that its smooth surfaces seem to lose their rigid edges, as if even they had been moved by her charm. Not that he tries to make an impression – on the contrary. If he is conscious that everything keeps reflecting the radiance of his being, he seems rather embarrassed by the fact, and the expression on his face manifests his regret at imposing despite himself a presence that while not immodest is at least out of place. He looks at the young woman, who tears herself away from the spell this vision has cast upon her.

Filled by a certainty that gives him total self-assurance, David goes to the sideboard intending to set the table. There is a note of authority in his voice when he addresses his mother again:

'We'll give you a hand, won't we, William?'

The young man walks round the table, approaching the young woman with his arms hanging at his sides. He offers her his services as if he were offering himself. She dodges out of his way, lays on the table the three tomatoes she has been rinsing.

'I fell really embarrassed, receiving you again in such a poor way,' she says. 'What on earth can you think?'

She has some trouble thrusting the blade of the knife into the soft part of the tomato, and then guiding it so as to produce perfect slices. William puts out his hands, forcing her to abandon the job to him. After a brief hesitation, she gives way. She moves away from him at once, and busies herself washing the lettuce at the sink.

As he is setting the table, David keeps exchanging glances with William, and whenever he passes near him, he touches his body with furtive pressures, secret strokings. Some inexplicable impulse urges him to rise up on his toes, almost impelling him to start dancing.

'We could go back to the river tomorrow,' he suggests.

'I want to avoid annoying the others,' the young man replies. 'Let's go at the end of the afternoon, if you like, after work.'

The young woman raises her head suddenly, her eyes looking at William with a fearful, concerned expression:

'I must tell you, Dieter doesn't want David to be with you men any more.'

The boy lowers his heels to the floor, the young man frowns.

'According to him, the work is getting too dangerous. He's afraid of accidents.'

'That's not the reason,' William retorts. 'Why would he accept Renato, and not David?'

'He doesn't want to take the responsibility.'

'Then I'll take it myself. He can just keep his mouth shut!'

She lowers her head, puts the salad bowl in the centre of the table. David looks sideways at her.

'You really want to go back there? Is it really sensible?'

'As long as William wants me there!'

A hint of tears he forces himself to restrain glints at the corner of his lids. William feels as if the slightest gesture on his part would make the boy burst into sobs of happiness.

XX

I have always been struck by the fascinating presence landscapes assume in moments of anguish, during the few seconds following the announcement of a catastrophe or of a failure, or when some disappointment in love, some grief, some pain afflicts us. The finite then is never more perceptible, yet at the same time more remote from us. Some incapacity holds us at a distance. We sense the power of such moments whose depths of silent vision, unlike the sentiments that accompany them, never alter, never cloud over with a veil of uncertainty. Confronted with this inertia in one's faculty to mine, as it were, the solidity of things; given the obtuse, stubborn, indifferent appearance matter takes on in the organization of its impassive resistance, thought is annihilated in favour of a more elemental reverie, more primitive, composed not of questions, phrases, images, but of an all-encompassing, stupefied sense of loss.

Throughout all the morning of his return to the forest, David remains in a state of prostration caused by the violent altercation between William and Dieter concerning him. When the foreman arrived at the farm and found him there among the other lumberjacks, he became furious. At once he attacked William, charging him to take David home at once. The young man pointed out that the boy was there under his responsibility.

'So you're not going to take David back to his mother?' Dieter had exclaimed. 'Very well. But I do not want to see him at the felling site.'

William had retorted that such a decision was not logical unless it also excluded Renato: his presence at the felling site was no more justified than David's.

'He's with his dad,' Dieter had protested.

'Well, David will be with me,' the young man countered.

Without the intervention of Quintarelli, they would have come to blows. But Dieter refused to be beaten: 'I'll make you pay for this,' he retorted. 'From now on I don't want to see David in the forest. Renato neither, since it upsets you.'

The noises coming from different parts of the building now bear witness less to the continuity of existence than they confirm a latent irritation, underlining, in the image of Renato whom David has vainly attempted to approach, a withdrawal of things, a closing, a determination to ignore him. Dieter's anger has left behind it a tension modifying the colour of the light, awakening menacing glimmerings here and there, or suddenly recalling the violence that the face and the words of the foreman had aroused.

At noon, although less enraged and even embarrassed, visibly, at being at the origin of the climate of discord that only contributes to an exacerbation of the sense of suffocation and congealment produced by the heat, Dieter still strives to impose his presence. However, the hostility leaguing them all against him is dying out, resentments are subsiding into somnolence, rancour is swamped by a nauseating slackness.

Giving him a nudge with his shoulder, William invites David to leave the dining room. They leave the table and cross the room, barely attracting the attention of the others whose glances they draw behind them as if focused into a wake left by swimmers, producing by their displacement an effect of deliverance strong enough to prompt the loggers to sit up and engage in movements that will make them leave the room in their turn, each one making for his own bed.

Though it is torrid, the heat of the courtyard seems to them less oppressive than the humid semi-darkness in the dining room. Even though saturated with sunlight, the open space offers their senses a possibility of expansion that overwhelms them. William lays an arm round David's neck. It is the first time he has made that tender gesture. The boy gazes up at him with an incredulous look on his face. The young man, presenting an energetic and sibylline profile, seems to be warning him not to trouble with his curiosity the link between them that this contact confirms.

They walk up the road, keeping in step. The arm weighing on his shoulders communicates to David the firm attachment William is devoting to him. The young man is pressing with all his weight on his back, tensing his arm to forge their bodies closer together. They do not speak, but seek only to consolidate this union that resists the violence of words as they pass through the fields, through the tall waves of grass.

They do not go right up to William's secret refuge. The young man suddenly sits down. He curses Dieter, is furious with him for spoiling everything. Then he holds out his hand to David standing there in great distress. He draws him down so that he is lying beside him, and tells him not to lose heart. This evening, he will come and they will go to the river, just the two of them.

At the sound of the light truck's muffled roars through which pierces a strident note re-echoing from the sides of the blind valley, David had gone to the open door. The amplification of the engine's throbbings, above all its modulations that now grow louder now almost die away, give some idea of the vehicle's progress and seem to allow him to guess its position at bends in the road. Finally, a sort of sudden gust of noise, distinct and close, is heard behind the farmhouse, and the arrival of the truck is no more than a matter of seconds away. Accompanying the hum of the engine, the creakings of the springs and the metal bodywork, together with clatterings and rattlings that are not so easily identifiable, constitute this sonorous personality which, like the timbre of a voice, would make it recognizable among thousands of others. As usual, Quintarelli breaks contact before reaching the bottom of the ramp and in neutral lets the truck roll of its own accord down to the shed, making a scarcely perceptible rustling from which emerge only the squealings of springs and the crackle of gravel beneath the tyres.

William and Mario unbolt the back flap on their respective sides and let it drop before jumping down. Mario moves over to Renato who is engaged on some mysterious tinkerings, while William goes towards David who in his turn comes to meet him. They advance towards one another without hesitating but in a restrained manner, avoiding each other's eyes as if they were afraid to reveal, through the eagerness or commiseration their mutual observation might be prompted to betray, something indecent in their feelings. When they are standing face to face, one would say that, suddenly awakened, with no memory of the causes that had brought them together, they are wondering not only why they find themselves united again and to what purpose, but also what they can be expected to feel at the sight of each other's features, the aspect of their physiognomy, the pigmentation of their eyes, all those superficial elements that confront them like enigmas. So they stand there, out of contenance, forgetting to smile.

Suddenly William lifts his head, the skin round his eyes creasing under the sun's rays that hit them full in the face, but the flash of his gaze is still brilliant between the eyelids, piercing the eyelashes. Dieter is coming towards them. His figure silhouetted against the sun is not threatening, but David feels a certain purposefulness in his step that prompts in him a reflex action bringing him closer to the young man. The foreman shrugs his shoulders and says mockingly he isn't going to gobble him up, he only wants to have a few words with him. He signals to him to approach, and is already turning away for a private conversation, but as the boy does not move, Dieter puffs out his chest, sighs, shakes his head. He wants to make peace with David. He would agree to his returning to the forest if he would discuss the matter with him and his mother.

'Discuss what?' David asks.

Dieter is trying to ignore William's gaze. He addresses the boy more vigorously. He says certain things are far from clear, and he insists on an explanation.

'We have nothing to discuss,' David cuts in.

The foreman gestures to show he will not insist upon the point, but having turned away he turns back again and reminds the boy that after all it is thanks to him that he is here at all, and that he has a right to expect a different sort of attitude on his part. He assures him that he holds nothing against him: though he seems to have reached the age of reason, it is obvious that he is allowing himself to be manipulated. Upon which he walks away, passing through the dining room to get his haversack before departing on the tractor.

Plunging his gaze deep into David's eyes, William once more seems a prey to conjecture. The thick blond forelock hanging over his brow, a few tips of which are brushing his nose, gives his eyes a profoundly worried look. His expression intrigues David who cannot resist asking him what he is thinking about. William raises his eyebrows:

'I'm trying to find a path through the clouds,' he says.

And as this reply leaves David looking baffled, he smiles, gives him a playful pat on the shoulder and invites the boy to follow him. They go up to their room intending to get towels and a change of clothes for their projected bathe. But first, William feels he wants to lie down a while. David hastens to assure him that their trip to the river is not all that important. He sits on his bed while the young man stretches out on his, holding an abandoned attitude, one arm across his brow, the other trailing beside the bed. In order to feel more comfortable, he has unbuttoned his shirt, and his deep chest is swelling out of the loosened cloth that falls on his flanks, marked by the thoracic cage that his posture is forcing to stand out more clearly.

In a voice whose trembling he cannot quite control, David asks if he would like something to drink or eat, and offers to go and get whatever he wants. William removes his forearm from his brow in order to look at him, tells him he is very kind, but there is nothing he wants – he is just feeling a bit knackered after the day's hard work. His back is aching. The boy replies that they can go to the river some other day. Would he like him to take off his boots? William gladly accepts, and stretches out his legs. He suggests that as David is removing his boots, he might also massage his aching back afterwards – but he hastens to add that he is just joking.

David returns to his bed, lies down, sinks into the young man's fatigue as if it were his own. Evening peace spreads over the fields, entering the room like a distant echo, and covering them both beneath the tranquil contentment they feel with one another.

XXI

It is obvious that the relationships established between my characters are forcing them into an untenable situation. Probably only William is able fully to realize what an impasse the threads slowly woven by feelings and desires are beginning to drive him into. So I seem to see him trying to escape from the story: next day, in the middle of the meal, he roughly pushes his plate aside, steps over the bench and with all eyes fixed upon him leaves the room in a few great strides, disappearing into the brilliance of the yard without giving anyone a chance to react.

When David recovers from the stupefaction William's abrupt departure has caused in him, he is at first inclined to attribute it to some excess in his own behaviour. But he guesses that worries of another nature are doubtless the cause of the young man's state of mind. There is no way the boy can bring him relief because, unknown to him, these cares are dragging William into regions which David has not been considered worthy to enter – not mature enough, not self-confident enough, too much lacking in experience of life. But then he can bear it no longer – he gets up and runs out in his turn. He takes no notice of what the foreman shouts after him, but dashes over to the stable building.

When he arrives in their room, William is busy packing his things. He has already rolled up his sleeping bag, and now he is gathering up his clothes. He ignores the boy who on entering lets himself slide down the wall and sits leaning against it. The young man goes on packing using gestures whose calm is perhaps not without affectation, but David does not notice it. He is simply watching those movements William is making and that are dismantling the elements of the world they have built together: those movements suddenly reveal its illusory nature, like the panels of a roundabout, the backcloths and wings of a theatre. The magician is taking down his platform, packing up his spells: he is crumbling between his fingers the faeries that had sprung from them, and now only he is left, intact, heavier, more precious, even more prestigious than what he is recuperating and storing up for other places, other eyes.

Yet in the end William turns towards David.
'What d'you want?'
'Are you leaving right away?'
William crouches down to fold a shirt.
'There's nothing more for me here,' he replies.
'Has Dieter spoken to the boss?'
'Perhaps. It's of no importance.'
The boy lowers his eyes. He hesitates before continuing:
'Is it because of me you're leaving?'
William shrugs his shoulders, gives a faint whistling sound.
'Where will you go?'
'Don't know.'
'Will you try to cross the frontier?'
'I'll see. There's nothing to keep me anywhere. I'll just take off. I'm free.'
Suddenly his gaze becomes penetrating as a hint of gentle concern attenuates the harsh blue of his

eyes, giving his physiognomy an expression of the most profound confusion. He turns his eyes away, sits down, bites his fingernail.

'I need somewhere to stay the night,' he says. 'D'you think your mother would let me?'

'No problem,' David says.

'The friends who usually put me up are not expecting me until the weekend, you see.'

'We can put you up.'

'I'd have liked to go back to the river with you.'

David simply nods his head, for his throat is all choked up.

'Perhaps we'll find another one,' the young man adds.

So, a prisoner of circumstances or of his own weaknesses, or perhaps because of a conjugation linking both indissolubly, for him there is no escaping a profound turning of the wheels, that has engendered this story within me.

Under the glow of the bedside lamp, the dazzling whiteness of the sheet illumines on either side of the opened sofa-bed the faces of William and the young woman that draw closer when tucking the edges under the mattress. The young man's features take on a radiant, almost childlike expression. As he carries out his part of the task, he never takes his eyes of the young woman: his gaze, from beneath the heavy forelock, remains fixed on her face with an insistence so marked it is difficult to say whether it is caused by simple delight in watching her or denotes a patient expectation.

David's mother is not insensible to this look. Though it is occupying her thoughts, there is no reason for her to take offence or to feel uneasy, and even less to be embarrassed by a homage she knows is in the nature of things, without consequence, addressing itself not so much to her as to the image she embodies for a man. Her rather haggard eyes show she is preoccupied by more serious questions.

The quiet of night holds captive the soft rustlings made by their gestures, the faint brushings of linen on linen. Away from the cone of light, the rest of the living room is plunged in an expectant dimness. The french window, open wide, gives immediately on the opaque mass of night punctuated by the rare yellow rectangles of windows still lighted in the façades of buildings that are of a more matt black on the other blackness. There is no breath of wind, no sound except the distant, continuous plashings of the river over the full sluices.

His mother's voice brings David gently to his senses. The two faces turned towards him express the same amusement, the same somewhat cruel pointedness in their attention. As he hands her the top sheet they now have to spread, the young woman gently wags her head with that hint of reproach that her son's absences of mind inspire in her. William's gaze is more serious. It looks deep into the boy's eyes, trying to fit the image of the boy he knows with the unseen boy who, with such an obstinate and self-assured conviction, is governing their destinies.

The slap of the top sheet cast high over the bed interrupts their communion. All three of them start to stretch it. David, who is at the foot of the bed, has the job of tucking in the end between the mattress and the box-spring, while his mother and William pull it up to the bed-head, where, with a symmetrical and synchronous movement they carry out like partners attentive to one another as they perform a *pas de deux*, they tuck in the embroidered hems.

'With all this heat,' the young woman says as she straightens up, 'I don't dare offer you a blanket . . .'

All the same, she has taken that precaution, in case he should suddenly feel cold, and she points to the spare blanket she has laid on the armchair. The smile that flits across their faces barely masks the violence of the feelings underlying it, independent of their will, leaving them at a loss. As if in a reaction caused by fear and communicated less by William's immobile leap towards her than by the attraction she feels and against which she is astonished to find herself resisting, the young woman turns her eyes aside, staggers slightly before regaining her balance, when she stands with crossed legs, crossed arms, distracted gaze.

'All the same,' she says at last, giving her head an imperceptible shake, as she refers to the foreman who, the boss has told her, had made complaints about William, 'I should never have thought him capable of such a thing . . .'

She bites her lips, her eyes wide open on some inscrutable point in the shadows. Then she looks at the boy, giving a slight frown:

'It's all your own fault, you know that, don't you? I warned you to be more friendly towards him.'

She turns towards William. With a slight shrug of his shoulders he seems to be encouraging her to accept, as he himself is doing, this inextricable tangle of chance and blind necessity that, finding their focal point in David, have decreed that he, William, should be present here this evening, he rather than any other, a docile and obliging messenger, incarnation of an image she perhaps had never been conscious she was dreaming of, or had never envisioned in just such a form, and in which she does not dare acknowledge the personage who in the depths of her being that other she sometimes conjures up, because never could her imagination have been capable of formulating an identity so precise; because never would she have believed her personal preferences could tend towards this type of man, a man almost like a fictional hero in the way he satisfies strictly formal requirements: because, finally, she would never have considered herself as someone possessing the finesse to handle a creature still in the first flush of his youth.

And yet there he is, allowing his whole body to take the initiative in displaying its charms. Flexing a knee, shifting the weight on his long legs, placing hands on hips, he exhibits himself without reserve or false modesty, making the best of himself. The radiance of his flesh seems to soak the fabric of his clothes, in which the outlines of his anatomy expressed through the creases and the seams invest his body like a nimbus. There is no trace of arrogance in his attitudes, simply the acceptation of his true nature.

The young woman remains uncommunicative, incredulous perhaps, inclined to hold fast to her conviction that this is all a game – one that is inevitable in the circumstances, and certainly exciting, but played in vain. She returns her eyes to David, who is impatient to read in them at least a partial conquest, a beginning of acquiescence. But she suggests that they should leave the young man now. The boy thinks of going to fetch some magazines in case William should want to read. The latter tells him not to bother, and begins, this time with a hint of provocation, to unbutton his shirt. The young woman makes sure he has everything he needs and leaves the room just as the young man's torso, supple and golden under the lamplight, is delivering itself from its chrysalis. She casts a furtive glance at him through the glass door. The rays from the bedside lamp enhance the contour of the muscles whose firm bevellings stand out from the shadowy hollows of their junctions. Before she moves away, she meets his eyes that have been following her and gleam then with a brighter light.

I can quite see that it is inevitable it should happen thus: David, during the night, creeping towards the door of the living-room, not bothering to close his own behind him – for he does not intend to stay long in the corridor nor to venture too far simply to satisfy a mordant curiosity – hoping perhaps to find his longings fulfilled and for that very reason impelled to approach ever closer because it seems to him as if that will indeed be the case and – though he does not dare believe it – wants to confirm his anticipations. He can make out no shape under the whiteness of the sheet that seems to glow with a teasing absence.

Smiling, he pauses and listens in the direction of his mother's room, but no sound comes from there, so he wants to make quite sure. He continues his progress towards the living-room door with less hesitant steps, so certain he is now that he is right. No, William is not in his bed but, from behind the door, David cannot see if he is somewhere else in the room. He gently opens the door.

Barely has he passed his head through the opening than he discovers the young man leaning against a leaf of the open french window, his weight displaced on one hip, his body encased in a silvery aura formed by the light of the moon or the refraction of the street lamps and that emphasizes his outlines, making him stand out against the profound blackness of the night. He seems to be rocking to the rhythm of some tune running through his head and that gives his hips and his flexed knee a languorous oscillation, though perhaps the movement is caused by a shivering of the air around him.

David decides to enter the room, and closes the door behind him. The click of the latch, the soft steps of his bare feet as they brush the parquet, the creaking of certain blocks he tries to diminish but does not attempt to avoid, the stir that his intrusion provokes in the heavy stillness alert William who glances over his shoulder, suddenly incising his profile upon the powdery radiance; but he moves it away at once, he does not turn round, but displays a sufficiently obvious reticence to dissuade the boy for a moment from approaching any closer. David remains a couple of paces behind the young man's naked back, entirely absorbed in the contemplation of its only faintly gleaming shapes where the furrows and gentle depressions appear all the more darkly modelled on the shadowy flesh.

As William's very immobility suggests that he is waiting for an initiative on his part, the boy resolves to take the two steps that still separate him from the young man's nakedness. He raises one of his hands to the level of the youth's shoulder, and slowly places it there. He weighs on it with a pressure that he would like to make both suppliant and persuasive, asking forgiveness for the disappointment this night has caused his friend, urging him to be patient, assuring him of his support. Then, in a whisper, he asks him why he cannot sleep.

William's shoulder rises a little under the boy's palm, shifting it imperceptibly, allowing it to slide over the rounded richness of the warm muscle. However, with a deliberate slowness that could never be taken as a rejection, the young man turns away from him and pivots on his heel in order to go back into the room where, his nakedness paganly mottled with light and shade, he moves fairly swiftly to the bed. He sits on the edge with precaution and in an attitude that are all a little strange, theatrical, as if caused by a vast weariness or extreme discouragement. On the edge of the bed, his trunk leaning forward, shoulders raised, he squeezes his rigid arms between his thighs, and his face, barely lifted, appearing ghostly through the sooty veil of night, is betraying, beneath the casque of fair hair shot with coppery threads, a certain annoyance mixed with embarrassment.

Surmising what it is that he is thus trying less to conceal than to spare him the sight of, David recalls that engorged, purplish turgescence to whose imperious exactions he had surprised William offering up his entire body in ecstatic sacrifice, and the consciousness that behind the curtain of the young man's tense arms there is at that very instant in a state of erection, iron-hard, taut, blood-boltered, drawing on every fibre of William's anatomy, the tumescent burgeoning of his sex, produces within him such an overwhelming thrill that the boy at once feels his guts writhing and his own rod proudly standing erect.

Though convinced of the impossibility of William's noticing anything, since the boy, with his back to the moonlight, can only appear to him in shadow, he cups his hands over the swelling's cumbersome arousal and moves towards the bed, his steps hampered by the throbbing tensions in his vitals. He sits down cautiously, at some distance from the young man, and raises one knee against his chest, the better to hide his horny erection from a possible sideways glance.

They both sit gazing at the haloed moon's misty luminescence dusting the darkness beyond the french window, bright enough to cast a pale, phosphorescent veil over the cement of the balcony, the leaves of the plants, the cross-pieces of the window-frames. They keep gazing fixedly at it in order to avoid looking at one another, pretending a somnambulistic numbness that absolves them from the neccessity to speak; but they are well aware of their common attentiveness to one another in their present manly condition, and of their obsession with their prolonged state of embarrassment. The keen intuition they have of what is keeping them both so tensed up does not prevent them from focusing all their attention upon it and willing an accentuation of its dolorous manifestations – at the same time in the immobility and silence hoping and praying for a blissful easement of their predicament, a mutual release that alone would allow them to regain their peace of mind, their comfortable familiarity.

They become strangers again to one another, they are kept apart by the haunting apprehension of being discovered in a condition of which they are ashamed, as if they feared it might destroy the image they have of one another, might expose them to humiliation, subjugated as they are by a master whose total domination over them deprives them of the liberty to dispose of their bodies as they would wish. They experience the reflex of wounded beasts that defeat chases away from the light of open spaces. They cannot dream of showing themselves thus branded in the most intimate recesses of their disfigured flesh without running the risk of frightening others, of provoking mockery or inspiring opprobrium.

However, William, still bending forwards, is giving his trunk a slight rocking motion destined to dissipate the torpor that holds them in its spell. While still keeping a rein on the words now probably on the tip of his tongue, he casts a glance at David from time to time, then considers him more pointedly, waiting for the boy to turn his eyes upon him. David cannot bring himself to face his gaze. So then, removing an arm from between his thighs and holding it out towards him, William lays his hand on David's drawn-up knee, and tries to make him lower it by using a fairly powerful pressure.

'What've you got hidden there?' he murmurs to the boy.

David resists the pressure, perhaps in play, since

William is the stronger of the pair and he himself is no longer so determined to preserve his privacy; perhaps in fear, suspecting that William, at the sight of his whiteish member, well-developed certainly but still smooth, mottled, unfledged, might have the same reaction to it as himself, finding it repulsive, disgraceful, disproportioned, as if not really belonging to his body.

The pressure of the hand upon his knee becomes more insistant, and feeling he might displease William by persisting, he lowers his leg. All the same, he cannot bring himself to look at the young man, and he waits, in this total abdication and dereliction, the reaction that will either save him or condemn him. But William says nothing, makes a brutal advance, and comes so close that the bounce of the mattress beneath their weight brings them side by side. The young man spreads his thighs and stretches his legs in front of him, at the same time delivering his torso to the light that at once picks out the quivering arc of his horny member, its sides thickly swollen, its underside columned all its length by a tubular channel firmly distended, laced by tortured veinings that intensify the impression it gives of being on the point of bursting, the tender, frail orifice of the prepuce continuing to expand under the strong thrust of the empurpled glans, already half-uncovered, slippery, gleaming.

'You see,' William hoarsely whispers, 'we're both in the same boat!'

He is just as unsure of himself as David is: his eyes looking into the boy's even betray uneasiness, as if he were afraid of behaving too audaciously, or as if he felt overcome by some sense of remorse, the idea that he might be shocking the boy.

Divided between the emotion he feels at the confidence William puts in him, and the awe that grips him at the sight of his violently exhibited cock, David is at first paralysed. The vision of this body that has nothing more to hide and displays for him alone a power that is perhaps not vain but rather purposeless, distraught, ill-omened, leaves him feeling at a loss. It seems to him that this vision is demanding something of him. He is sure that William is asking nothing of him and that he is exposing himself to him thus stark naked out of a pure desire to be frank with him: but that body is calling to his own body. He guesses that his flesh, his skin, his palms have in their possession something that William is for the moment lacking, that he is clamouring for, and that to keep him waiting any longer would be to torture him.

Then he is gained by the intuition, by the conviction that he has to take William's prick in his hand. Although unable to descry any certainty in it, William's gaze is upon him, at once questioning and imploring him. The boy slowly twists his body round and begins to lift his arm, sensing the distance his hand must travel. William's shaft visibly stiffens, vibrates at his approach, seems to want at the same time to abandon itself to him and to withdraw, and now it is something pulsing with life, burning, springy yet hard as rock and of a monstrous size that he has between his fingers, that submits to his capture, that pours through his own body an intensely voluptuous fire.

William makes no move. On the contrary, he intensifies his immobility as he grows taut at the contact of this hand that arouses every fibre in his body. Head thrown back, he closes his eyes, parts his lips, concentrates upon these rushes of stabbing bliss that the to-and-fro motions of David's hand sliding up and down on his prick, at first slowly and hesitantly, then gradually more firmly and rhythmically, unleash like bolts of lightning in the very depths of his being, the furthest fathoms of his flesh. David wonderingly observes, in the passionate contractions of the young man's lips and eyelids, the almost puzzled knitting of his brows, the eager flarings of his nostrils, the ritual progression of the dark forces now taking possession of William. The boy has no consciousness of being in any way personally responsible for this voluptuous pleasuring: rather he feels he is just doing a job, compelled by some blind authority beyond himself and outside the young man's control to bring this task off, to be made use of in order to sustain the frenzy of this flagellation that keeps William in bondage to him, and which the young man, by his feverish contorsions, strives to exasperate ever more brutally, the chosen instrument and vessel of this mysterious chastisement he has to both provoke and suffer.

 The progressive hardening of the member tends to loosen the garrotte of his fingers, the pounding surges of blood in its adamant shaft, the convulsion of sinews at its root, the loaded testicles, the thrashings of the foreskin against the distended, inflamed corona of the glans, the fluid, crystalline, oily secretions that lubrify it, the shuddering paroxysms that keep jolting William, his accelerated panting, the feeling that the young man, in his ever more violent jerkings, is going to slip out of his over-excited grasp – all these things hold the boy in the grip of a delicious panic he cannot subjugate, caught up as he is in the machine-like beat of a rhythm that now utterly dominates his own flesh. Overwhelmed by the force of his own movements as they participate in the torture he is inflicting upon William, longing all the time to interrupt them for fear that the young man might die beneath his hand, he nevertheless both accelerates and throttles them in spite of himself, obedient to the deep groans and sullen growls coming from

William and which are interpreted by the boy as so many imperious and terrible commands. He feels the young man's whole body arching, he sees his face contorted in a grotesque grimace, the throat labouring in his abandoned neck, he hears this grave roaring that is rising from the depths of his chest and that his clenched teeth try to stifle but nevertheless are forced to release at last, as, at the same time as an ultimate convulsion arches his weapon to the extreme limits of endurance, an overpoweringly vigorous cataract of red-hot fluid shoots out, succeeded by others, weightier and creamier, pouring, under the pulsions of fresh spasms, from the tip of the shaft, and running down all over David's fingers, that are now dripping with fragrant sperm.

The boy only now begins to realize that the movements he has just been making and that he had been reducing little by little until their purpose was fulfilled were as nothing compared to the difficulty he feels awaits him at this crucial moment when he must look back again at William's face, questioningly, listening for his first reactions, begging to know if he has performed his task well and also wondering if perhaps he is going to be thunderstruck by the young man's anger. In those first few seconds, it is all the destitution, all the distress of a pathetic boy stripped bare of everything that he must lay before William's feet, and his anguish keeps growing as the time passes, as he feels between his clammy fingers the young man's member gradually softening, retracting into its thin sheath of skin, signalling that the culmination of all pleasure is now in the past.

Then he sees William's belly creasing under the tension of the muscles as he raises himself up, and, almost at the same moment, David feels his arm laid round his neck, pulling him against him, holding him tightly, dragging him down full-length upon him on the bed.

They lie there motionless, silent. His face crushed against William's warm breast as the young man plays with his hair, David closes his eyes. He listens to William's heart pounding slowly and gravely underneath his cheek, he hears the faint rustlings of his hair twining in William's fingers, their breath rising and falling in harmony, and these light sounds cradling his happiness, they almost fall asleep in the haven of one another's arms.

'And the lateness of the hour, the tranquillity of time slowly passing, the very silence around them produce a kind of profound throbbing in his ear, as if the slight noises he hears are coming from within his skull, as if the low hum of his own body were taking the place of all other sounds, enclosed as he is in the comforting security that comes from a common consciousness of their approaching slumbers.

Torn between this gradual numbing of his faculties that he is plunged in as he lies resting in William's embrace and the worry he feels at the prospect of having to return to his own room, David is being shaken by light spasmodic movements that prevent him from dropping off completely. He keeps his ears pricked listening for some indication that he might mistakenly have ignored William's suggestion that he should leave: but he can hear nothing but the beating of their two hearts, the mingled sighs of their breathing, the rustling of their hair troubling this ever-present, everlasting tranquillity. The boy allows himself to hope that he is going to stay there beside the young man, for William's arms are still holding him firmly clasped against his body, as if nothing could ever again come between them.

Despite the discomfort of their posture, he takes care not to make the slightest movement for fear of initiating any kind of change in the disposition of a world that has forgotten them. He prays that the sense of peace beginning to flow through him, patiently encouraged by William's tender fingers continuing to play with his hair, that this exquisite languor may go on for ever and ever.

XXII

David fell asleep against William. The young man waited until his sleep was deep enough to take him in his arms and carry him to his room. Thus, when he came to wake in his bed, late in the morning, David might have thought he had been dreaming – which could be said to be the case, for the relationships we have with others and the images we superimpose upon those we love are after all nothing more than chimeras.

Of course, it was not for William to make any allusion to the night they had spent together. Yet he was there, sitting on the edge of David's bed, and when the boy opened his eyes, the first thought that crossed his mind was that the young man must have been watching him a long time: under the blond forelock his gaze still had a contemplative gentleness, his eyes wide with wonder showed that they were still watching his face, taking in his features, thinking about the identity of the being who had taken his flesh in hand, and who was the same as the one who had shown him so much admiration, abnegation, such an absolute devotion. And what David felt next was the finger-tip William was passing over his cheek, a caress with which he was wakening him as if against his will and that he was continuing almost absently, no longer thinking of hiding his tenderness from him. In the look they exchanged – so long, so peaceful – there surfaced a common knowledge already blurring in their memories but dispersed within them, nourishing their cells, and from now on becoming a part of their being. Then William had started joking about David's laziness, making plans for the morning, saying that they must no longer delay if they wanted everything to be ready in time for his mother's return at noon.

    Loaded with shopping, they are now returning home, discovering in the atmosphere reigning under the plane-tree avenue bordering the square a holiday air that makes them want to linger. The travelling showmen's caravans have taken over the borders of the esplanade. In the middle they are busy erecting the roundabouts. Tarpaulins set a seal of secrecy that excites some curiosity as to the nature of the attractions. Children, adolescents, even grown-ups keep wandering round them trying to make out details that would satisfy their curiosity, while the fairground people treat them with indifference as they go about their business, not without a touch of arrogance, in the spaces separating the caravans. All this creates a sense of animation that diffuses in the midsummer air a feeling of amusement in total harmony with the golden light of morning and the faultless blue of the sky where some jovial and carefree spectator seems to be giving it all his full attention.

    David keeps looking up at William. He is careful to keep in step with him so that they walk side by side. The glances of passers-by cannot come between them, separate one from the other. Whether they are housewives going to the shops, young people belonging to William's generation or young boys of David's age, none can take in one without the other. David is beginning to think that their reactions put the seal on a relation he could never have objectified, and that he would never have had the audacity to imagine so perfect. But he is surprised that their eyes are not fixed more on William, whose noble physique David thinks must be plain to everyone in the T-shirt and white shorts he has put on this morning. With his blond hair, his free-and-easy walk, tapping his bare thigh with the folded newspaper he is holding between two fingers, looking straight ahead of him, he seems to David aureoled with a climate all his own, whose unchangeableness exhales the perfume of another world, the perfume clinging to his perfect body.

This impression is again reinforced in the way David looks at him in the sawmill, where William has gone thinking he might find Stéphane there. The boy watches him, surrounded by workmen he is questioning.

He has not dared follow him into the sawyard where the turbulent snowstorms of sawdust preserve a sanctuary for the machines which the spasmodic screechings of the saw frames slicing up the trunks fill with a dissuasive stridency: but, from the edge of the machine-shop where he is standing, he marvels at the immunity the young man seems to be enjoying from the very fact of the lightness of his attire, that seems to make his whole body send out rays of light, thrusts back the half-light around his well-knit, lissom silhouette. The sawyers have stopped their work. Respectful, they keep a certain distance and are sorry not to be able to furnish the information he wants. They ask each other questions to which they can only reply with a helpless shrug of the shoulders or by indicating, by movements of the head or hand gestures, vague and conflicting directions.

They follow him with their eyes after he turns away from them to rejoin David. The boy tells him they are not very far from the river. He takes him there.

Adjoining windowless walls and somewhat sinister buildings, a grassy open space occupies a few metres beside the river. They sit there out of the sight of prying eyes. William remains sitting but David lies face downwards on the ground, looking towards the young man who is partly hidden from his view by the newspaper he has unfolded and is reading. But the boy is still able to drink in rapturously the smooth firmness of William's bare limbs, whose bent attitude, knees apart, are alive with a vigour all their own. The boy observes their zones of tension, the spaces in which power is contained, the relay areas where fibres are gathered into a final culminating point from which they transmit their energy, before it becomes exhausted, to other fibres that pick it up again, renew it, use it in tracing other curves, in unfolding other shapes. His eyes linger over these vast concave expanses where the relaxed flesh, though still within the firmness of its contours, suggests the softness of sand dunes: the inner flanks of the thighs spreading towards the groin, which is reduced, at the fork of the crutch, to a triangle of wrinkled fabric forming a gore that cups the weight of the member and the scrotum's heavy balls. He feels light-headed with amazement at the possibility of being able to dispose of William's body as he pleases, and in doing so to provoke neither his embarrassment nor his anger, to be henceforward so at one with the young man that no look they might exchange could ever again present some dubious or illicit aspect in their close relationship.

Nevertheless, he notices from the frowns and the fixity of the eyes that William casts on the newspaper whose pages he keeps shaking so as to alter their reading position, that the young man is bothered by something. Almost at once he folds the paper and stands up. He admits to David who cannot conceal his concern that he prefers not to keep himself informed on certain subjects. He suggests that they should go home.

She had appeared mortified when she had to tell them that the *gendarmerie* had telephoned the office. The boss had been in a rage all morning. Of course he had questioned her, asking her what she knew about William. She realized then that Dieter, better informed than they had suspected, had set the boss against him in no uncertain manner. If William were to go on staying with them, he would certainly be arrested.

In a deserted alley down in the working-class quarter of the town, a boy is standing beside a young man who is straddling a motorbike. The latter's white T-shirt and shorts stand out against the black shapes of the engine. They do not speak: they both keep their heads lowered, hugging to themselves the stupefaction of this heart-rending separation. David is running his finger over the swollen mass of the tank: William is holding the handlebars with only one hand, and the other is lying on his thigh so that David can reach the tank easily. His forefinger tracing ephemeral arabesques on the lacquer is invading a territory that William now feels David has every right to explore. He is suddenly conscious of an emptiness there at the pit of his being, an empty space where, against all reason, he would be only too glad to cast all prudence to the winds and install the boy.

'I'd be glad to take you with me,' he says at last, 'but you know it's impossible.'

The boy takes his finger away from the tank, and nods his head.

'Just let me find some place for tonight, that's the

most urgent. Then this evening we'll see if you can stay on with me, if your mother is agreeable.'

He leans forward and seizes the other handlebar. He plants his boot on the starting pedal: a single vigorous kick is enough to start the engine that is still warm.

'She may find a solution,' David says.

The hard look on William's face intimidates him, as does the severity of the profile he has already turned away as if he was in a hurry to leave the boy behind him. The motor is throbbing softly within the fork of William's broad thighs as he releases the brakes and begins to roll forward slowly. David walks beside him.

'You sure you've got it right about where to meet?' the boy asks him as the bike, now running faster, forces David to start trotting beside it. 'Can you find your way?'

'I'll be there,' William shouts.

The boy breaks into a run in an attempt to follow him but he is left standing and all he can do is watch the white T-shirt fluttering in the breeze, seeing it grow smaller until a turning hides it from sight, though the final echoes of the throbbing engine are curiously amplified, reaching him like an exhortation.

They reach a plateau where the evening light gilds the tall grasses that crackle beneath their feet and rustle against the young woman's dress. She is still worried about William's new lodgings: has he found a safe place? Will he get enough to eat? Will he be sure no one will betray him? William does not answer her questions; the face he turns towards her is radiant. She repeats her questions: she knows from experience that the more one depends upon friendship, the less dependable it becomes. She speaks in a confidential manner David had never heard her using before, an urgency as flustered as when it concerns himself, and he can sense, beneath the tedious accumulation of advice she unloads upon him, that she is a prey to unreasonable apprehensions. He is afraid that William may feel as annoyed by them just as he is himself, but on the contrary it all seems to encourage him to treat her more boldly. He jokes with her before laying a hand on her shoulder in a gesture as grateful as it is affectionate.

They push their way across the grassy plateau whose tall stalks rise up again behind their passage, covering up their tracks, and isolating them by extending all round the couple they form an ever-widening zone of solitude, as if they had moved into another epoch. The more reserved attitude of the young woman finds itself opposed by the young man's ardent, all-conquering eagerness that urges him on, exalts him, makes him jump for joy, as his blond hair sparkles in the sun, the movements of his head giving it iridescent gleams. Walking just ahead of the young woman, he opens out for her the landscape curving away beyond the grassy plateau into a wide dale where no visible road, no fence divides the meadows. A few massive buildings in the distance are the grave custodians of a secret and restorative intimacy. The sombre bands of the forests on the heights frame the dale without shutting it off completely. Overhead, the sky looks timeless, eternal in its original colour and purity.

Holding out an arm, William guides the young woman to a stony little plot planted with elms and beech trees. He invites her to sit down here on a smooth stone that serves as a seat and suggests that David sit on the grass between him and the boy's mother. The breezes stirring the topmost branches keep up a gentle rustling that for a while takes the place of conversation.

Returning to his usual grave demeanour, William asks David's mother if she has again been bothered at the office because of him. She does not conceal the fact that there has been further discussion about him, but this time from a strictly administrative point of view. On the other hand, she has had to invent a pretext in order to bring forward by one week the recruitment of truck drivers, the only chance she has to visit people likely to have a solution to their problem. In fact, everything had gone well and now she is able to tell him that if he wishes he can find a job with some farmers who need extra hands during the harvest season. They are people she knows personally, and she trusts them completely. Their farmlands moreover enjoy the advantage of being relatively isolated and close to the frontier. With a little help from her friends, he should have no trouble in crossing it. All the same, she does not know if the accommodation and the working conditions will suit him.

William declares that he could never have found anything better. He just regrets having to be far away from her and from David. The frankness of this statement disturbs her. David starts quoting names, but a negative shake of her head dissuades him from continuing: she says he does not know the farmers in question, but that they are in fact just as helpful as the ones he has been citing.

'Perhaps they could take me on with William,' he suggests. 'You could come and visit us on Sundays.'

She tries in vain to suppress a smile.

'Don't you think that William already has enough on his plate taking care of his own affairs?'

'Your mother's right,' William says. 'I'm fed up with having you always under my feet.' He gives the boy an exasperated look that the sparkle in his eyes shows is make-believe, then throws himself upon David and hugs him to his chest.

She adds that the farmers will not be expecting him until next week: will he be able to find lodgings somewhere until then? Still hugging David, William assures her that it presents no problem and that whatever happens he is not likely to die of frostbite if he sleeps out of doors in this high-summer season. He gives her a more pointed look: he does not know how to express his gratitude.

'Give her a kiss!' David shouts, removing William's arm from his neck but holding on to it to drag the young man towards his mother.

She protests that what she has done is nothing out of the ordinary: she is fully aware of all that David owes him. She would have continued, interposing a frail veil of words between herself and William's approach, but he doesn't wait for her to finish, and presses his lips on her cheeks.

'I'll go and get the basket,' David says.

He runs back to the car and does not turn round until he has reached it. They are again almost face to face, his mother with her arms crossed over her breasts, William sitting cross-legged at her feet. The leaf shadows blend their figures flecked with moving spots of sunlight.

They are still in the same position when he returns with the basket. His mother asks William what he will do until Monday.

'I'll be missing you,' he says.

'Let's all go to the fair on 14 July!' David suggests.

His mother thinks it would be taking too many risks.

'No one will notice us in the crowd,' the boy insists. 'We'll put on disguises!'

William thinks it's not such a bad idea. He'll wear a hat, let his moustache and beard grow.

'People will think you're fiancés,' says David.

'A fine reputation I'm going to get!' his mother sighs.

'I'll be the one making everyone jealous,' William says.

The young woman remains silent. They agree to think the matter over and to meet here again the next evening before making a definite decision. David is worried at the young man having to spend a day all alone. How will he occupy his time?

'With you, naturally!'

'Really?'

'Your mother can't leave you without supervision, you know very well!'

'It would be wiser not to show yourself in town,' the young woman says.

'Take him a little beyond the level crossing, at the crossroads. I'll come and pick him up there. We'll be seen only by the birds and the bees . . .'

XXIII

After a dead-straight hundred metres or so, the road along the hillside opens on the hollow formed by the shadowed end of the valley, but David knows that at this point it cuts off into a steeper slope and so descends to the level crossing, beyond which stand the town's first houses. He can make out a part of their roofs through the halo of mist that veils them and that is pierced only by the glint of what are probably dormer windows, or the edge of some tiled roof iridescent with dew, or some new length of guttering – glints like those cast by mirror fragments. Suggestive of the underlying swarm of life caused by the revival of daily activities, a quivering passes over the downy layer which is taking a long time to dissipate.

From the bank on which he is perched, David now lets his eyes travel upstream: the road on this side climbs with many a twist, appearing and disappearing several times before vanishing beyond the shoulder of the hill it encircles. It is from that direction that William should appear.

In his impatience to see him again, it seems to him that the precision taken on by the landscape's contours is the result of some special effort, as if it were definitely disposing itself to receive the young man, was tensing itself in preparation to welcome his arrival on the scene, beginning – alerted in this respect by distant vibrations – to lay plans for the settings that will be organized around William's entrance, and that in this way they prefigure, await, and find indispensable to their self-composition.

David is not sure if he should go to meet him. That would remove him from the crossroads where begins another road along which William could just as well be coming. He is careful not to dissipate his energies in frivolous gestures, in exuberant and uncontrolled demonstrations of the joy that is accumulating within him and diffusing itself in distracting pins and needles all through his limbs. Faced with the length of time that has been promised and all the hours in William's company lying before him, he is expecting a pleasure that, just as much as any pain, is beyond the means he disposes of to bear it.

The young man should not arrive too late. It would be best for him to arrive at this, the most powerful moment of the boy's waiting, at this moment in which his yearning for the young man takes him right out of himself. William ought to appear now, to coincide with his image and assume the royalty the landscape is conspiring to confer upon him. Punctuality is the politeness of kings, and also their privilege. It is a characteristic of commoners never to be on time, detained by their deficiencies and restrained by their limitations, held back by their subjection to events and things.

But apart from the rattling of stalks in the fields, that are lifting up their heads under the heat and the dispersal of dew absorbed by the earth; apart from the more remote, haphazard, indolent chinkings of the little bells round the necks of the herds scattered over the pasturages, no sound comes to trouble the immobility of space, no hint of a sound even to reduce space to a point towards which

David can direct his ear. The heat of the sun's rays is already robbing the air of the underlying freshness that made it so alive. The morning is overtaken by that dense, stifling heat in which the day will gradually be slowed almost to a halt. Already beads of sweat are standing out on his brow, on his upper lip, and moistening his palms.

David keeps walking to and fro on the ridge of the bank, letting his eyes slide along the field he dominates and which lower down slopes upwards, forming a shelf in the valley where the river is hidden in the channel it has dug for itself. He does not want to let himself be overcome by the disappointment he is beginning to feel. He chides himself for doubting William's word. It makes him feel ashamed just to imagine the young man might have dismissed him from his mind, or found some other occupation sufficiently attractive to allow him to neglect his friend.

Space remains devastated by an absence all have abandoned. No premonition of some foreign intrusion lends its outlines the expectant trembling announcing an arrival. David cannot accept the possibility of William arriving late because of having had a sleepless night or having overslept. The insistent immobility that from all parts of the valley seems to counter his hopes convinces him that the young man cannot be driving towards their encounter on any road or country lane. It is then that a brutal, destructive fear begins to grip his heart, tightens its claws round his throat, makes his face grow pale. Could William have met with some misfortune? Had the *gendarmerie* been tipped off and nabbed him the minute he got up, leaving him no chance of escape?

A dull throbbing comes from behind the hill's shoulder the other road winds round but, judging by the broken-winded, sputtering sound it makes as it draws nearer and grows louder, it could never be mistaken for the exhaust of a motorbike. In fact it is only an old two-stroke Vierzon* tractor David sees coming round the bend and rumbling towards the crossroads. The farmworker driving it looks down upon the boy in the lordly manner his elevated and isolated position seems to confer upon him in the deafening racket of the engine. Little puffs of black smoke keep popping out of the upright exhaust pipe, and though the tractor has now stopped, the fly-wheel regulating a steady operation of the motor is still turning. The man makes no secret of the distrust the presence of the boy arouses in him: he radiates a proud familiarity with the surrounding fields to such an extent that the boy almost begins to feel he is a trespasser, as if he were impudently invading private property. The tractor moves off in the direction in which David had been expecting William to arrive, and its progress destroys one by one all the anticipatory signs in which nature had decked herself to celebrate the young man's appearance in her midst.

David returns to the milestone at the crossroads and leans against it, trying to distract his thoughts by kicking with the toe of his shoe the gravel chips covered with tar still not integrated with the road's surface. He no longer feels either disappointed or worried: he is now in a sulky, almost comatose state. But as he lifts his eyes in the direction of the town, towards the still-misty hollow at whose edge the road seems to end, he has the huge surprise of seeing a man's figure waving to him excitedly. He rushes forward, but either because a surge of fresh emotion takes the wind out of his sails, or whether he feels he must preserve a certain dignity, he

---

* Named after the French town where they are manufactured. (*Translator's note*)

controls his impatience and advances towards the encounter with the young man making an effort to give his steps the same carefree swing as his friend's.

William comes towards him bare-chested, holding with one finger the shirt he has cast over one shoulder, chewing a blade of grass, and seeming to be suffering from the heat. A sudden access of timidity or modesty prevents David from looking at him too directly or too continuously; he is unable to seek his gaze when they meet, and his confusion almost turns to dizziness when he feels William's hand falling on his shoulder with a firm pressure that makes the boy swivel round towards him; then an arm encircles his neck, crushing him to the moist coolness of his breast, bathing him in the spicy aroma of his youthful sweat.

In a voice somewhat breathless with effort, William explains that this morning his bike would not start, so he had to shove it and roll down into town in neutral. The garage had promised it would be ready by this evening.

'Were you scared?'

David simply nods his head. William crushes him to his breast again. He wants to take him to meet the people he is lodging with. He has told them about David, and they can't believe he has a son.

No, William will never make the girl believe it; but, flinging her head back in a movement that stretches the neckline of her black blouse from which her firm breasts seem to threaten to pop out at any minute as she is shaken by great spasms of laughter, she keeps repeating William's joke as if for a while she had taken it sufficiently seriously to be worried about it.

David cannot take his eyes off her. He is completely conquered by this face whose regular oval, enhanced by two plaits of glossy black hair severely parted down the middle and framing the rounded temples, is so different from the common mould, and it is even more surprising to hear coming from it a voice without accent or faults of pronunciation.

The girl cannot keep still. She inundates the vast kitchen with her gestures and her speech, with her intangible, indefatigable, overwhelming presence. She scolds her little brother, a two-year-old parading bare-bottomed round the table, shoves him away to play somewhere else, returns to her handicapped sister who is jerking incessantly in her chair, showing David a radiant face that grows hilarious as soon as he looks at her. The girl in the black blouse and red skirt is coaxing her, trying to make her eat.

Turning towards her visitors, she shrugs her shoulders. With the frankness of people living in intimate contact with this type of malady, she talks to them about her sister as she would to describe the character, the habits, the reactions, the little triumphs also, of a cat or a dog. She indicates her mother with a jerk of the chin, explaining that she had held back too long at the moment of giving birth to the baby. She goes on to something else.

The woman in question is busy at the oven and shows as much reaction as if she were deaf. She still looks young, her fine features contrasting with her corpulent figure, her luxuriant breasts covered by a shapeless blouse that is also too short. A prisoner of her native dialect, she takes on the role of servant, and only the clatter of her wooden soles from time to time on the flagged floor remind one of her presence. Again and again, in a gesture that expresses a certain weariness, she smoothes the mass of her dark hair combed straight back. When they smile at her, she responds with her own fainter smiles, and, when she has nothing to do, she sits in a chair beside the window, where she remains motionless, her hands crossed on her knees.

Stella's vivacity, her clothes, her vigorous movements that make the pleats in her ample skirt swing from side to side, create a false note in the austerity of the huge room whose whitewashed walls and stone-flagged floor make noises and voices re-echo in a harsh way. The sighs, the complaints, the lamentations she indulges in have an affected, suspect character, as if, despite all the things justifying them, she was more concerned with the image they allow her to present to the world than with the expression of authentic rebellion. She curses the life she leads here, she says she has to take the responsibility for everything, she threatens to drop everything and go for good, then suddenly she bursts out laughing or dashes over to her sister to steady the hand holding a cup she is on the point of spilling, and almost at the same moment snatches out of her little brother's fingers the knife he has managed to get hold of.

She has eyes only for William. She takes every opportunity to come close to him. When she pours for him, she lays her hand on his shoulder, presses her pelvis against his back, lowers her head over his, and when his hair brushes against her hand transforms the movement into a kind of caress. She adopts languorous, provocative poses, simpers girlishly. When she asks him if he has slept well, her eyes sparkle. The veiled look she gives him seems to be a reminder of promises not kept, of an engagement she does not want him to forget. She is sorry she cannot offer him anything more comfortable. Of course, if only she had her way, she would suggest some more suitable arrangement. Alberto, who also comes here to sleep from time to time, has nothing to complain about: and how is Alberto, anyhow?

She runs to the door, she chases away a hen that has ventured inside, she shuts it with a resounding slam. She turns round, hands on hips, to scold the little boy:

'Salvatore, just you watch out! If you ever open the door again, I'll put you to bed!'

He looks up at her, a finger in his mouth, with a candid air not without a touch of mischief, and when she advances upon him threatening to smack his bottom, he bursts out laughing and takes refuge with his mother, on whose knees he lays his head.

She comes back to William and David, stands at the other side of the table laden with dishes, bottles, fruit. She seizes the frying pan her mother has placed there a moment ago and with the help of a large fork lifts out a breaded veal cutlet which she offers the boy, saying he's going to enjoy it. She serves William, then her sister who is getting impatient, and finally herself. She sits down. She sighs. She puts her elbows on either side of her plate, holds her head in her hands. She says she's not hungry. She looks at William. As he does not respond to her look, she consults her nails. She raises her eyebrows.

'How are you proposing to take me dancing this evening, if you don't have your motorbike?'

'I'm afraid you'll have to find some other means of transport,' says William.

'We can find some solution, can't we?'

'There's only one I can see: ask your father for the light van.'

She gives a start:

'Can you see us arriving for the dance in that heap of old junk?'

'There's nothing to stop us decorating it with garlands of flowers,' says William. 'And some paper lanterns would look well on it.'

'The truck's not my father's, that's one thing.

And for another, I'm not going to the municipal rubbish dump, I'm going to a dance! Couldn't your rich friend come and pick us up in his car?'

'I don't know where he is.'

She does not seem to be terribly put out. She says she doesn't mind missing the dance, but she is sorry not to be able to wear the dress she had run up for the occasion. Her face becomes animated. She jumps up. She is sure William would like to see her in it. She waits for his reply that does not come, then agrees to let him see the dress. She puts the fork back in her sister's hand. The walls resound with her laughter and the whirwind of her skirt as she jumps from one foot to the other.

Her disappearance leads to an embarrassed silence in which each of them feels isolated in the even more vast emptiness of the room. A ray of sunlight coming through the window falls on the mother's hand gently stroking the little boy's head on her knees: this slow massage is sending him to sleep. In the continual buzzing of flies only the little trills of laughter from the handicapped girl can be heard accompanying the creaking of the chair she incessantly rocks.

'*Buono,*' says William, looking at the mother. '*Molto buono!*'

She smiles, shrugs her shoulders, lifting a hand in the air.

'We could have asked Stella to come with us,' David is saying.

His voice takes on a tremulous quality in the echoes coming from the tall cliffs of grey rock rising above them in the river's narrow chasm. Except for a few branches whose scanty leaves on black stems accent the walls with their rare touches of green, vegetation is almost absent from these depths that are scoured by the rapids and that the reverberations of light against bare rocks bathes in an unreal radiance. David and William are talking to one another from two huge blocks fallen into the middle of the river and on which they are resting, hidden from all curious glances, with the feeling of having reached a 'somewhere else' made especially for them.

'She wouldn't have accepted,' says William. 'Even if her mother had agreed.'

The close contact of his flesh and the rock emphasizes how different the outlines of his body are from the lifeless consistency of the great boulder on which, at points of contact, his frame barely shows any signs of resistance, and at the same time reveals, even in the fine texture of his skin, a kinship with the granulated material, despite the unevennesses, the twisted shapes that inform it. Half-reclining, motionless, he almost looks as if he has issued from the very stone he is lying on, sculpted from it, and needing only a few blows of a chisel in order to release him from it completely. He closes his eyes, his arms lying along his sides. His hair is no more than a brighter vein mined from the rock.

'You're not bored?' David asks him. The boy is sitting up, limbs clutched to his chest, his chin resting on his knees.

William glances at him before replying:

'We're all right here, aren't we, just the two of us together?'

The boy nods his head eagerly.

'Let's stay a little longer,' William goes on. 'We'll have to find another place for swimming.'

'I'm in no hurry,' the boy replies. 'It was just that I was beginning to think . . .'

'You're lucky I can't get my hands on you. I'd soon chase them away for you, those thoughts of yours!'

David smiles, gazes a moment at William, then, overcome by so much security and gratitude, he finally stretches out also. It is then probably difficult for him to distinguish the dull throbbing of the blood through his veins from the pulsing of water over the pebbles, a sound so transporting, so neverending, it has a hypnotizing effect as soon as one begins listening to it.

He again questions William about the girl. He is still intrigued by the playful attitude she adopted towards him. He suspects that the young man does not find her attractive, and he would like him to explain why. He feels it is a disquieting sign that he himself has fallen under Stella's spell: he imagines he should not have allowed himself to do so, and thinks himself at fault, as if he had committed some mistake. William declares that she is the sort of girl one finds attractive only in relation to the degree of detestation one feels for them; and they do everything they can to provoke such a reaction. They build up for themselves an image they know is closest to the image aggravating the anguished desires of men when they want to make love.

With a shake in his voice, David cannot help asking him if he has loved a lot of girls; and, as the young man's replies are evasive, he ventures to use more precise terms: had he already slept with a woman when he was David's age? His question, uttered too faintly, is lost, or else William is thinking of something else. He sits up.

'Tell me about your mother,' he says. 'You know, I didn't realize it at first. It was only gradually, without knowing why, I felt the need to, you know, to protect her.'

The effect that would be made by the young man's forearm covered with fine blond down on the rounded smoothness of his mother's shoulders, the shells of his hands barely curving round her breasts, the comfort the hollow of his neck would offer her face are some of the images that pass through David's mind, and which he truly feels would bring him an unspeakable sense of peace if only they could be made reality.

'You should just tell her . . . tell her you like her.'

'She wouldn't believe me,' William answers.

He sits cross-legged, brushing with a finger the down on his thighs.

David goes on to encourage him to be less timid with her.

'When she comes to pick us up presently, kiss her, put your arm round her neck. In front of me, she'll never dare to resist. We'll get her, the two of us!'

'You talk as if she were Stella,' William says.

They look at one another, united by the sounds of water that enfold them. David tells of his wish that William should marry his mother. William lowers his head, then raises it and points at the boy.

'I'd make you mind your p's and q's! I'd give you some stick!' he threatens.

David just laughs.

'You wouldn't have to go wasting your time in the woods,' William goes on teasing him. 'I wouldn't want you associating with every Tom, Dick and Harry! Absolutely no question of allowing you to laze by the river with a deserter! I'd forbid you to leave the house, first off.'

'And I wouldn't leave you alone for a minute, number two!'

'You would have to devote yourself completely to me!'

'I'll lock you up in my room.'

'You'll take off my boots and socks!'

'I'll tickle your toes!'

'You'll massage my back!'

'I'll scrub it with steel wool.'

'You'll serve me my drinks!'

'I'll give you methylated spirits!'

'I'll throw it in your face,' shouts William, slipping down off his rock.

'You'll miss me,' retorts David, standing up on his.

'I'll catch you,' says William, trying to grab him by the heels.

'I'll . . .' exclaims David, but the icy blow of the water William splashes over him stifles his voice.

And to get his own back he rushes at the young man who holds him helpless in his arms. They fall upon one another amid wild bursts of laughter and the river's leaping jets of foam.

XXIV

Framed in the opening of the car window that has been wound right down, the face of the young woman emerges from the dark background of the passenger space illumined only intermittently by flashes of sunlight. A smile is hovering round her lips and even seems to animate the lenses of her dark glasses. On their mirror surface, David can see outlines, distant and deformed yet concise, the double silhouette he forms with William against whom he is clinging closely on the back of the motorbike. His face is set sideways on the hunched back of the young man whose head is standing out against the sky, the fluttering flame of his hair uplifted by the wind of motion. He cannot make out the words being exchanged between William and his mother who are not succeeding, even though they are forcing their voices, in overriding the noise of the engines nor in piercing the wind barrier dividing the bike and the car.

As the road now starts some sharp bends, William suddenly accelerates and roars past the 203. All David is conscious of is the roadside streaming past, the flying carpet of asphalt, the swoon of turning trees and, further off, the fields or the mountains, depending on whatever inclination William gives the machine, from one side to the other and back again, the roarings of the motor between his legs, its vibrating pulsations that resemble the reactions of a wild beast trying to dislodge a burden weighing on its back. The boy closes his eyes and concentrates his whole attention on the vibrant pressure of William's back against his clinging torso, clinging to it as if he wished it could stay like that for ever, his one safe anchorage in all the world.

After the hairpin bends, William slows down, lets the 203 catch up with him, whose chrome fittings, the wide space between the headlights, the curvaceous sweep of the wings, the pointed beak of the bonnet seem to be reflecting the amused smile which must be the expression on the young woman's face for the moment obscured behind the rushing reflections on the windscreen. The car leaps forward, overtakes the motorbike that then catches up with in on the left, again slows down on a level with the driver, and the same image of David and William crouched close together is mirrored in the lenses of the sunglasses. The young woman's smile widens a little, and she slowly shakes her head as she looks at the young man, unable to decide whether to disapprove of this game that amuses her but that she still cannot help feeling is unwise.

William goes on playing it right on the outskirts of the town where the narrowing of the streets and the traffic make it impossible. They cross the bridge, and reach the temporary parking lot around the war memorial. William chooses a vacant space where the young woman can also park her vehicle, which she does after he has stopped his engine and David has got off the back seat, still light-headed with the excitements of the trip.

His mother takes more time than necessary to collect her belongings and leave the car. The adventure she realizes she is being invited to share arouses in her an apprehension that forces her to postpone the outcome. David urges William to take the initiative. The young man takes the few steps that separate him from the car. He succeeds in giving the gesture he makes to open the door and offer his hand to the young woman a sufficiently burlesque touch to disarm her fears. She gives him a still undecided look: one might almost think she is on the point of asking him to give up this outing, but she puts her hand in his, William moves aside a little and discreetly helps her to get out.

They do not continue the game as they have to make their way one after the other between the vehicles. Reaching the broad main road, which they have to cross in order to join the rest of the crowd moving towards the fair, confronting the dazzling pavements whose reflected sunshine makes the ground vanish under a blinding sheet of light, they perhaps begin to realize more vividly the nature of the test they are about to undergo. They do not retreat, for they can no longer do so, but they move ahead separately, each of them with head lowered on thoughts in confused disarray.

They are now proceeding side by side, barely brushing against one another, wondering what the point is in pretending to be a couple of fiancés. William is not sure if he is alarming the young woman by adopting towards her from the start a more tender behaviour. David follows a few steps behind them, divided between impatience to see them coming closer together – to precipitate the event indeed – and the feeling that he should make himself scarce. The gravity of the emotion he guesses is unsettling them, the intensity he supposes their experience, their age, their physical maturity lend their sentiments, the complementarity with which despite themselves their reality as man and woman imbues their beings, the anxiety that gives their limbs a slightly drunken tremulousness are all for him so many clear signals, making him feel that, in any case, they have entered upon a sort of understanding that unites them and from which he is excluded.

The blaring music and the announcements bawled out over the loudspeakers override the sonorous base continuo of footsteps, words, cries, laughter, murmurings. The young woman turns round, the flash of her sunglasses betraying her fear of having lost David. He gives her a reassuring sign. A group of brawling adolescents passes close by them, throws handfuls of confetti. William and the young woman receive a fistful full in the face. They are tangled in coloured streamers from which William hastens to free David's mother.

Above the rumtitum of the roundabouts, the bitter-sweet sonorities of the accordions and the no-nonsense clamour of the singers' voices can be beard the pop-farts of the shooting galleries, the rattling racket of the lottery wheels, the blasts of mechanical organs. Odours of sugar, caramel, peanuts and nougat swamp the air, seeming to give it a scented humidity.

The young woman turns back again towards David. Her face, partly masked by William's arm around her neck shows she is divided between remorse at leaving her son on his own and astonishment at finding him so agreeably disposed to her companionship with William. She waves him closer.

'Where should we go next?' she asks him.

He tells them not to worry about him, as he wants to make a tour of the roundabouts and will meet them again under the plane trees where they can wait for him. He moves away, turns round after a few steps. Through the moving shadows of the passers-by, he sees them standing motionless, face to face. William has laid his hands on his mother's shoulders. She is looking up at him. Then he disentangles a piece of confetti from her hair.

Jingling in his palm a few coins whose chinking underscores his feeling of jubilation, David plunges into the dense crowd in the fairways; he is full of the thoughts of the happiness he has left behind him, restraining the rapture he feels in anticipation of the new relationships that will spring up between the three of them when he returns home: he walks along lost in a nimbus of joy that gives him only a blurred impression of the flashing colours and the dark shadows surrounding him.

But gradually the setting becomes clearer. He finds the roundabouts from preceding summers, notices that they are laid out in the same way. He has no trouble finding his way in a universe that holds no surprises for him and for that very reason loses some of its seductive charm. The fact that now he is enjoying the fair all on his own gives him perhaps a sense of responsibility hardly propitious to the reawakening of his former enthusiasms. Indeed, in front of the roundabout on which he never failed to ride – swan-shaped boats floating on waters whose green tint was all the more fascinating because it clashed with the magenta tones of the surrounding wooden railings – he feels a sort of shame at having been attracted by what now appears to him as rubbish fit only for kids.

He is at an age to desire stronger sensations, to ride on the grown-ups' carousels, like this jet plane racer that his mother had always forbidden him to try and towards which he now makes his way between the stands. In a hissing of the hydraulic jacks that activate their articulated arms, the crudely made gondolas whirl across the sky, forming a starry bouquet whose elements rise or fall according to the way the occupants manipulate the 'joysticks'. Some of them block their jets in the highest position and the contraption's steep incline gives the impression that they are holding on only by centrifugal force, while others laugh and utter loud screams at every fairly brusque change of speed. David then has second thoughts as he approaches the cashier. He is perhaps thinking that after having rejoined his mother and William the latter will agree to share a ride with him.

He wanders away, more detached, picking out in the crowd the couples holding each other round the waist. He looks more closely at the girls of his own age or a little older, trying to see which ones might please him and at the same time meet William's standards; that is to say, asking himself if what he feels when he looks at them can be the symptoms evoked by the young man which, according to him, are so significant. The fierce look his scrutinies give his features does not seem to indicate that the experiment is conclusive, especially as it provokes in the young ladies concerned startled or even frankly hostile reactions that do not show them to their best advantage.

The stacks of caramels on the display shelves, the cornets of peanuts enrobed in soft nougat, the marzipans and the marshmallows, the boas of caramel that the candy-makers knead, scramble, stretch, calibrate before chopping them with their scissors; the barley-sugar twists, the cotton candy gathering on a wooden stick passed over the walls of a cone in which the sugar is spun to create in a few seconds the monstrous distaff of candy floss – all that brings back to his mouth memories of tastes he would like to rediscover; but he hardly sees himself going back to meet William with the stupid look of those who wander around licking the stuff.

He does not waste any time beside the bumper cars, although their flashing rumblings, the shocks when they bump and above all the rattling of their trolleys on the wire mesh overhead from which they draw sparks still have power to attract him. He goes straight to the 'Caterpillar' which has always fascinated him and arrives just at the moment when, to the scream of a siren, the ring of cars is gathering speed, forcing back on their seats the occupants who are lost in a cloud of dust. Already the covering above the cars is half-raised but suddenly it slams down, creating an annulated green sausage that rushes round the undulations of the platform. The chance it gives sweethearts to exchange their first kiss has given this roundabout a rather bad reputation, at least so his mother has told him. David couldn't expect his mother to let herself be embarked on it by William, but he cannot help dreaming of the chances it would give the young man to strengthen his conquest.

Someone suddenly calls his name and grabs him by the arm, and he finds himself face to face with Dieter. The laughing face of the foreman, highly amused by the fright he has given him, produces the impression in David of a counter-blow, as if that laugh deprived him of the pretension of being a grown-up, and thrust him back into childhood.

'Has your mother abandoned you?' Dieter asks him. 'How could she have let you wander around alone here?'

The boy does not reply. His situation already seems to the foreman to be suspicious, and the slightest reaction could deepen his suspicions. Nor can he run away from him, because he would be capable of pursuing him. He tries to resist him simply by glaring at him.

'Still just as talkative,' Dieter sneers.

But he straddles his legs and crosses his arms on his puffed-out chest.

'So your blond has left you? He didn't waste much time over you!'

The boy holds his tongue, afraid of over-reacting.

'He's been to your house, it seems? I hope your mother locked her valuables away.'

He tittups on his heels, showing signs of impatience.

'Fortunately he didn't stay long. If he had, he'd have been enjoying a different kind of festivity . . . and you, too.'

David's obstinate silence unsettles him, but he does not give up without a parting shot:

'You're lucky I'm not the spiteful kind. By giving him shelter, you've broken the law, you could still be brought to court for it – just tell that to your mother!'

He wags his forefinger at the boy, gives him a long look, and finally turns on his heel. David stands rooted to the spot. He waits to make sure Dieter is not going to follow him, waits until his figure has been swallowed up entirely by the crowd.

Of all my wanderings in fairgrounds that I attribute here to David there remains the memory of an impression I was then unable to explain, of course, but that deprived me of part of my enjoyment. Perhaps the news broadcast on the radio, the climate of insecurity that dominated everything in those days, the fear that was so obvious in the sombre and nervous attitudes of people, all that had finally left me with a permanent feeling of apprehension: not for one moment did I feel free from a menace against which the fair offered only a pitiful sort of defiance. It paraded without shame the vanity of its means, the inoffensive nature of its fantasies, the insubstantiality of its decors. On the roundabouts, nothing masked the fragile structure of their installation; the stalls were only big trailer-trucks whose wheels, barely concealed by the lowered backs and sides, suggested their temporary set-up; the mountains of dolls, the feathered baubles, the tinselly glitter of the treasures displayed in these itinerant Ali Baba caverns hid nothing of their rubbishy nature; the curtains, the decors, the gildings, the medallions, the mirrors, the garlands and the scrolls that overburdened the panellings with their capricious profusion, branches, flowers, fruit produced only by human imagination and depicting a world without weight, delirious, necromantic perhaps, did not try to lay claim to any reality, any permanence – it was all a castle of cards, a palace of the winds, a parody of paradise.

The depths of squalor and loneliness the music was intended to cover up persisted in oozing through the notes and the scratching of the sapphire heads in the microgrooves. Like the paradoxical sonorities of the accordion that were the dominating tones, flabbergasting in their agility and at the same time reedy, nasal, trivial, joy itself here presented the character of sadness, the euphoria one was supposed to feel could not divest itself of a profound distress.

That *chanson* by Brassens* broadcast in those days from one stand or one carousel to another encapsulated for me this melancholy condition:

Les amoureux qui se bécotent sur les bancs publics,
bancs publics,
bancs publics,
En se moquant pas mal du regard oblique
Des passants honnêtes,
Les amoureux qui se bécotent sur les bancs publics . . .[†]

---

* Georges Brassens, poet-composer of popular non-conformist *chansons*, 1921–81.
† *The sweethearts kissing on the benches in the park,*
in the park,
in the park,

The singer's fleering voice, the hidden smile that vibrated through its hoarse timbre, the tenderly mocking tonality of the two musical phrases repeated again and again succeeded in evoking those couples, whom I had not failed to notice in the very situation where the *chanson* placed them, with a complaisance that first made me doubt the seriousness of their emotion. Above all the melody, mischievous, carefree, accompanying a subject that I thought merited greater seriousness, exacerbated the bewilderment I used to feel when I saw them; it seemed, beneath its ironic surface, to express heaven knows what sad fatality linked with their condition, heaven knows what despair underlying their reciprocal attentions, heaven knows what anguish in their desire. Yes, that is what it was: an element of disappointment and regret from time to time loosened their embrace, they did not really believe their vows and they themselves were not deceived by their false promises: they were glimpsing perhaps the limits of a liaison that cut them off from the same sort of adventure with others, and above all with the ideal being of their dreams they could not stop thinking about. That would explain the girls' air of resignation, their often reticent and sulky behaviour, the boys' eyes grown suddenly haggard, their bafflement when they could not make a go of things, expending endless patience to bring their companion out of her shell, never discouraged, as if the misunderstanding were part of the game, as if their disputes formed part of a rite they were obliged to pass through.

Doubtless it is because of that song by Brassens

And caring nothing for the sideways looks
Of respectable passers-by,
The sweethearts kissing on the benches in the park . . .
                    (Translator's notes)

267

and his vision of the sweethearts that I cannot place William and David's mother anywhere but on a park bench. That is how he finds them just after leaving the fairground. Whether it is because at that very moment a roundabout is playing the song, or because the boy is familiar with the words and the music after hearing them so many times, he gives them a look fraught with the latent anxiety the song used to create in me: so he stands to one side, away from where everything is in the balance, over there, in the shade of the foliage of two plane trees that mingle their branches above the couple – all is in the balance there, his present, his possible future evolution.

He cannot judge what progress William and his mother have made in their relationship: he is waiting for some gesture that would let him know, some sign of their desire, of their complicity, of their love – even if it means his own exclusion. He needs this confirmation of the happiness of the two people he feels closest to, in order to have some guarantee that this happiness also is for him – if not a promise – at least a possibility.

He sees them only from behind. The young woman is sitting up straight, her back against the cross-piece of the bench supporting her shoulders. It looks as if she is sitting with legs crossed, head lowered, looking down at the clasp or the strap of her handbag her fingers are playing with in an effort to resist some other movement that would unbalance her if she did not in fact restrain herself.

As for the young man, his whole upper body is leaning forward, his elbows on his parted knees, his clasped hands beating out a rhythm perhaps intended to calm his impatience. He keeps turning his face towards the young woman, talking to her, pursuing the same argument time and again, doubtless in a somewhat plaintive tone. Although they are so close to the fairground that is pouring out its hubbub of shouts, bangs and music all round them, they seem isolated from it all as if they were under a bell-jar, and 'the sideways looks of respectable passers-by' do not bother them – these are not the cause of their indecision, the reserve they show one another, their anxiety.

And then, suddenly, William straightens up, raises an arm already curved to fit the shape of the young woman's shoulders but, in that movement that twists the top half of his body, he sees David standing there, smiles at him, and simply lays his arm along the bench's wooden support, while at the same moment the young woman turns round and smiles also.

XXV

She stands out against a background of flowers, garlands, lanterns, of moving figures steeped in the restaurant's ruddy glow: her face emerges from the rhythmic clatter of cutlery, plates, glasses as if in a bubble of silence, her features smooth and pale, lit by an unmoving, broad, blinding smile that is not the result of a more or less sudden exaltation bordering on movement, announcing a word or a gesture of gratitude: it expresses rather a mysterious sovereignty, the possession of a knowledge she will never reveal.

She sits away from the table, leaning against the back of the chair, one arm across her breast, the other bent and raising to her lips the cigarette she has accepted from William, that is held between her lifted index and middle fingers. The thread of smoke at first rises vertically then twists, sways, with the same suggestion of amused sagacity as her smile, before spreading sideways in lascivious, carefree undulations. Thus she considers them both, the boy and the young man, uniting them in the same somewhat distant tenderness, unable to enter into their togetherness and happy with the effect it produces, finding herself overwhelmed by their certainty of their own happiness.

Never before has David seen in his mother this

dazzling light that sets her apart from him. A woman's features have probably never aroused in William a more agonizing emotion. He asks nothing of her, he is trapped in his desire, he has stopped – if he had ever begun – paying court to her. His arms on the table, body leaning forward, he observes her with that patience David could comprehend only if he were to assimilate it to his own behaviour at the sight of the blond hair, the features, the body of the young man: this inexplicable possession of all one's being by the words, the motifs, the melodies swirling up from the lines of a face and a body, the relationship of their elements, their colours, their voices, the uniqueness of their appearances on the breath of life that bears them onwards.

Though he cannot hear the music that enslaves William in the presence of his mother, David has never before perceived with such acuity the purity of the song that surrounds William's illuminated profile on the red half-light: the outward qualities he had until then been able to appreciate in him were still only vague presentiments compared with this discovery, as if he had been attracted to the young man, from the moment he had first seen him, by an intuition that this love was possible. It could only be the effect of his blondness, the shape of his eyebrows, the form of his nose, the fullness of his lips, the jut of his jaw, his blue eyes: and yet there is something more, like a secret or, lost in the farthest reaches of his being, a memory that belongs to him alone and that only William could take possession of.

Under William's enamoured gaze his mother no longer belongs to David, she is no longer his mother but, although it makes him acutely aware of his own solitude, he is glad that it should be William stealing her from him. Deep down inside him, that is really what he wants. It is his fate to live on the verges of life: his heart is so constituted that it can beat only in proportion to those emotions he guesses the hearts of others are beating to.

He would be so happy to see – as he sees other couples in the room doing – William and his mother holding hands, linking their fingers across the table, breaking the brilliant carapace that holds each of them in separate perfection, and, through the pressure of their palms, beginning to disturb each other, to set themselves apart from the crowd, to disappear from the common world in order to give him, through the certainty of their own, the jubilation he does not have the power to attain.

He is growing impatient. By holding back as she is doing, his mother is persisting in depriving him of William. By refusing what the young man is offering her, she is robbing him of what he had been expecting. What is she waiting for? There is no doubt she has begun to enjoy the game and that, in this parenthesis to ordinary daily life, far from the voices on the radio, the prying eyes, the constraints of the times, she is welcoming without reserve and even with encouraging signs the young man's declaration. From the sparkle in her eyes, her animated movements, the smile illumining her face, it does not require great perspicacity to realize that she has been seduced, anticipating the pleasure she supposes William capable of giving her. Why do the words she refuses to address to David not break forth from the mask of her face? Why do those words remain scattered over every inch of her skin that is animated by their embryos with incessant scintillations – why do they not gather all together on her lips where we have been kept waiting for their appearance? For a moment, the boy thinks his mother is on the point of proffering that word which would resolve everything, for she lowers her eyes, leans forward from the back of her chair, bends over the table – but no, it is only to crush the half-consumed cigarette in the ashtray, and she insists on extinguishing the embers with repeated nervous tappings as if she were squashing an insect, unwillingly, disgustedly.

The boy proposes a return home. She is astonished that he should have forgotten the firework display.

'You never liked it before,' he says.

'It will help us to pass the evening together,' she explains.

'We could pass it together at home,' he insists.

She gives William a helpless look. She is waiting for him to use his influence to persuade David to be reasonable. He turns towards the boy and says it would be a pity to shut themselves up indoors when the weather is so fine. He suggests a stroll.

They walk away from the restaurant. The light is dying out over the town, sucked in by the spaciousness of the evening sky on whose silvery backcloth the angles of the façades and the edges of roofs are silhouetted as if cut out with a razor. Their three figures move undecidedly in the open spaces of deserted roads, looking small and lost, their outlines assaulted by gusts of air that seem hostile to their presence. The breeze is taking advantage of the emptiness of the streets to strengthen its force, blowing down the centre in a turbulent stream that throws off, along the asphalt or the gutters, crazy squalls that whirl up greasy papers, handbills, newspapers, tangled streamers, snowstorms of confetti. From time to time it bears along with it the echoes of fairground brouhaha that prove the fair is still in full swing, though on a smaller scale, limited to a certain almost private area beyond whose bounds the real has already reasserted its rights.

They wander through outlying districts, under mean, shabby façades like the back lots of movie companies, along blind walls of factories, the shut gates of workshops and garages. Here and there an open window sends out a narrow beam of light, an atmosphere of reclusive, solitary existence entirely turned in upon itself. Cats seem to be the only guardians, indifferent and self-sufficient. Disconnected from the young woman's actual footsteps, the clicking of her high heels echoes high up, like the inexorable march of time itself.

In these lifeless lanes and alleys they walk side by side, not touching, not speaking. William and the young woman have the same lost look, arms hanging limply at their sides, heads lowered, the slowness of their steps sometimes making them off balance, like people overburdened by their bodies after they have talked themselves out completely. They do not have enough past life in common to be able to converse like an ordinary couple, and desire takes up too much room in their encounter not to leave them wordless, at a loss. They stroll along like two lovers who can only fill in the last moments of their rendezvous by adopting this listless companionship, when time is too short before the imminence of their separation for them to undertake any further action, too long for them not to begin to wish those moments would pass as quickly as possible.

Against the mauve veils of the sky the lighted street lamps begin to clothe themselves in night, to create in the vanishing perspectives long arcades of shadow and light, to sparkle as if it had recently rained. Firecrackers, followed by shouts and cries, explode from time to time. It seems to David as if William has drawn closer to his mother. Or else it is the result of the falling darkness enveloping their figures in the same zones of shadow, or filling with shade the gap separating them. In front of them, couples more or less reduced in size according to the distance between them reflect their silhouettes. The young woman accepts William's offered arm, but she at once asks David to take the other. They return to the main street, mingle with the strolling crowds: they cannot be distinguished from the rest of all those gathered on the site of the firework display.

They are swept up in the sound of footfalls and in the enormous rumbling of voices that at times swells up in a stronger wave or releases, at isolated points, around a shrill cry, fountains of laughter. Dark forms have occupied the balconies of the surrounding façades, and only a flash of eyes or the sparkling of a jewel or the flame of a cigarette lighter shows them to be spectators.

The young woman keeps turning her radiant face to William and David on either side of her, and on their arms her fingers emphasize, with more explicit pressures, how happy she is. Then the boy and the young man look at one another, and thus confirm again their contentment, their delight in one another. The more the crowd grows, the more it shelters them, brings them together, encloses them, reunites them.

As David's eyes are scanning the crowd, not without a hint of defiance in them, as if he were expecting to discover people looking at their trio with envy, jealousy, astonished admiration, it so happens that he thinks he has glimpsed the foreman's head, and suddenly he drops his mother's arm. He would like to have it out with him, and hopes also, if possible, to distract his attention, but he does not have time to get away from the couple; the street lamps are dimmed, night swamps the crowd that now is nothing but one vast sigh, rising like a ground-swell quickly subsiding and leaving behind it moments of intense anticipation that scattered shouts, tending to increase as the expectant crowds are kept waiting, do not succeed in destroying. Then it is the whistling hiss of the first rockets which, followed by ear-splitting detonations, unfold across the heavens their multicoloured and expanding blossoms of fire.

That is about all David will see of the fireworks. Having spotted among the brightly lit and blissful lifted faces of the crowd those of William and his mother, he does not let them out of his sight. He sees them, barely hidden from time to time by dark silhouettes coming between, radiantly lit with more or less brilliance by the pulsing rays of the fireworks, at first transfigured by a rush of childlike wonderment, then, irregularly, because of the reflected light's visible variations, rapt in a sudden spell of anticipation, and sometimes obliterated by blackness pure and simple: he sees William's head lowered, and that of his mother shaking with the effort she is making to keep facing the spectacle, then William turned towards her, then, her eyes raised to his, the young man bending over her at last, with a pleading look, his trembling hand plunging into the young woman's hair, his full lips meeting her lips as she closes her eyes.

At the sight of this kiss, David has not noticed the end of the display; he only notices, suddenly, the movements of the crowd around him, people getting out of his way, crossing one another, bumping into each other and making off in different directions, William and his mother looking for him. He loves them in this display of parental concern that binds them more intimately than ever, and he would like to go on watching them like that. They will soon see him there, the texture of the crowd is thinning out, and soon there will be no one between him and them.

They form in the midst of the retreating flood a portal whose arching tenderness he already feels round his shoulders, but as the last remnants of the crowd disperses, he makes out one motionless figure, far back, round which the withdrawing flux divides like waves on a cutwater stem. The alarm on the boy's face alerts William and the young woman who turn round. They in their turn discover the presence of the foreman. He is smiling, keeps nodding his head; the white tips of his shoes on the pavement consolidate his unwavering stance, the hands in his trouser pockets lift up the front of his jacket alive with a shot-silk effect, one of the hyphens of his moustache is higher than the other.

Belated spectators slow down, in their eyes that spark of hope struck by the expectation of a scene, and they move away as if regretfully. Then the space is open between Dieter and the couple, and the pace at which the foreman advances, first one step, then another, finally begins to narrow it in a way that seems to make the night swim around them. That is when David dashes forward, but his prompt interception is not enough to impede Dieter's progress: his eyes fixed now upon David's mother, now upon the young man do not notice the boy.

His deep voice is heard, its resounding timbre wounding, stinging. David wants to throw himself upon him to make him shut up, to thrust him away, to exterminate him. But as in a nightmare of helpless flight, he remains rooted to the spot, he can do nothing against Dieter's all-conquering, screaming, deafening voice – he sways, does not feel the earth rushing towards him.

Each one of us carries within himself a promised land he is unable to describe on his own, that he loses consciousness of as soon as he approaches it. Why deny it? I have attributed to David an attitude

I may have had myself: the fields and the roads, the countrysides and the woods he has traversed are not unknown to me; he has found himself in a situation that evokes what memory suggests to me as a personal story. He has conducted me to the threshold of that interior world that I feel to be my own and which is not comprised of actual moments I have lived through but of fleeting impressions, evanescent sensations, bafflements in which my actions and gestures, my emotions, my thoughts, my very desires were only fortuitous events. Perhaps we never really live except in the realm of memory, having at our disposal no other means to realize ourselves in our entirety, when the very act of casting our minds back into the past delivers us from our fatal evanescence. David is now abandoning me at the precise moment when, on the point of being separated from William and being reunited with me, he is no longer capable of embodying what has always been within me, and in the Word ever since the dawn of time. I am compelled to leave him here, along with all that may appear inexplicable, and also many an enigma.

Here is what I can still make out: William has noticed the boy's abnormal tenseness, the figure drunkenly swaying before him, and he has rushed forward in time to catch him in his arms. Under Dieter's dumbfounded gaze, he lifts him up, feeling a little light-headed himself. The young woman is not too concerned, she knows that a fainting fit is nothing serious, she understands what this, the only possible action, has meant to David. She refuses to call help, she lives just a few steps away, and William is strong enough to carry the boy that far.

He lays him on his bed, removes his shoes. David turns his head on the pillow, as if he is about to awaken, and smiles. His mother puts out the light, two shadows leave the bedroom. The roar of a motor starting, helped two or three times by bursts of the accelerator, fills for a moment the space that is striped with rays of moonlight filtered by the shutters. A narrow band of light falling across the boy's eyes appears like the slit in a helmet on his shadowy face. He presses his head against the pillow that he hugs in his arms as the motorbike's roaring gradually moves away, and dies out on a final rolling echo.